SPRINGTIME IN MAGNOLIA BLOOM

A MAGNOLIA BLOOM NOVEL BOOK 3

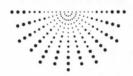

PAULA ADLER

DRAGON DREAMS PRESS, LLC

ISBN – 978195128059 (e-book)

ISBN – 978195128011 (paperback)

ISBN – 978195128158 (large print paperback)

ISBN – 978195128066 (audio)

ISBN – 978195128295 (library audio)

LCCN – 2021911375

Cover Design by Hang Le

Copyedit by Joyce Lamb

The Magnolia Bloom series:

This series is being produced in audio,

available from Chirp, Audible, and many other audio retailers

Magnolia Bloom Beginnings, A Three Novella Box Set – the Origins of Magnolia Bloom

Return to Magnolia Bloom, a Magnolia Bloom Novel Book 1

Mistletoe and Magnolia, a Magnolia Bloom Novel Book 2

Springtime in Magnolia Bloom, a Magnolia Bloom Novel Book 3

Moonlight in Magnolia Bloom, a Magnolia Bloom Novel Book 4

Sweet Dreams in Magnolia Bloom, a Magnolia Bloom Novel Book 5 –March 2021

If you enjoyed *SPRINGTIME IN MAGNOLIA BLOOM,* please leave a review on your favorite sites (Amazon, Goodreads, BookBub). It's the most amazing thing you can do to help an author! THANK YOU!!

Please sign up for Paula's newsletter at https://www.PaulaAdler.com to receive Eunice Greene's famous Chicken Salad recipe, updates, and information on all future publications. You can find her on Facebook at https://www.facebook.com/PaulaAdlerAuthor, and by email at Paula@PaulaAdler.com. She answers all emails personally.

CHAPTER ONE

ALLY

"I think I was abducted by aliens."

"Recently?" My agent doesn't look up from the papers she's arranging in the briefcase resting on her knees.

"No, no, a long time ago. I was looking at my baby pictures and I was hella cute, but I don't fit. It's just some days I look in the mirror, and I see this woman who's all of five-foot-five tall, most days feeling five-foot-five wide, and I wonder why my sisters got Mom's Scandinavian genes, and I stayed firmly in Dad's Scotland. So maybe we're not really related after all."

There are many days I envy my sisters' tall, sleek blondness. Both of them should have been models instead of a doctor and a lawyer. With my couldn't-be-a-water-girl-for-the-WMBA height and naturally dark hair currently a golden honey, I feel like I'd have to polish my résumé to be considered for Cinderella's understudy.

"Sooo…. Did they return you by sneaking you into the nursery like those cuckoo birds that put their eggs in other bird's nests, or did they put you under a cabbage leaf?"

I ignore the twitch of her lips at her not-so-subtle joke. "I'd guess cabbage patch," I mumble around the hair tie held between my teeth before taking it and wrangling my long, wavy mess away from my face. "I'm not sure how much of it we grow in East Texas, but I think it would make a better ballad."

"Agreed. I don't recall many ballads about aliens, but considering you haven't written one in over five years, maybe you should start making notes." She looks up from her papers and gives me a squint complete with pursed lips. "Come to think of it, that's good advice."

"Sometimes I think you missed your calling as a therapist."

"Don't worry, this job often requires me to pull double duty, though you wouldn't know it since this is the first time you've ever let me focus negotiations on something *you* want."

While I wait for Sarah to finish whatever she's doing, I glance around my magazine-worthy living room in downtown Nashville and tuck my security blanket in the back pocket of my plain ol' Levi's jeans. No bling. No strategic rips or frayed hems. I'm pretty sure I bought this pair at the Trader Days in Atlanta— Texas, not Georgia—the last time the Terrible Trio had gotten together. As radically different as we are, both physically and in temperament, I miss my sisters, but Bailey and Cammie have their own lives, which seem thousands of miles away instead of mere hundreds.

I feel marginally silly that the only time the little secret packet isn't with me is when I'm in some sequined Spandex nightmare and about to go onstage, but even my therapist has stopped trying to make me leave my woobie at home.

I resist the urge to tell Sarah to hurry as my nerves are already about shot, and try to keep my coffee-and-bagel breakfast from making a reappearance. She doesn't need to know how many hours I stayed awake trying to decide if now is the right time to be pushy. I've been hesitant to rock the boat, letting old fears keep me silent, but I'm trying to break out of ancient patterns. Still, it took a concerted effort to finally ask for the ballad album my soul needs to put out into the world.

And who knows? Just because there aren't any space alien cowboy songs doesn't mean there shouldn't be. I might start a whole new sub-genre of music we didn't know we were missing.

Sarah's a friend as well as my agent, but I'm a master at hiding my jitters when we're together. Unless there's craft beer or Jägermeister involved. Then all bets are off, but thankfully I lean toward happy in those moments and tend to channel my inner Cammie and my baby sister's talent for humor.

Still, I turn away so Sarah doesn't realize her offhand remark has scraped the scab off a wound that doesn't seem to heal.

Five years. Five years since I wrote from my heart. Five years since I did what I once believed was my calling, my destiny, my duty. I don't know why the gods of music chose my ears to speak to, but they do.

They did.

The words, the notes, the rhythms, the cadence, the essence of something spiritual used to make it to the blank pages of the notebooks never far from my hands. There may have been days it was an ugly wrestling match between my brain and my pen, but eventually the song would take form and bloom. Now it's been so long, I wonder if I've abdicated all chance of finding that creative space again.

Whether I actually started out under the broad green leaves of a garden vegetable, I'm a bona fide country music superstar, or so people like to tell me. Sadly, the accolades aren't from the ballads that have been my signature, but because I gave in to Zane's insistence that we needed to get established with a more popular up-tempo subgenre first.

Then the charts exploded. I still feel like a sellout with every new top ten, much less the number ones, but it's hard to argue with success. Or, in Zane's world, the *ka-ching* of dollars hitting the bank.

My name's on the title to this luxury penthouse in the heart of country music's Mecca... but only because I felt I owed Zane since I'd just bought five hundred acres of raw land abutting my family's estate in Texas. There's barely a speck of me in this place. He wanted this fancy-schmancy address, and I... caved. Again. There's nothing in this hoity-toity palace that speaks to my soul, except the perfect replicas of my family's Valais Blacknose sheep flanking the hearth, made with wool from our flock. Their little black faces and ears, with requisite knee patches, are so lifelike and adorable, they take the tiniest edge off the nausea rising in my throat.

I glance at the marble mantel over the ridiculously huge fireplace, the soft scent of verbena wafting from the atomizer reeds on the far end. I count the Grammys Zane and I've won both as Country A to Z— or just AtoZ all mushed together by the radio jocks—and the ones with just my name on them. But it's the Tony on the end that's my favorite.

Best Performance by a Featured Actress in a Musical
Ally King

SARAH MOVES up beside me and gives my arm a squeeze.

"You were magnificent." She's obviously followed my gaze, reading me better than I give her credit for.

I feel my face heat and curse the telltale blush of my not-alien-Scottish ancestry that prevents me from hiding what I'm feeling. "It was amazing. I've been in front of a thousand crowds, but that play, that night, was... heaven." I brush off my reverie and nod toward the little statue. "I've been meaning to ask them to remake the plaque to read Alyssa MacInnes King, but I haven't gotten to that particular item on my endless to-do list."

Sarah lifts a brow. "You want me to get your assistant on that?"

Oddly, I don't. "Thanks, but I'll handle it."

She gives her head an aggrieved shake. "I don't know why you even have an assistant, since you do everything anyway."

Okay, maybe not so odd, since she's not wrong.

Turning, I tuck her arm around mine and lead us away from my distraction. "The entire country music world may think I'm some snotty princess and can't even cut my own food, but deep down, I'm still a little girl with big dreams who's afraid she's never quite made the grade so yeah, the assistant thing is still hard."

"I think you can put a big ol' checkmark in the "made it" column."

"And I think my Freudian slip is telling. I've never gotten the degree I always said I'd go back and finish. Bailey and Cammie did pretty good fulfilling the higher-education demands in my family, though, so only one daughter's a failure."

Sarah blinks in disbelief. "Are you kidding? I've met your dad tons of times. I've never gotten that vibe from him."

"Ah, but you've never met my mom, and then you'd understand." I wave a let's-change-the-subject hand between us. "I'd rather focus on the fact that I was lucky enough to be a crazy MacInnes who grew up around a Scottish castle in the wilds of East Texas. Having a personal assistant always makes me think my grandmother's going to pop out from behind a door and tell me I'm getting mighty high-falutin' or, her other favorite, too big for my britches."

Speaking of, I give my back end a pat to triple-check. To be fair, my security blanket is little more than a tiny bump in my pocket. Just a leather cover holding four things: my driver's license, a debit card, a hundred-dollar bill, and the key to my truck.

My truck.

The '69 Chevy C10 Stepside I repaired with my own two hands over the summer of my junior year of high school… with a metric crapton of help from my surrogate dad. Brian Steele had been a mainstay on the estate and in my life, teaching me so much more than how to wield a wrench. Over the course of his quiet lessons in mechanics, I got grease in places I hadn't known grease could get into, busted my knuckles more than once, and for months, my fingernails were ragged and never completely clean. I have no regrets, as I know now how to set a dwell, check timing, gap spark plugs, and adjust a carburetor, although sadness whips through me as I realize I'll never again get Brian's barest nod of approval for a job well done.

Thinking about the castle reminds me that Bailey and Cammie are going to be at the family compound this weekend. They asked me to join them for a long-overdue reunion, and I push regret and disappointment away with a firm hand. I love my sisters, but I don't have time right now.

Unhitching herself from me, Sarah collects her briefcase and checks for her sunglasses and cell phone. "Let's leave your impostor syndrome here, shall we? I need your A game while we put the screws to one of the biggest labels in this industry. I know you don't want to do another pop album, but it will get you your ballad project green-lighted."

"I just wish every step of this wasn't such a fight."

"You and me both, baby. We can't fix the insanity that is the music business, but there's still time for me to add a vital-records search to the attorneys' agenda, if you want. And on a side note, you should wear pink every day. It's awesome on you."

I look down at the V-neck cable sweater in a blush primrose I chose as much for the color as because it's one of the most comfortable things in my closet. "Thanks, but we can nix the birth investigation. Just having a momentary existential crisis."

I don't doubt my talent. I love it, appreciate it, and hold it to me like a precious gem. For me, true joy is when the words are coming and I hear the notes before I can get my hands on a guitar. I don't doubt I've been given an immeasurable blessing. Where I get wonky is that I don't just believe—I know—people don't see the real me. The public loves the glitz and glamour, the hype. The parts I hate. But it'd be a lie to say there aren't advantages to fame.

There are enormous disadvantages, too, but no one believes that.

Snapping her fingers in front of my face, Sarah pulls me from my navel-gazing. "I've been your agent for ten years, and we've discussed ad nauseum how painfully shallow most people are in this business. I don't know a single other performer who refuses to follow even a hint of social media, making you one hell of a unicorn."

"I just can't deal with the constant negativity and cruelty. The things people post behind the anonymity of being online makes me sick, but I assure you I have my own bag of crap. Don't anoint my head with holy water just yet."

Sarah pats her briefcase. "Don't worry, no applications for saint-hood await, but the big thing is, in an industry obsessed with knowing every inch of your business, you've trained everyone from real journal-ists to the scummiest of the paps to leave your family alone."

She's not wrong. If anyone wants an interview with me, they better not have anyone on their staff who has searched out my family. If I hear a whisper of any of them buying images from the blood-sucking ticks hiding behind the long lenses, they're on my dead list forever. I've infuriated Zane and Sarah both, but I won't do an interview with those kinds of reporters no matter how much money it might earn us. It's one of the few things I have absolute control over. It doesn't stop the gossip rags, but my life's pretty boring by their scale, so they have to be desperate to give space to me.

Sarah squints against a beam of sunlight cutting through the spotless wall of windows. Shifting away from the glare, she diverts me again. "I'm a little worried Zane isn't here yet."

The acid I've kept tamped down does an Indy-car lap up my esophagus. I wish I could fake unconcern, but Tony on the mantel or not, I have a poor poker face. "You and me both."

A blush tinges Sarah's cheeks. "Honey, I'm sorry. Things still sucky?"

I swallow to get the lump in my throat to back off. "Zane didn't come home last night, and his absences are becoming too common for comfort. We've fought more in the last ten months than we have in the preceding ten years, but I'm hanging on to a thread of hope that it's just a phase."

"That has to be it. You two got together so young, and you said you didn't have two nickels to rub together back in the day. That gives you strong roots." She leads the way to the arched front doors with their stunning leaded glass panels. "Let's head over. I'm sure he'll meet us there."

As we've done dozens of times, Sarah and I walk out of the condo and wait for the elevator doors to glide open. We enter the beautifully appointed, mirror-lined car serving as one of many pieces of evidence that I'm far and away from anticipating scullery work in my future. We'll be whisked down thirty floors and deposited into the marble-floored lobby—white Carrara being a theme in this high-rise. Then we'll exit into the glorious late spring sunshine to take a short walk over to the conference room of country music's most prestigious record label.

I try to put on a brave face, but I don't have time to worry because the instant we step out onto the sidewalk we're swarmed by people with cameras and microphones. Everyone is talking at once, and several flashes fire. I blink against a moment of blindness despite the fact that it's a brilliant-sky, eighty-degree Nashville day.

When my vision clears, I see Rex Chum, a horribly yet aptly named greasy-haired camera tick who, for some reason, has a particular hard-on for me. He loved the old days, before the body-positivity movement, when he could splash my picture highlighting any six-ounce weight gain, making sure the angle provided the least flattering print of me possible.

"… you find out about the affair—"

"Will you be divorcing—"

"What will happen to the new album—"

"… betrayal by your own publicist—"

"How long… sleeping together—"

Sarah faces me, away from the cameras, and talks through her teeth. "Go. Back up to the apartment. I'll take care of this and be there in a minute."

When she turns back, her face remains grim, but I catch the screw-with-me-I-dare-you light in her eyes.

I don't argue, but I don't obey. I do go inside the building where I can't be followed, but instead of heading for the elevators, I walk straight to the private door to the garage. For seventeen years, I've kept Blue Beauty parked anywhere I've stayed for any length of time. It's the one crazy-rich-person thing I do, and I'm sure my assistant curses me soundly for having to make arrangements to have BB hauled around, but who's laughing now, hmmm? Who's not crazy for having an escape plan after all?

I put my cellphone on the roof and dig into my back pocket, my fingers shaking as I pull out the little case and remove the key that has created an imprint in the brown leather. I slip into the driver's seat but can't reach for the ignition yet. My vision is blurry and my pulse is racing too fast, and despite the fact that there's no one to see, I'm blushing so hard I feel the heat radiating from my face.

If I had to learn my suspicions about Zane were correct, did it have to be on a downtown sidewalk while on my way to the first meeting with the label execs I actually felt good about, that I actually believed might be the start of a new phase of my career? Instead of being on a natural high with ballad lyrics pumping through my brain faster than I can get them written down, I'm sitting alone, in a parking garage, my heart breaking because what I'd feared has come true in a spectacularly public fashion.

At least my heart can break into a thousand pieces in a spectacularly private fashion because no one would think to look for me here, nor could they get here even if they did, but knowing my luck, that will last for another five minutes, tops.

Damn it, Zane. Our publicist? Really? Not that who she is matters. What matters is I truly wanted to be wrong. I wished upon stars that this was just a rough patch. Lit a candle in that little church I'd passed driving home from Kentucky, whispering, "Please," into the echoing stillness. Threw pennies into fountains, needing to believe we'd get through this, whatever it was, together. Like we always do.

Did.

Used to.

Gulping in long, deep breaths, I cross my fingers as I turn the ignition. All eight cylinders purr into gas-guzzling action, and I suck back tears of gratitude.

At the last second, I curse a streak and climb out to grab my phone off the roof before throwing it onto the passenger seat. I press in the clutch and put the truck that has a special place in my past, and now my present, into first. The three-on-the-tree probably serves as its own antitheft device these days, but my gut is too knotted up for me to laugh. It doesn't matter, because this rhinestone girl learned to drive in a pickup much like this one, except I'd been broken in not only with a standard transmission, but manual steering and brakes. Add in my experience on every piece of equipment on the MacInnes estate before it was legal for me to even apply for a learner's permit, and I've earned my country-girl bona fides.

It's not that BB needed this long to warm up, but it's taken these few minutes to get myself together and get her moving.

There are plenty of people lurking around the garage's exit, but every one of them is trying to spy Ally King in a shiny Mercedes or my signature red Tesla. No one is looking for Alyssa MacInnes in a pickup built when Nixon was president.

Ha! Suckers…

I turn left out of the garage and laugh as the jerks don't realize it's me until it's too late. All they get is a snapshot of my rear license plate.

BLOOM

Someone might extrapolate my home town from that, but I don't care. I'm not headed to Magnolia Bloom anyway.

Wait. Why not?

My immediate thought had been to head for my farm a mere hour-ish from here just across the Kentucky state line, but it's too obvious and no doubt the first place the nest of vipers, and Zane, would look. Then I consider my best friend's place in Montana. She has three hundred acres of mostly wild land, and I can hole up in her cabin for a year if I want. I know the security codes and where the secret key's hidden.

But as I merge into traffic on I-40, I realize something.

I don't want to go to Kentucky. Or Montana.

I want to go home.

CHAPTER TWO

CAMMIE

THE LATE SPRING weather seems rudely chipper to me. The sun shouldn't be brilliant, the air crisp after the deluge yesterday, the temperature a lovely seventy-three. If the world were fair, as I sit in the cell phone parking lot at DFW airport, waiting for my sister's plane to land, it would be raining to beat the band, with lots of jagged cloud-to-ground lightning strikes.

I'm certifiably crabby with a slow simmer of pissed off, ranging from despondent sadness to boiling mad, depending on where my mind settles. I am personally and profoundly aware that the process of grief isn't linear, no smooth movement between stages. My journey looks more like a monkey overdosing on caffeine was let loose with a Sharpie and a sheet of butcher paper.

At the moment, instead of doing a simple breathing meditation my therapist has suggested 11.7 million times, I'm torturing myself by studying the business card with my name engraved in black script that I've been rubbing like a talisman, or a really flat genie bottle.

Cameron Eileen MacInnes, Esquire

Law Offices of Johnathan Arthur Dallas

THE THICK VELLUM, the perfect typography, the discreetly small address shouting *offices in the heart of Dallas, Texas's most affluent business district* are from my past life. The life that ended two years, one month, and four days ago, but the final nail wasn't pounded in until I had to spend two hours waiting on roadside service to come jump-start the car. I barely made it to the airport on time, and I'm afraid to turn off the engine, as I don't want to put Bailey through a repeat of the indignity.

What makes my obsessive rereading of these minuscule facts about my previous life even more sad is I'm doing it behind the wheel of a 2009 Corolla with a leather-scented air freshener doing its job but fooling no one. The Toyota's hood is a different color than the rest of the resilient little beater, and the car burns oil, though it runs well enough… usually. Quite a fall from an ebony Mercedes AMG GT C, no hanging deodorizer required.

My phone buzzes, but instead of a text saying my sister has left baggage claim and is waiting for pickup, it's her daughter. Even if Lila wasn't my only niece, she'd still be my favorite. The image on-screen is one hundred percent Bailey's mini-me. Shorter, true, but graceful and beautiful, with a pale blond Nordic vibe at odds with our usually dark or redheaded Scottish genealogy. No one has ever explained why Bailey and I look like we were smuggled into Mom's delivery room from Copenhagen, while Ally looks top-to-toenails like our MacInnes side, but I put those stray thoughts aside and answer the call.

"Hi, love bug. How are you?"

"Hi, Aunt Cammie."

I touch the screen, wishing I could hug the beautiful creature who has defied all the teenage stereotypes and is simply an amazing human being at seventeen years old. "Have you heard from Princeton yet?"

"Not yet. I'm wait-listed so I'm excessively refreshing my email, but nothing so far."

"Fingers crossed for you."

"Thanks. Listen, I have a favor to ask."

My inner radar pings, but I keep my expression fixed. "Of course. What can I do?"

"I need you to keep Mom in Magnolia Bloom until graduation. I know it's two weeks away, but she's going to decide in a couple of days that she needs to get home for me. I'm totally fine, and she needs the time off. You have no idea how long it took me to get her to take that many vacation days in a row."

I nod as though I understand. "Oookay."

"I'm serious, Aunt Cammie. Keep her there if you have to hogtie her and lock her in one of the turrets."

That image threatens to make me risk the snort-laugh that I'm teased for to this day. "I hope such drastic measures won't be necessary, but I'll do my best."

"You're a lifesaver. I'm staying with my best friend, and Jenny and I are on top of everything. Mom's stretched so thin she's breaking out in hives. She doesn't think I know, but I saw her slathering on anti-itch cream, and she's got to get some rest."

"Will do, honey. I have my marching orders, and I'll keep your mom here, but we'll be present for the big day with bells on."

"Perfect! You're the best, Aunt Cammie. I love you."

"Love you more, darlin'. I need to go. Your mom's text just came through, and she's waiting on me. We'll talk soon."

Lila throws me a kiss, and I toss one back before I tap the red button, slipping the phone into the cup holder, whispering a little prayer that the whole thing doesn't fall through the floorboard. I scold myself for being melodramatic, but today's been a bad day. You'd think after two years of processing, I'd be in a better place. Most days I am, but my final stop before heading to the airport was at the jewelers. The sympathy in Mr. Landau's eyes as he gave me the money from the consignment of my Cartier Tank Française nearly did me in. It was the last thing Johnnie gave me, for our eighth anniversary, the week before he decided to have a coronary after swearing to me he'd gone to his physical and passed with flying colors. It was the last thing I had, the last resource I could tap to get enough cash to leave Dallas and return to Magnolia Bloom.

To come home.

I maneuver through the insanity just short of bumper cars to pull into a spot near the curb and park. I step out to wave to Bailey, knowing she's looking for the Mercedes as I haven't mentioned my dramatic downgrade. It's inevitable that I have to shout to get her attention. Even from thirty feet away, I can see her frown as she heads toward me. The fact that my sister has only a rolling carry-on for a two-week vacay tells me Lila has an accurate pulse on her mother.

She walks slowly, like a dog warily approaching someone who sounds familiar, looks familiar, but all the other cues are wrong. She joins me at the rear of the car, where I've popped the trunk and left room for what I'd hoped would be at least two suitcases, then gives me a tentative hug filled with unasked questions. After putting her bag in the too-big space, she gets in the passenger side, again with the hesitancy of someone who's wondering if her sister's been replaced by a clone.

"What's the joke?" She tosses a thumb toward the back seat and the elegant dollar-store laundry baskets stuffed and stacked beside my two Goodwill-purchased suitcases. You'd be amazed how much money Louis Vuitton luggage can snag on Amazon Marketplace.

"Sadly, nothing laugh-worthy. I'll spill the gory details, but it'll take most of the drive." I check my mirrors and pull out into the endless stream of cars, keeping my focus on getting us out of the small city comprising the airport. Bailey sits with obvious impatience but determined silence until we're on the highway, as if her concentration alone will ensure the Corolla gets to merging speed in time.

I hide my similar worry until we're a comfortable leg down I-30.

Bailey shifts in her seat, and I detect the laser focus normally reserved for her patients. "All right. Spill."

I let go of the wheel with one hand to rub my temple. "The short version is these last two years have been pretty challenging."

"Yet whenever we've talked, the most you've said was, 'Settling big estates is always a pain in the ass,' which I'm now assuming is code for nuclear meltdown. And if so, why didn't you tell me and let me help?"

I cut her a glance. "Your expertise is in Texas probate law as well as how to replace a heart?"

"Not a heart surgeon, and you know it. I just know when they're broken and try to fix them before they head over to the operating room." She holds up a don't-do-it finger. "What's going on?"

"It turns out Big Johnnie Dallas was overextended a thousand ways into the next century, and without him around to keep the plates spinning, everything crashed around me in a giant blaze of humiliation. I stand before you—or rather, sit beside you—the proud owner of a 2009 Toyota Corolla, a few thousand dollars in cash, and the shattered remains of my pride."

"But—"

"I'm aware that Johnnie was a multimillionaire and, by extension, I supposedly was, too. The keyword in that sentence, in case you missed it, is 'was.' By the time I settled everything, I'm just grateful I'm merely unemployed and not hitchhiking to Magnolia Bloom."

I can practically hear Bailey's teeth grinding. "Let the record show I'm repeating my question. Why didn't you call me?"

"And do what? Pile more worries on your shoulders? Good golly, Miss Molly, you're practically transparent. If you lose any more weight, you'll have to buy your clothes in the preemie department."

I don't dare tell her the reason I truly have nothing is because I paid Johnnie's daughter from his first marriage as much as I could of what she would've been due if her father hadn't been so financially irresponsible. He'd always been sure he'd be able to fix his latest loan to cover the last loan, which he managed to roll into the one before that... All the while whisking me off to Zurich or Adelaide or wherever he'd decided our newest adventure lay. My own attorney called me nine kinds of fool, and a few more explicit names, for my determination to do what I felt was right. Even though Johnnie's daughter and I probably say twenty words a year to each other, she's his only child. I couldn't make the estimated amount completely whole, but I did an admirable job trying, if I do say so myself. Thankfully, Johnnie never changed her as his beneficiary on his life insurance policy, so my racking guilt that I never even tried to get to know her is somewhat appeased.

I've mostly dealt with my anger over my belief that, if he'd just told me, I could've helped him. I would've been more than willing to forgo vacations and jewelry and remodeling an already gorgeous home to be financially solvent. I'm a small-town country girl. I enjoyed the high life, sure, but I never asked for it, never demanded it, never needed it.

Bailey deflects my concern about her vampiric white skin and paper-doll-thin body. "But didn't you get a decent buyout? You were with that firm since you graduated law school."

"I was a senior associate, not a partner. There was nothing to buy out. I never pressed anything because, you know, the whole married-to-the-boss thing."

"But didn't you have retirement?"

"Liquidated, at a horrendous penalty, but it is what it is."

"That was—"

"Stupid? Probably. But the mountain was overwhelming. Remember, Johnnie was twenty years older than me, and the majority of the assets were his prior to our marriage."

"I wasn't going to say 'stupid.' You're brilliant, you nut."

"Not so brilliant I knew any of this was happening." I hold up a hand to stop her response. "I was in my last year of law school when I met him, and yeah, I was swept off my feet. I came into the marriage with nothing but student loans, so no, I had no standing to demand a prenup, since that's what you're about to ask."

"Well, this sucks."

"Trust me, the *Schitt's Creek* references started a long time ago. There's been endless fodder that a probate and real estate attorney— and I'm a good one, current evidence notwithstanding—got caught in this mess."

"Guess that makes you human."

"Says Wonder Woman and Supergirl all rolled into one."

Bailey snorts. "Hardly."

I don't bother arguing. Despite the fact she's my sister, I don't know a lot about what she does except she's a cardio pulmonologist or something close to that. I mean, really, how many people truly know the details of what their siblings do?

I make an adventurous move to pass a semi and restart the conversation. "Is Ally coming this weekend?"

Bailey gives one of her signature shrugs. "She offered the usual 'I'll try,' but you know what that means."

"Yeah."

I point to an upcoming road sign. "Stop for coffee?"

She glances at her watch, calculating our arrival at the estate. "Sure. On me."

It's pointless to argue, and besides, I'm too tired. I'm just happy to have Dallas in my rearview mirror and a new horizon ahead. I honestly have no idea what I'm going to do, but the only thing on my agenda this week is settling into the arms of my crazy family and remembering how to breathe.

Or at least pretend. I don't have much faith I'll ever feel light, or whole, ever again.

CHAPTER THREE

BAILEY

I CONCENTRATE on my pistachio latte and let the miles roll by, thinking about Cammie's bombshell. Shells, plural, actually.

I have so many questions, but can't get my brain to focus. Like, how could she have not known? But I'm sure she's tortured herself enough. And what about her future? Does all this stuff affect her law license? I don't have a clue how all that works.

I mean, I know Cammie's a great lawyer. And that's not just proud-sibling talk. She won Most Up-And-Coming Lawyer, or something close to that, by the Texas Young Lawyers Association. Lila and I were proudly seated at the front table to watch her accept the award. Ally would have been there, too, but she'd said that, right or wrong, she would have stolen some of Cammie's spotlight. We both loved our big sis for always being the thoughtful one.

Cammie's voice jerks me out of my reverie. "Do you want Fam One or Fam Two?"

"Huh?"

"I talked with Kiki, and she said both family suites are free until the games. I'm more than ready to watch hot Scottish guys in kilts throw heavy stuff around and eat faire food until I bust."

"You take One, and I'll take Two. If lightning strikes and Ally comes, I'm happy to share with her."

"We'll be lucky if we see her at the games, although she's promised she'll be at Lila's graduation."

I nod, recalling Lila's cartwheels when she and Zane agreed to do a set at the reception. "At least she can come as herself. She's hardly the only celebrity or government big shot who'll be there. Lila's almost immune to having Very Important People around."

"Yet she defies stereotype and stays grounded and sweet. I think she may be a mutant."

"If so, I'll take it. As for Ally, she said she'd come incognito if she had to. She wants everyone centered on Lila."

"Our much, much older sister is a good bean."

We laugh at our ancient joke. Ally is twelve months older than me, and I'm ten months older than Cam. All our lives, we've endured endless teasing that we're really triplets. Mother glacially ignores any pointed remarks. It doesn't help I contracted meningitis in sixth grade and got held back, so Cammie and I not only look more alike, but we were also in the same class through most of school.

"Enough avoiding, Bailey-Boo. What the heck is going on that you've gone from your usual sky-high levels of cortisol to meteoric?"

I frown, but try not to distract her from the road. "Seriously? I get the third degree, and we haven't even had a dip cone yet?"

"Dairy Queen can wait. I, however, cannot, and I will ask the witness to please answer the question."

"Now you're starting to sound like Lila."

"She's practicing cross-examination? I didn't know she wanted to be an attorney."

"I can't get her to tell me what she wants to be, but that's not the point. It's not your job to be worried about me, and it's *really* not hers."

"Maybe, but if you don't chill out, I'm going to toss you into one of the turrets and blockade the door until you have to escape, Rapunzel-like. Maybe by the time your hair gets that long, you'll weigh more than my feather pillow."

Equal parts love and worry flood me. I went into labor with that child during finals in college, and she's never quite gotten over her tendency to quietly go about her business and then—*BAM!*—surprise me with something and throw me completely off-kilter. She doesn't mean to. It's just she's so darned determined and diligent. Even though she looks just like me, her temperament is pure Ally, all quiet and contained. Holding everything in.

And being hella tenacious behind her still smile.

I love my baby girl, but I'm terrified she's working on an ulcer before she hits double-decades.

"There will be no tossing of anyone into the towers."

Cammie coughs. "At the moment, I could throw you with one hand. All that aside, my goal's a little more self-centered. I'm gonna make you walk every square inch of the town with me and give me an excuse to make you eat all the honey-buttered croissants Vivann can make."

Ah, Vivann's On the Square. Best soup and sandwiches in East Texas.

"Which means we can spend hours in the Emporium, or trying on boots at Henry's, or seeing what new artsy-fartsy stuff Emmett has in the gallery."

"Endless hours. We both need it."

My baby sister doesn't know the half of it, but I'm not about to unload my problems on her, not now that I've been read in on the surface of what she's been going through. Which makes a T. rex of guilt rampage through my insides. The three of us are close, but we aren't joined at the hip. Months can go by without us calling one another. We're all professionals, but to know Cammie's world utterly imploded, and she brushed it off as "just legal stuff" makes my acid reducer completely useless.

I should have sensed it, should have—

"Stop it, Boo. I mean it."

I attempt an innocent expression, but she just rolls her eyes at me. "It's just—"

"It's just you think you somehow should have known how far my life has devolved, just like I should have known you're literally disappearing."

"I promise I don't have an eating disorder."

"No, you have a stress disorder, and it manifests in you working twenty hours a day. If you grab a pack of peanut butter crackers out of the vending machine, you tell yourself you're getting protein. Now, to quote you, spill."

We're only about thirty minutes from the castle now, and the city has long given way to fields dotted with harvesters bringing in hay. It's an idyllic part of spring, when everything's in bloom, especially our beloved magnolias. We're coming up on a huge grove, the sun behind us casting them in afternoon brilliance. As if we're both longing for the reminder of better days, we roll down the windows to inhale the glorious fragrance.

The warm air gliding over my skin blows away the edges of the constant shadow of sadness woven around me. "I missed this."

"Me, too. And you're stalling."

I heave an intentionally exaggerated sigh. "I'm worried about Lila. She's so determined to go to Princeton. If those suckers don't answer her soon, I'm driving to New Jersey and shaking someone's teeth loose in the admissions office."

"No one says no to Lila. She'll get in."

Cammie's mama-bear tone lifts my heart. She might be Lila's aunt, but hoo doggy, my baby couldn't ask for more fierce champions than my sisters. Ally's just as protective, but doesn't get to see Lila as much, so Cammie takes her role with ridiculous fervor.

Amusement forms in equal parts with chiding. "We'll see. She was disappointed in Columbia, but shrugged it off." I smile to myself, realizing Lila shares Cammie's determination to keep moving forward, no matter the circumstances.

"They don't deserve her." Cammie sniffs haughtily. "You know, getting into Rice ain't chicken feed. *Forbes* ranked it ahead of Cornell, Dartmouth, and Brown."

"True, but she's lived in Houston her whole life, so she's not real keen on going to college practically in our backyard."

Cammie shoots me a give-me-a-break glare. "Like you wouldn't move to Timbuktu if she got accepted to whatever school might be there."

What? I'm not one of *those* parents. "I'm not going to be a helicopter mom—"

"Continue to be, you mean?"

"You hush." I flap a hand at my bratty sister, determined to not be a victim of her courtroom persistence, although, honestly, I don't know if Cammie is ever in a courtroom. Once Cammie gets the proverbial bit between her teeth, she doesn't let go. "I won't follow Lila to whatever school she picks, although... *fine.* I might do a little dance if she relents and accepts Rice's offer."

I throw the bone, hoping my sister will back off.

Cammie checks her mirrors, signals, and changes lanes. I note the motor home taking its sweet time and cross my fingers, throwing up a quick prayer to stifle my concern that my sister isn't getting overly ambitious with her new acquisition.

She gives me a quick glance, but thankfully returns her eyes to the road. "All of this discussion about my amazing niece is awesome, but you're deflecting. Again. So, what's up? For real now."

I don't want to sigh, again, but my lungs have other plans. "I'm just tired."

"No shit, Sherlock. Skip the patently obvious and get to the good stuff."

"Quit riding my butt. It'll all be settled pretty quickly." I recross my fingers. "I just need to get Lila situated and—"

"And then you'll be facing tuition that would make some small nations blanch."

"Yeah, but it'll be worth it."

Cammie goes so quiet I look away from picking at my cuticles and stare at her. "What?"

"Is it worth it? I mean, I know Lila's a genius, and I'm not saying that because she's my niece, but is chasing the brass ring really worth an ulcer or seven?"

Argh. She's not giving up, and my upper lip's lost the will to remain stiff.

"It's not just Lila. My life's a whirling blender of issues right now. We lost a whole set of talent at the hospital. Some of our sharpest and best broke off to form their own group, and it's adding up."

I can't keep doing the work of five people.

"Which begs the question of how you managed to get off this many days in a row. Not that Memorial Hermann can't do without you for ten consecutive seconds."

I don't want to tell her it's because I nearly made one hell of an error, and my boss said if I didn't take the vacation time, she'd fire me. The thought that I nearly harmed a patient bothers me far more, but in truth, I'm not sure I could get over the humiliation of being let go.

"I just needed some time with my baby sister, and I put my foot down."

Does it count as a lie when only the second half of that statement is pure BS?

"All right, all right. I'll get the whole story out of you tonight after we've had a bottle of Cab on the balcony." Cammie gives up with more grace than usual, and my pride's a bit stung knowing she pities me.

She's probably right, but for now, I slide my sunglasses into place, even though the glare is behind us, and try to convince my ulcers that this is all we need. Rest. Family.

And the healing power of Magnolia Bloom.

CHAPTER FOUR

ALLY

DIVING straight west means I'm in danger of wrecking the effects of my last Botox appointment. Even my killer shades from the Emporium, from my last trip to Magnolia Bloom with my sisters, can't stop me from squinting. I'm not a diva, but I'm not completely ambivalent about my looks and do what I can to mitigate damage. I wear sunscreen, I moisturize, I try to keep from frowning.

That last one has been a lost cause lately.

I know I'm driving too fast, but once the destination's set in my mind, I'm afraid my lead foot takes over. Brian used to give me a quiet headshake when I'd race down the road to his garage.

"What I want to know," he'd say, wiping the back of his neck with one of the endless supply of blue bandannas tucked in his pocket, "is how the good Lord gave someone as quiet as you such a loud gas pedal."

I'm not sure, either, but at least I've managed to keep from losing my license. Barely.

When I see Sonic listed on a sign for nearby eateries, the need for some chomping ice hits hard. After I pull into one of the slots and wait for the carhop to bring me my cherry limeade, I make the mistake of looking at my phone, then force myself to put it down when my blood pressure starts rising. I stare out the windshield, concentrating on wishing I had my cooler with me so I could buy a bag of their famous frozen pellets.

Lord knows I'll need something to work out my stress for the rest of the drive that won't risk my molars getting ground down to nubs.

Of course I cave and grab my phone again, noting screen after screen of missed calls and messages. I text Sarah that I'm fine and promise to call her later, and I do a group delete of Zane's many messages.

The arrival of my order short-circuits the urge to hurl my phone out the window and into the next county. Instead, I mute all notifications and put it back on the satellite channel that's been keeping me company.

I give the young girl a tip twice as large as my order, and she beams one of those pure Southern thank-yous. "Anything else I can get you?"

Know the name of a good divorce attorney? seems inappropriate, so I demur. "This is all I need to get home."

"Drive safe now, hear?"

Clearly, this young lady has no clue as to my vehicular reputation, so I nod and pull out, humming along as I mentally count down the remaining miles. A glance at the gas gauge reassures me I can make it to town, but I'll have no more wiggle room on stopping.

I should call Bailey and Cammie, but I can't. Not yet. Luckily, when I saw Kiki a few months back, she told me Brian's place was at my disposal, as they weren't in any hurry to reassign it. At the time, I wanted to escape to a place with zero marble in sight. Those weeks now seem like years. Back then, I was feeling a little lost after losing a man I didn't share a drop of blood with, but who felt every bit like a second dad. His passing was nearly catastrophic on my emotions, but I never imagined I'd have to get my head around my marriage publicly imploding on a sidewalk in downtown Nashville. It's like a few pieces of me didn't make it off the concrete, that somehow the flashes of those cameras stole little bits of my soul.

Zane and I have our problems, but I was embarrassingly blind to believe we were different than other couples. God, how could I have been so naïve?

I'm so wound up I almost forget to stop at Everson Auto to get gas. I'm not sure which member of the family with almost as much history as mine in Magnolia Bloom will be behind the counter, but it's another signal that I'm home. I pull up to the pump and note the juxtaposition of the modern fueling stations against the well-tended but weathered building all but shouting *small town*. Each time I return, part of me feels I've outgrown the place, and another believes there's a level of calm and care in this tiny corner of Texas that I need. The little sign tacked to the pole reading "Press here for full service" and pointing to a red button pretty much says it all.

I'm more than capable of pumping my own gas, even if I haven't done it in a while, and start fueling before I head inside.

Hyped up from too much limeade, I go for broke on poor calorie choices and grab a bag of Gardetto's Special Request garlic rye chips, a PayDay, and a bag of Munchies Flamin' Hot peanuts. I'll have to stop by the pharmacy, as I'll need the basics of skin and hair care, so I add antacids to my list. Groceries can wait until tomorrow, and a quick dash into the dollar store will cover undies, sweats, and cheap tennies. I won't need much else, and if I do, I'll hit the Emporium for something cute.

Although why and for whom I'd want to be cute, I don't know…

Which makes me grunt in frustration that those won't-take-but-a-second errands will require a visit to the bank at some point. Turns out one simple fill-up shows a hundred-dollar bill doesn't go very far these days. It won't take Zane long to figure out where I am, but thanks to my account at the Magnolia Bank and Trust, I don't have to worry about a debit-card trail showing up on our joint account.

I'm still writing a mental shopping list when I reach the counter and stop short. The reason for my race into the sunset with nothing but the clothes on my back glares at me from a flat-screen television.

Great. The latest breaking story is me and the disastrous did-you-know-about-the-affair? sidewalk bomb from this morning. There are many things country music fandom doesn't believe about me, and one is that I despise watching myself on television or film. I can change a channel at light speed, but I don't control the remote today.

"... music star Ally King was met with a shock this morning outside her exclusive Nashville condo. Country fans haven't been shy about their opinions on the matter."

The camera cuts to a young woman with dubious taste in makeup leaning too close to the microphone being held toward her. "I'm not surprised. I was telling my friend Katrina, like, you know, who could blame Zane? Ally is such a snob, I bet he just couldn't take it anymore. She thinks she's so much better than him..."

It takes the man behind the counter about two seconds to recognize me, and he mutes the sound, but that doesn't stop the closed captioning from revealing a series of quick cuts from other man-on-the-street interviews, the general consensus being Zane is some kind of saint, and I'm the stone-cold bitch who drove him into the arms of another woman.

"Hey, you're—"

"Yeah, but let's keep it a secret between us, if you wouldn't mind. I'd really appreciate it."

"No problem, Mrs. King—"

"Just Alyssa, please. And you are?"

"Jerome Everson, but everyone calls me JJ."

He's tall and slender, maybe all of twenty years old, his skin rich and dark, and he has those amazing gray-green eyes like Traycee's. She's the Everson I know the best, as I'm an ardent customer at her store when I'm home.

"It's good to meet you, JJ."

"I hope I don't sound like a crazy person telling you you're my dad's favorite singer. I'm sure you get that a lot."

"Not yours?" I tease.

"I'm more of a dubstep guy right now, but your stuff is great, for country."

I bark a laugh, appreciating his kindness as well as his honesty, but anything related to music feels like a stab. I know I'll get over it, but that moment is far in the future. "It might surprise you to know I listen to a bit of dubstep when I'm playing Beat Saber."

His face lights up, and I can see I've inched away from *old lady* in his eyes.

"Cool! Oculus or PlayStation?"

"Oculus. The new Quest 2 games are pretty sweet."

"Right on!"

"I should get going, but it was great to meet you, JJ. Tell your family hi for me."

"I will." JJ looks toward the cash register, then nods toward the television. "I'm sorry to hear about… you know."

Boy, do I know.

"It's been a heck of a day. I'm just anxious to get away for a bit."

"Nothing like coming home when your heart's hurting."

I shrug a shoulder. "I'm still a bit numb, but this seems like the place to be. I'm hoping I can have a few days with the illusion of invisibility, even though I know it won't last."

"Your secret's safe with me, but you're a MacInnes. You know the Grannies probably already have their binoculars focused on you."

I'm thankful for the unexpected touch of humor. "Indeed, and since your Grannie is the squadron commander, I'm guessing you'll be making a phone call when I leave."

His expression is sheepish, but he doesn't deny it. "She'll have my hide if I don't."

"Don't worry about it. It's not like I can disappear from public life for long. I may have hated not being able to get away with anything as a teenager with the Grannies being the neighborhood watch on steroids, but I have to confess them circling the wagons for me doesn't make me sad."

"Magnolia Bloom takes care of its own."

It does. And deep down, my internal compass knows it. Which is why I'm here. This town is magical, and even with a few warts, it's an amazing place to live. It was certainly a great place to grow up.

The bell dings, announcing another customer's arrival, so JJ takes my money and hands me my change as a tall woman comes in. An itch of recognition starts at the base of my brain. I glance at the TV before I look her way, grateful the story has changed to some other poor person under the paparazzi microscope.

JJ raises a hand. "Hey, Diana. Welcome back."

"Good to be back."

My head jerks to the woman's face as she looks up from her phone, and our eyes meet.

Time slows to a stop and shifts into reverse, and for a second, I'm at lunch in sixth grade. My memory may be faulty, but I think it was exactly this time of year, not long until school let out for summer, and I see a girl at the table the farthest from the door in the outside picnic area. She's tall, doing that hunched-shoulder thing trying to appear smaller, even though she's sitting down. Her nose is buried in a book, and a brown bag sits untouched at her elbow.

I usually take my tray to the choir-and-drama-geek table, but for some reason, I keep moving and stop by the edge of the otherwise empty space.

"Can I sit here?"

Diana looks up at me, trying to hide shock and disbelief, but then she nods, and I slip into the seat opposite her. I open my orange juice as if we do this every day. I comment on her book, saying I love *The Handmaid's Tale*, and she says her mother told her she's too young to read it, and I say I'm not supposed to read *The Godfather*, either, but guess what? Then we talk nonstop for the rest of the break and become best friends.

We stay that way through our first two years of college. She's maid of honor at my wedding. Then I go on the road with Zane, and we lose touch.

It hits me like a punch to the solar plexus from a prizefighter as her eyes widen, and her hands drop awkwardly to her sides. Time has been exceedingly kind to my friend, who seems to have overcome teenage acne and now embraces her naturally wavy, raven hair. Her makeup is understated but beautifully applied, and for the first time, I feel like the awkward one in our friendship.

"Hey." My brilliant opener comes out soft.

"Hey."

We stand there for a long, awkward moment and then fall into a hug that erases time and distance.

Diana swings her hair off her shoulder in a gesture that makes me smile. I'm not sure what's happened to her since we last saw each other, but it appears good. "I've missed you."

The low, choked up voice is all I need to break, too. "Ditto. You in town for a visit, too?"

She shakes her head. "I came back five years ago. I'm the head librarian."

I give her a playful punch on the arm. "Look at you plowing through stereotypes. I bet with you at the checkout desk, applications for library cards have blown through the roof, all male, of course."

She gives me a raised eyebrow. "Why all male, necessarily?"

Then she grins, and I give her a hell-yeah nod.

"The harsh truth is, the only reason membership is up is because I pushed for a new computer lab, but whatever gets bodies through the door is good with me." An awkward silence descends after she glances at the television screen and then back at me. "Are you okay?"

I wonder why people always ask that, when, on what planet, would someone be okay right now? "No, but being with my sisters will make things better."

"Uh oh, the Terrible Trio rides again?"

"For a short while at least."

"Can I claim some time on your dance card while you're here? I'd love to catch up."

A little sliver of the ice encasing my insides chips off. "I'd like that."

We trade phone numbers and goodbyes. I wave to JJ as I head out, feeling slightly lighter as I take the nozzle from the gas tank and close everything up. BB purrs to life like a good girl, and I head on toward my destination. Coincidentally, my path takes me by the five stories of

Gothic beauty on the edge of downtown that seems more suited to being a city capital than a mere library. We have our matriarch to thank for both the design and the monument to knowledge. Evajean MacInnes was nothing if not obsessed with books and architecture, and now I can add my thanks for reigniting an old friendship to all I owe her.

I put my mental wanderings aside and glance at my phone for the time. I have no regrets over the minutes I spent chatting with Diana, but I have to hurry to get to the bank before it closes.

"Thank you, Daddy." There's no one to hear my whisper, but that's all right. Daddy know. He'd opened an account for each of us girls when we were still teenagers, a man ahead of his time who believed a woman should have a safety net. My dad may not be a scion of feminist activism, but he has a few issues he's fierce about, and he made us swear we'd never reveal our secret accounts to anyone.

I decide I'll tell Daddy my appreciation in person later. For now, I can be holed up at Brian's before sunset. Considering that's around nine o'clock these days, I'm in good shape.

With my plan in place, I head Beauty straight toward downtown.

CHAPTER FIVE

BAILEY

CAMMIE and I reach the stage where we've talked ourselves out and are now playing the grownup version of the quiet game. We reminisced, discussed Lila's college prospects and our mostly illegal plans if anyone breaks her heart, and mused about the upcoming games. We've both missed far too many of the annual event, but Cammie's determined I'm going to eat my weight in kettle corn and turkey legs. I'm not opposed to this plan.

As we hit downtown, I see Cammie glare at the dashboard, and her lips compress. Luckily, we're close enough we can make it to the city center with a minimal hike if it's anything catastrophic.

"What's up?" I keep my tone light.

"Just calculating how many miles we've driven. I think we can do all our errands and make it to the estate before I have to add one of the quarts of 10W-30 stashed in the trunk."

"It won't take me but a sec at Palmer's Drugs, and I'll meet you at the bank. That's the plan, right?"

"Thank goodness your memory hasn't disappeared along with your hips, butt, and bust."

I don't bother with a rejoinder as she pulls to a squeaky-braked stop. I unhinge myself and get out, trying not to groan from the stiffness that settled into my lower back somewhere after we hit Highway 77.

I slam the door shut with more force than might technically be necessary and add ibuprofen to my mental list. I love my sister, but she can tap-dance on my last nerve like no one else. Then again, if I hadn't been so distracted trying to get out the door for my flight and left my makeup bag containing my medicine on the kitchen table, this would be moot.

Palmer's Drugs hasn't changed a bit, except for maybe the surprise of faux-wood planking replacing the industrial carpet and the previous incandescent lights being upgraded to fluorescent. Otherwise, I take a nostalgic trip down the snack aisle, ridiculously gratified that the rusty chest-style freezer is still stocked with Push-Ups and Crunch ice cream bars.

On the way out, I'll buy one of each and stuff them down until I get brain freeze.

It takes about ten seconds to get the things I need, including a tube of mascara, a cheap blush, and some lip gloss. Even though I should hurry, I can't stop wandering the aisles, thinking that only in a small town can you buy tea towels to embroider at the local drugstore.

"As I live and breathe, if it isn't the famous Bailey Anne MacInnes, head of pulmonary arterial hypertension at the vaunted Memorial Hermann Heart and Vascular Institute."

I turn, warmth and amusement spreading from my heart all the way across my face. "Doc, that's a whole lot of words for a girl with bunions from doing plain ol' rounds. You're giving me a tad too much shine there, and you know it."

"Only a matter of time."

I step into the hug of the man whose letter of recommendation is largely responsible for me getting into med school and eventually having my white-coat ceremony. His barrel chest feels like home, the smell of pipe tobacco Mrs. Doc harangues him about lingering on his plaid flannel shirt. His long, corded-muscle arms seem more suited to pulling an engine than giving babies their shots or doing a solid week of physicals before the start of the religious holidays known as Friday night high school football. He kisses the top of my head, which says a lot since I'm five-ten.

"Girl, you're gonna blow away in a stiff breeze." He peers into my shopping basket. "If I can perform a diagnosis based on what you're buying, you need to see a gastroenterologist."

"I might." Truth. "I'm fine." Lie, or at least a stretch of the truth, but I don't have time to worry about situational ethics, and I don't have the energy to fend off another wave of well-intentioned but exhausting concern.

Doc might be known around here as a small-town doctor, but in the halls of Columbia Medical School, he's the professor who never has an empty seat in his classes when he guest-lectures. His confident, shoulders-back posture inspired by his years in the Navy combined with his rugged good looks were part and parcel of his sharp-witted and ruthlessly intelligent presentations. To those eager students, he might have been Dr. Carter, but to me, he'll always be just Doc—eagle-eyed and missing nothing.

I'm saved from any additional half-truths when a man comes toward us, talking on his cell phone.

"Yes, Uncle Lem, I promise. I'll get the real aspirin, no fake stuff."

I can't see any more as Doc throws himself in front of me, but I'm assuming the dark-headed man pulls up short, because there's no evidence of a collision. That's just an assumption, as the only thing in my field of vision is red plaid flannel.

"Oh, shi—uh, sorry, Doc."

"Jake, you trying out for defensive lineman and haven't told me?"

I'm revealed from behind my savior's back as Doc returns to my side, and I find my irritation dissipating as I wait for an introduction. Mostly because this Jake's cheeks are a delightful shade of pink, and he looks sweetly chagrined.

Doc gestures toward me. "Jake, do you remember Bailey MacInnes?"

He offers his hand, but shakes his head. "I don't think we've met. I'm Jake Broder."

I accept the warm clasp of his fingers around mine. "I don't think so, either. It's a pleasure."

Doc is clearly calculating ages in his head before he finally nods. "Sorry. Jake's a few years behind you, and he's been gone a long time, building skyscrapers in the big city. The older I get, the more the same age all you young'uns become."

Jake and I share an eye roll at Doc's ancient-and-decrepit shtick. He's seventy-six and still going gangbusters, but we let him have his small-town-doctor, paid-in-chickens routine. Unfortunately, the way he said *a few years behind you* all of a sudden makes me feel cougary. Which then makes *me* feel ancient and decrepit, because I haven't had a lascivious thought about a man in so long the only reason I know my lady bits still function is my gynecologist tells me everything's working fine. And my southern hemisphere decides now to get tingly at the dark, warm, and yummy eyes Jake Broder has trained on me?

I thank all the celestial beings I can name that Doc appears unaware of my bizarre physical response to a complete stranger. In fact, he frowns and turns to the unexpected lust-producer who's still smiling at me, although Doc's expression is morphing into a bit confused.

"Jake, I've got your uncle on a blood thinner. You can't give him NSAIDs."

"I know, Doc. I was going to ask the pharmacist, but I'm glad I ran into you, although I hadn't planned for it to be literal. I'll get whatever you say and buy a bottle of the brand he likes, then switch them out and hope he won't notice."

Doc's expression firms, but there's sadness in it. "I understand your motivation, but that could be dangerous. If something happens and someone besides me treats him, what's in his medicine bottles has to be accurate."

"Maybe if I tell him it's what I take, he'll go for it."

"It's worth a try." Doc turns and looks at me. "Lemuel Broder is Jake's hardheaded great-uncle and my best friend... who doesn't always remember me these days. Jake's doing a fine job taking care of him these last few months, though, I'm grateful as hell to say."

"I'm so sorry to hear that." I feel a blush heat my cheeks. "I mean, I'm sorry to hear about the memory issues."

Jake's mouth is tight, but I know the reaction isn't directed at me. "Lem's always been... unique, but this all happened so fast."

A series of questions queue up in my head, but I keep them there. Doc's a fine physician, so he doesn't need the pipsqueak he helped get into medical school second-guessing his diagnostic skills. Needing to extract myself and meet Cammie at the bank, I step back.

"I'll get out of y'all's way. It was a pleasure to meet you, Jake, and, Doc, I'll—"

"Wait a sec, Bailey." Doc holds up a hand. "I have an idea, if you're willing."

Oh no. Please, no. *Time off* means *Time. Off.* I haven't been in town thirty whole minutes.

"Sure." I look around. Yup, that was my voice. Clearly my mouth is moving in spite of my brain.

For his part, Jake appears confused.

"I'll discuss more details if you're on board, but the short story is this: Lem's a stubborn cuss, and he started acting a little off about six months ago."

Jake makes a so-so gesture with his hand. "For Uncle Lem, acting off isn't always an easy thing to gauge. I love him, but he's been a recluse for so long, he's... forgotten some social graces."

Doc's eyes are sad. "I don't know what I did, but he got his dander up about me and won't let me come check on him. He's still sharp most of the time, so Jake doesn't have any grounds to step in on a legal front, and besides, the last thing Jake or I want is to take away his autonomy. But I'm thinking that if you went out with Jake and checked on him, he might be more amenable to coming in and getting some tests run. Hell, even if you have to take him over to Atlanta, that'd be fine."

"Doc, I don't have privileges anywhere in Atlanta, and my

specialty is PH, not dementia. Heck, I don't even have a stethoscope with me."

"Come by the clinic, and I'll loan you one, and I've got friends in Atlanta, Texarkana, and Dallas if we can just get his butt to any of the above. I'm thinking maybe this could be oxygen loss due to PH and not dementia at all. I mean, we know he has regular hypertension, but it's not severe. Yet." He runs an agitated hand over what's left of his short, gray hair. "I can't get close enough to him to get a good look. He wouldn't even let me check his feet for edema, so maybe he'd tell you if he's taking his vitamins and prescriptions, and you could charm him into revealing an ankle."

"Look, I appreciate the vote of confidence, but—"

Jake takes a half step closer to me, and I try not to see the pleading in his eyes. "Please, Dr. MacInnes—"

"Bailey, please."

"Bailey, then. I know we've just met, and it's really awkward of me to impose, but I'm worried about him."

Argh! Any of the possible answers, good or bad, are time-sensitive. I try to sigh silently. "All right. Cammie's waiting for me, so I really do have to go. Have Doc give you my number, and we'll make a plan to see if I can help."

Relief floods the melted-dark-chocolate eyes framed by ridiculously long lashes. I'd bet good money he could be a Hollywood leading man if he were so inclined.

As clearly as if he'd been freezing and I'd poured warm water over him, his shoulders relax. "Thank you. I really appreciate this."

I nod at the two of them and head for the front checkout. The two men continue talking as I hurry away, only to realize the relief I drained from Jake has transferred right onto me.

CHAPTER SIX

CAMMIE

I HOLD the door for the little old lady exiting the lobby of the Magnolia Bloom Bank and Trust, head inside, and step back in time. The décor isn't excessively outdated, although the desks are huge and dark wood, the offices have real doors, and there isn't an inch of chrome in sight. No Plexiglas divides the three teller stations, but there's only one person waiting expectantly behind the long counter. The walls are polished paneling, the grain beautifully preserved and beeswaxed to a glossy shine. It's all exactly as I remember from when Daddy brought us three girls in to open individual accounts and receive a lecture on compound interest.

It's more an energy, a feeling that the esteemed Dean Whitson—descended from our matriarch's side of the family—is probably sitting behind the door marked President. Evajean's father established the first bank in this town, and a Whitson has been in charge of the branch ever since. I'll bet what little money I have he still wears three-piece suits and has the same wire-framed glasses from twenty years ago. If he comes out, he'll pat my shoulder, call me darlin', and ask me how things are over in the big city. Hopefully, Mr. Whitson has already gone home for the day so I won't have to face that question.

"Welcome to Magnolia Bloom Bank and Trust. How can we help you today?"

A young woman in a high-necked white blouse and a name tag that says Lanie Whitson smiles at me from behind the counter. Daughter, granddaughter, or niece, I'm sure. While not generally abused, there's lots of nepotism in Magnolia Bloom. That's a stone we MacInneses can't throw.

"Hi, Lanie. Just here to make a deposit."

"That's wonderful. I'd be happy to help you."

If Lanie's surprised to be handed a thick envelope of cash, which she has no idea represents a sum far less than what a Cartier Tank Française is worth, she hides it with a professionally bland expression.

She checks my driver's license and looks from the card to me. "Please forgive me for not recognizing you. I know most MacInneses around here." She clears her throat softly. "And I'm sorry about your husband."

I shouldn't feel insulted, but I know that busybody tone. "No need to be sorry. They just kicked me out of Dallas because my hair's not big enough."

Lanie laughs at the old joke and lifts a hand to check her teased bouffant. "Higher the hair, the closer to God, darlin'."

I'm grateful she taps a few keys and turns away to put the bills into a high-speed counter. Or rather, I'm happy the financial transaction's nearly over as I have the sudden need to tear out of the bank, find the nearest gym, and take out my frustrations on a punching bag with a series of roundhouse kicks.

"Here you go." She tears a piece of paper from the thermal printer, and I glance at the total available.

Huh… Daddy's right. Compound interest is a helluva thing. The slightly smeared line isn't Big Johnnie Dallas money, but it'll keep me from parking the Corolla in a pasture and turning it into an RV.

"Thanks." I skip the pleasantries and head for the doors, slowing when they open. A slightly older version of my date to the junior high

Sadie Hawkins Dance enters with an eye-pleasing, lean-physique confidence, and parts of me I thought had died with Johnnie take notice.

"Trey Greene." The inside of the bank is so quiet, I don't need to raise my voice.

He looks up, the hello-old-friend expression creasing his face easing the vise grip of sadness and anger around my heart.

"Cameron MacInnes."

He's one of the few people who calls me Cameron. Always Cameron. As if calling me Cammie would make him like all the regular people in my life, and we both know he's always had a special place.

Trey didn't want to be regular when we were kids, and I'm assuming the trait hasn't changed. There's hunger in him I've always understood. The difference between us is he stayed, and I got the hell out of Dodge before the ink was dry on my diploma.

Still, he whispered my name under the bleachers or in the shadows of the many illegal bonfires we had by the lake in high school. I barely resisted his quiet charm then, but in these few seconds of setting eyes on him, I remember the calm he exuded—and the wildness. There's a little devil behind the gentlemanly face that has become ridiculously handsome since I left for college and never looked back.

I don't regret my time with Johnnie. I don't need a psych eval to understand why I was drawn to a man two decades my senior. I was the stereotypical wild child, and while he was big and bold and brash, there'd been a stone-solid center to Big Johnnie Dallas.

I loved him with all my heart.

But seeing Trey wiggles something to life in the still-shut-down parts of me. I step into his open arms without a second's hesitation, resting my head against his soft gray golf shirt and breathing in his signature spritz of Polo cologne. The grassy, spicy scent isn't fancy. It isn't expensive or pretentious. It's pure Trey.

"How the hell are ya? Home for a Terrible Trio weekend?"

His voice rumbles in my ear, deep and melty and evoking memories of bad jokes and sarcastic asides in home room that made me laugh, or more accurately, snort indelicately and loudly. Like the time I threw my pen at him and hit him on the cheek, not hurting him, but the thing popped, and ink dripped down his face and onto his white shirt like a demented artist had flicked a brush full of blue paint in his direction.

Somehow, I was the only one who ended up in the principal's office for the disruption. He mastered the innocent face and winked as I was escorted out of class.

I get control of my expression before we break apart and he can see my face again.

Swallowing around a sudden lump in my throat, I step back. "I might stick around a little while. Maybe we can get lunch and catch up?" Of course, I'll be too busy when he calls, which I guarantee he will. Even so, it's the right thing to say. I might not be able to buy much more than two-for-one tuna right now, but Mrs. Greene always said manners are free. Eunice Greene might be Trey's grandmother, but she's second-in-command of the Grannies and head cook at the castle, so she's part mine, too.

I'm not afraid Trey will judge me when I dodge him. Attorney or not, that's never been his nature. I'm much more terrified I'll see pity in those gorgeous brown eyes. That would destroy what little hold I have left on my crumbling inner scaffolding.

"What's wrong with right now? If you'll give me two minutes, we can get to jaw-jacking before our shadows hit full length."

I know for certain this aw-shucks, good-ol'-boy business is way overdone. Trey has a just-perfect-Texan accent, but I've never known him to fall down the hick well.

I'm saved from weaseling out when Bailey sweeps through the doors, coming to an almost comical halt when she sees who I'm talking to.

She pulls a full Bailey-watt smile and punches his bicep. "Greene Bean? Dang, dude, you've been working out."

I roll my eyes and shoot her a dirty look. "You'll have to forgive my sister. She's overdosed on simethicone and isn't in her right mind."

Bailey doesn't cut me any slack. "Be impressed my sister's playing doctor instead of me, but seriously, how are you?"

"Busier than last call at the Magnolia Moon, but it keeps me out of trouble."

"Your grandmother still clogging arteries but sending people to the big restaurant in the sky with a satisfied grin on their face?"

His chuckle is a ripple of perfect to my ears. "She's actually been binge-watching this cable cooking show, and she says she's gonna re-write all her recipes to be heart healthy. On top of that, she started lifting weights at Quinton Everson's gym."

I perk up at the mention of a place to work out, as I dearly need to indulge in some iron therapy. "Isn't your grandmother—"

"Eighty-eight, yes. Or is it eighty-nine? Regardless, she read this article about a lady her age who's winning bodybuilding competitions, so she's decided she wants to, and I quote, 'take her down.'"

I laugh, but the sound is equal parts surprised and impressed. "We all know where your mom and Fina get their gumption. Good for Eunice."

Trey's impressively broad shoulders slump. "Yeah, except she's started talking smack down at the gym, and Quinton called to ask if he needed to worry about a corporate takeover. Why couldn't she pick yoga or Jazzercise or something? I'm afraid she's gonna one-rep-max me in front of half the town."

There's nothing ladylike in my snort, but then, that's my curse... as my family never wastes a chance to remind me. "You obviously failed theater, because you're so proud you're gonna bust outa that shirt."

Not that I'm noticing to the point I'm in danger of drooling.

"Just promise you won't tell her."

"Scout's honor." I hold up two fingers. "Listen, Boo and I have to get to the market and grab groceries before we head to the castle. It was great to see you."

Bailey's glare at my public use of her nickname earns her a paybacks-are-a-bitch grin.

"Good to see you both." Trey's eyes stay on me. "I'm going to hold you to lunch, though."

Of course he is.

"Sounds great," I lie.

But it's also not a lie. I'd love to see him, reminisce. I just don't want him to know what a screw-up I am, at least for a while. I'm sure the story about my late husband will follow me through the grapevine, if it hasn't already.

The halo of concern showed toward me didn't last long after Johnnie shuffled off this mortal coil, as evidenced by the fact that cards and calls and flowers were followed quickly by silence. As I expected and welcomed, people went on about their lives and didn't give me a passing thought. I was too busy to notice since I was being blindsided by the wave after wave of claims by creditors that came within milliseconds of me filing the Application for Probate. Fortunately, only the estate attorney and I cared about any of it. Well, the two of us and the numerous claimants metaphorically standing in front of me with their hands out.

Houses and cars and boats and vacation properties get sold all the time when someone dies. Widows who aren't law partners have to find new jobs every day. Point being, I cleaned up every bit of the mess of Johnnie Dallas's financial empire illusion so nothing salacious got out. Johnnie deserved that, even if I am still mad at him.

But Trey doesn't need to know any of those details. And the easiest way to keep him from knowing is to just stay away.

CHAPTER SEVEN

ALLY

THERE'S ONLY a beat-up Toyota and a new Ford pickup in the bank parking lot, which means there's not a huge crowd inside. Not that there's ever a huge crowd anywhere in Magnolia Bloom, except during the week of the games, which I realize is less than a month away.

I've missed so many over my lifetime, but I'm going to put on a floppy hat and sunglasses and attend this year, blending into the barrage of folks who want to put on five pounds from turkey legs and kettle corn and stare at ridiculously strong men heaving hammers and tossing cabers. My stomach clenches in a good way in anticipation of the family tradition going back generations... and of just being home.

I park and hop out, *oofing* as my hips remind me I've been driving nonstop for hours, but my stride returns to normal by the time I breeze inside, only to jerk to a top at the little gathering in the entry area. I note my sisters in a millisecond, but it takes another blink before the identity of the tall, handsome man clicks into place. Trey Greene sure has come a long way from beanpole high school nerd, although the only sure conclusion I make is he's conquered macros and bench presses.

"Do I have to buy a ticket to this reunion?" I'd happily pay top dollar for a backstage pass just to stare at Cammie's hand on Trey's tanned arm.

Cammie's squeal at my voice lifts my spirits, and Bailey's arms wrapping around me is like a dip of warm chocolate over an ice cream cone.

Trey steps back, waiting until I'm freed from the welcome trap of my sisters to offer his hand.

"Ally, it's good to see you."

"You, too, but I guess I don't get to call you Greene Bean anymore."

His blush is delightful, but in his Trey-like way, he turns it into an endearing, self-deprecating smirk. "For several hundred dollars a month and Quinton Everson's ruthless workouts, you, too, can build muscles you never knew you had while trying not to cry like a baby as you beg for mercy."

We all laugh, but I answer. "I should sign up tomorrow, but I need to catch up with these two hooligans first."

"Let me know when you're ready. It's always good for my ego to bring someone to the gym who gives me the illusion my hard work is paying off."

"I'll be happy to help as soon as I can."

I always liked Trey. Even as a kid, he was deep and quiet, a still-water kind of guy, even though he hid it behind a sharp wit and keen intellect. I catch Cammie giving his pecs and biceps a last once-over, noting I'm not the only one who's made note of his transformation.

And I'm going to tease the hell out of her about it.

Trey extracts himself with goodbyes all around, but his eyes stay a few seconds longer on Cammie, and he didn't extend a future lunch date to the elder MacInneses standing right there.

I hurry to the counter to complete my withdrawal, ignoring the curiosity written all over Lanie Whitson's face, and we leave the bank.

Cammie hauls me in for another hug. "I thought you weren't coming?"

This confirms my suspicion she and Bailey are unaware of the predicament I definitely don't want to talk about it in a parking lot. "Change of plans. I thought you'd be happy."

"I'm ecstatic. Just surprised."

I'm happy my deflection skills still work.

We make a quick plan for them to head for the market to get provisions while I use my infusion of nontraceable cash to head to the discount store for the basics to see me through until more serious shopping ensues. I'm good with maintaining my everything's-fine illusion for a few minutes longer.

It's barely an hour later when I pass under the massive MacInnes arch, thankful the gate is open and not the tiniest bit ashamed of the tear leaking down my cheek. There isn't enough breeze to stir more than a ripple from the giant Texas flag hanging off to the left of the castle front, but that's all right. I have plenty of memories of the pride-inducing five-pointed lone star on a field of blue, flanked by red and white stripes. I park in the back lot by the kitchen door, disappointed Eunice isn't at the stove, as that image is the first thing that pops into my mind when I come home. It's my sign from above that everything's going to be all right.

While I don't get to see Eunice, I swipe a homemade cookie from the jar, and in short order, the ABCs are on the east balcony, each in a cast-iron rocker where generations of MacInnes butts have rested when in need of a family confab.

Bailey caves first. "Holy cow, I needed this."

Cammie turns her gorgeous blues on me. "What she needs is an IV filled with butter and a three-month nap."

To her credit, Bailey refrains from throwing something from our hastily prepared but still delicious charcuterie board. That would have been a tragic waste of a gargantuan olive, which I have to admit Bailey needs to eat.

"I need to hire four new doctors so I don't have to do the work of five people." Bailey stares Cammie down and makes a show of shoving two cubes of cheddar in her mouth.

As I'm sitting between them, admiring Cammie's talent for serving up sarcasm, I can't deny Bailey holds her own at returning fire, skills they honed in their middle school catfights. "I've obviously missed something. Catch me up."

"Our youngest sister's under the impression I don't eat, don't sleep, and an alien has taken up residence in my translucent body." Bailey lifts a brow at Cammie. "Tell Ally about your new car."

Cammie's fire dims, but she cuts Bailey an I'm-coming-for-you glare. "Let's stop with the verbal dodgeball. The short version is Johnnie had debts when he died, and I had to sell most of what we had to cover them. I'm broke, but fine, and I've got a ton of earning potential. You all do remember who's got the sharpest legal mind on this balcony, right?"

My sister and her nonstick defensive armor. Cammie sells one helluva everything's-peachy story, but I didn't buy it in the past, and I don't buy it now.

These moments are the ones making me glad I've got a top-notch investment team. "How much do you need?"

Cammie pushes up from her seat, her fire blazing anew. "I need your support, not your money. Don't push me, Al. I've worked my ass off to get through this, and I came here to move on from being the poor widow of Big Johnnie Dallas."

"And I came here to eat ice cream and funnel cake and not take a buncha lip from my sisters." Bailey crunches a gherkin, doing her best cow-chewing-the-cud impression. "So with Cammie looking to rebuild and me chasing a spike in my cholesterol, why, exactly, are you here out of the blue?"

I almost go with the I-needed-a-break deflection, but it's only a matter of time, likely minutes, until the scandal makes its way to the castle.

I go to spill it all, but bite my lips, wondering how to tell my two highly accomplished sisters that my life's become a tawdry mess. "Basically, Zane decided our publicist is more alluring than I am, and while I'm not sure I can refute that, I just wish he'd divorced me first and then moved on to greener pastures."

My attention shifts between my two speechless sisters.

"He cheated on you?" Cammie's legal mind takes off like a greyhound after the fake bunny.

Bailey picks up a carrot and tosses it back on the tray. "Wow. I liked Zane, even had the crazy notion I knew him, but I guess people aren't always what they seem. They also make mistakes. What do you plan to do?"

"Screwing our publicist wasn't a mistake. It was a choice, and one that I've always been really clear would render our relationship dead." The anger I put a lid on froths through the cracks. "Our marriage wasn't perfect, and the last eighteen months have been... terrible." I swallow against the knot trying to block my throat. "When Zane bought into a NASCAR team a few month's back, and I was relieved he had a shiny new toy. He loves everything about racing. The noise, the crowds, the adulation."

Bailey picks up a sliver of brie, using it as a pointer. "And you'd rather walk through a trough of Legos blindfolded and barefoot."

"Pretty much. But I should have—"

Cammie's hand slices through the air. "Do *not* defend him. We can state for the record that you aren't perfect, but now's the time to roast the stupidest living man on earth."

"Hear, hear." Bailey raises her glass.

I'm choked up at my sisters' instantaneous rally and support. I expected it, but the cargo straps cinched tight around my heart loosen a bit. I'm not quite sure how, in thirty minutes, I go from bound in eight hundred knots to stretched back in a rocker, my feet up, and a glimpse of peace trying to nip at the edges of the ropes hogtying my guts. I haven't watched a sunrise from this balcony in far too long, but the sun setting on the other side of the castle is almost as good. Sunsets over Lake Maggie are gorgeous, regardless of the vantage point, especially to a hurting heart.

I guess that's why I can breathe in Magnolia Bloom. Here, I'm no one special. Or, from a different perspective, I'm very special. I'm one of generations of MacInneses who benefit from an endless stream of love and acceptance and grit and determination.

"I'm not ready to talk about him. Not yet. I just wish I got to do this in anonymity like most people."

Cammie winces. "Yeah, that won't happen."

"I'm not a hypocrite. I've benefitted greatly from fame."

"And borne the accompanying burden, too." Bailey stands and takes the second bottle of wine from the center of the table, expertly removing the cork. Through the years, I've been grateful for the beauty and joy of Castle MacInnes, but tonight, I'm thankful for the wine cellar.

Cammie takes up the thread while Bailey pours. "The more you're a public figure, the less people think you're human, that you're immune to having your feelings bruised and battered. Somehow, you don't deserve common courtesy and kindness, and what people say doesn't affect you. But we know you. The higher you climb, the more you second-guess yourself."

"It's more accurate that the higher you climb, the less honest people are with you. I—"

Bailey stops midpour and frowns. "We're honest with you."

"True." I take my glass and indulge in a long, slow swallow of Cabernet. I'm usually a merlot girl 'cause I love me some tannins, but this one checks all my boxes. Rich, woody, silky finish. It's my second glass, and I'm relaxing ever so slightly, which is why the next bit slips. "I should have been honest with myself a long time ago."

"What do you mean?" Cammie sits forward, and I see why she's so good at what she does. In addition to her sharp legal mind, she cares. She's always cared and gives her all. For her clients. For her firm. For her husband. And even though all that's now gone and she's lost everything, she's still right here, caring about me.

"I'm a singer-songwriter married to a guy who wants to be a country-pop crossover. At my roots, I'm Ford, and he's Ferrari. I'd be fine in a fifth wheel, but he needs a marble mansion." I look between them, deciding to air my dream to the two people who won't look at me like I've lost my mind. "I want to write ballads again, just play my guitar for crowds of ten, not ten thousand, and I won't be with someone who doesn't support me to the same degree I support him."

Bailey's brows climb toward the dusk-shadowed sky. "Okay!"

Cammie raises her glass. "About time."

My nerves are shot, and I stand to excuse myself, but Cammie draws us together in a circle.

Bailey, not known as being the cuddliest of creatures, plants a kiss on my temple. "Whatever happens, you know Cam and I have your back."

"And if you want his bank account to be millions lighter, I know some people," Cammie teases, but I realize there's more truth than humor in her pledge to help me.

We raise our glasses, but most of all, I feel the rise of something much stronger: family. Sisters. Who have each other tonight and always.

Cammie smirks. "I've got a toast."

"Here we go," Bailey mutters and sneaks a quick sip.

"Here's to the ABCs. We may annoy the hell out of each other, but anyone messes with you, and they'll find out just how crazy a MacInnes can be."

"Amen, Sister," Bailey and I echo together.

We drink, then hook our pinkies and press our foreheads into a triangle. Love for my siblings nearly overwhelms me, but I stay silent, mostly because if I say another word, I'll completely fall apart.

CHAPTER EIGHT

BAILEY

THE ONLY REASON I don't throw my phone across the room when my old-school ringtone jars me into consciousness is because I don't want the hassle of replacing it. Shielding my eyes against the sunshine trying to sear my eyeballs, I grab the device that never sleeps and swipe blindly at the screen.

"Dr. MacInnes, how can I help—I mean… hello?"

"Bailey? It's Jake Broder. From the pharmacy?"

My eyes are wide open now, as I do indeed remember Mr. Tall, Dark, and Concerned. I'm a sucker for kindness, and Jake has it in spades for his uncle. I guess *great-uncle* is more accurate, but my few functioning brain cells aren't caffeinated enough to parse that level of detail.

"Hi, Jake. Yes, I remember. How are you?" *And why are you calling me at this insane hour?*

I squint at the clock. I guess nine thirty doesn't exactly qualify as insane, even on a vacation day.

"Did I catch you at a bad time? Should I call back?"

My overcompensation genes flare, and exhausted or not, I have to help. I throw off the pillow and force myself to sit up, bracing my head in my hand to shield myself from the blaring sunlight.

"No, not at all. What can I do for you?" My lie comes out with the seasoning of a professional. All doctors become accomplished prevaricators. We learn to say *it's not a bother* and *I'm happy to help* with perfectly straight faces. It's a required class in med school.

"I'm on my way to see my uncle, and I was hoping you could come with me. Doc gave me his medical bag and said to tell you he sterilized the stethoscope."

Of course he did.

"Listen, Jake, I—"

"Please. I know I'm asking a lot, but the thing is, Uncle Lem sounded worse when I called, and I'm worried. I hate to play the sympathy card, but I barely mentioned Doc, and it took me thirty minutes to get permission to come out. I figure I can stretch the invitation to you."

I hope my sigh is silent. I don't blame Jake. I blame Doc, the sentimental do-gooder with steamroller persistence masquerading as a hokey, small-town doctor. Sweet and well-intentioned, but unstoppable.

"Let me grab a quick shower and a cup of coffee."

I sense Jake's relief even with his silence and feel worse for hesitating.

"Thanks. I'll pick you up in front? In an hour?"

"I'll be waiting by Penny."

"Thank you so much. I really—"

"It's my pleasure. See you in a few."

I swipe off before he thanks me again. Even after all these years, it's hard for me to accept people's gratitude.

By the time I exit through the front doors, I don't need a thermometer to tell me it's nearly eighty, but the granite surrounding the giant water fountain is cool. The taps aren't turned on, which I note but don't spend any time worrying about. Instead, I perch on the rim and reach over to stroke Penny's nose, wondering for the millionth time how many fingers have smoothed over her long snout, wishing she could open it and talk to us.

"Hi, Penny. You look beautiful, as always."

Her inability to answer doesn't bother me. Somehow, I'm sure she knows her just-about-to-furl wings are magnificent, and she's as gorgeous today as she was more than a century ago when Alisdair MacInnes hired the artist who created the magnificent dragon monument for Evajean.

My one-sided conversation with our family mascot is cut short by the crunch of tires on gravel, and I know my ride to a destination I really don't want to go to has arrived.

"I can't thank you enough for doing this." Jake walks toward me and offers his hand.

Of course he's a true Southern gentleman.

I give him my neutral, professional, doctor expression and take his hand. It's nice, warm like his smile, and I wonder if I left my good sense back in the bed in Fam One. There's a Broder Engineering logo emblazoned on the side of his spotless extended-cab truck, and I'm enough of a Southern girl to appreciate his courtesy of opening my door and waiting until I'm settled before he closes it and heads for the driver's side.

"It's about twenty minutes from here, so I was thinking I could tell you a little bit about Uncle Lem, if that's all right?"

"Sure. That'd be great." I'm pretty sure I'd be struck by lightning if I said no, but I need the information to evaluate the man, if he'll let me, and give a report to Doc. Then I'll get busy vacationing. I will. I feel like a heel to even think it, but my sweet Lila's right. I'm tired. I'm burned out. And I do need a break. Yet, here I am, in town barely twenty-four hours, and I'm five inches from a stethoscope.

"Uncle Lem's seventy-seven. He and Doc have been best friends their whole lives, and Doc took care of Aunt Hannah while she was dying of breast cancer. Back in '88, Doc got her into a trial and, in the end, secured compassionate-care drugs we'd never have been able to get for her without him."

"That sounds like Doc. He's a hell of a guy."

"That he is. Anyway, these days you'd probably say Uncle Lem's on the spectrum, but don't underestimate his quietness. He's a thinker. Tack sharp, and he was a tremendous engineer for the railroad, but he gets riled if you throw too much at him at once. He and Aunt Hannah didn't have any kids, and I was born after she died, but Uncle Lem gave us plenty of his time and affection."

I think of my own extended family and know exactly what he means. There are times when being a part of the massive MacInnes clan can be overwhelming, but the benefits far outweigh any frustration.

"Our families have so many ties, but I confess I don't know your uncle. I probably met him at some MacInnes-Broder picnic or function, but I apologize for not knowing more about him."

"Nothing to be sorry for, because then I'd have to be sorry for knowing so few MacInneses. It's just life, even in a small town. We're all busy with our own comings and goings, so other than ribbon cuttings and, as you said, picnics and such, we're not exactly in each other's pockets."

"True. Life goes on, and we grow up. Some of us move away, some stay." I look left and appreciate he's a careful driver, watching the road instead of me. "Where did you end up?"

My segue's an expected conversation extender, but it serves the dual purpose of him not asking about me. True curiosity's at the root of my question, though, as I'm wondering why the very handsome Broder heir is still single. I know his status only because I told Ally and Cammie about the meeting at the pharmacy, and for some odd reason, Cammie knew that little factoid. Living in Dallas, she made it back to the estate more than Ally and I did, so I guess it's good one of us keeps an ear to the gossip creek.

"I went to school at Cal Tech. I wanted out, but didn't go north because I truly hate the cold. I loved California, but came back to SMU for grad school. It made Mom happy, and to be honest, I didn't exactly apply myself in undergrad. Had to work my butt off in Dallas, but I did grow up a little bit."

If his lines are well-practiced, he's convinced me with his deep voice, kind eyes, and the care I already know he has for an elderly relative. Every little thing I learn makes me like Jake Broder. Not that I didn't like him before, but there's something about a ridiculously good-looking, privileged person having a solid dose of amused humility that makes this one relatable. Most people assume that because I'm a MacInnes I come from great wealth. Far from it. Our branch is mostly plain ol' blue-collar types, and I still have the medical school debt to prove it.

Jake spends the rest of the trip pointing out landmarks I'm more than familiar with, but I don't mind. Much like the MacInnes estate has grown south, west, and east of town, the Broders have bought and developed the land northward and out from the place where they built their first factory in 1873.

"You know I grew up here, right?" I inject a healthy dose of teasing into my voice so I don't sound rude.

That aw-shucks drop of his head is back. "Sorry. When I shuttle visitors around, I tend to stick to my rehearsed spiel."

"No need to apologize. I promise I know the Broders are every bit a part of the heart and soul of Magnolia Bloom as the MacInneses."

We arrive at a beautiful home on a street lined with stunning hundred-year-old oaks shading the road. A long driveway leads back to Lemuel Broder's stately Victorian. More ancient oaks hide the well-tended mansion from view, and I admit to being a bit jealous as we pull to a stop. My house on the outskirts of Houston is nice, no doubt, but it has none of the charm or peaceful quietude of this elegant masterpiece with its mansard roof, gables, ornate pillars, and wraparound porches on both stories.

Jake catches my appreciative glance. "Uncle Lem and Aunt Hannah poured their hearts into this house. After she died, Uncle Lem's world became his trains, which you'll see in a sec."

Using his key to let us in, Jake yells up the stairs. "Uncle Lem! Come down. I have someone I'd like you to meet."

We both hear footsteps, and I feel my blood pressure rising. I'm not angry, just uncomfortable. Out of my several areas of expertise, house calls aren't on my CV.

A white-haired gentleman who's undoubtedly related to Jake joins us and extends his hand. "Good morning."

I'm pleased his grip is strong, his hands warm as he uses his left to cover our joined right ones. "It's a pleasure to meet you."

"All mine." He looks behind me and then to Jake. "Why isn't Wyatt here? Not that I mind having a pretty lady doctor in the house."

Jake's mouth opens, then shuts, and his brow furrows. "You said you didn't want Doc to come over."

"That's nonsense, Jakey. Wyatt and I have been best friends for almost seventy years. Why wouldn't I want him to come over? Is he too busy today? I've been telling him to slow down. Get a hobby like me."

He turns and leads the way into an enormous sitting room that feels a bit cramped with model trains on every flat surface except the chairs. Jake looks at me and shrugs.

Lemuel Broder is the picture of courtesy, allowing me to check his vitals and note his prescription bottles lined up in a precise row on his kitchen counter and chatting amiably the whole time about the history of the railways in Texas and the rest of the United States. His numbers are mostly within the normal range, and as I repack Doc's bag, I make notes on the pad conveniently stashed in a side pocket.

"I've got something to show you." A spark lights in Lem's eyes.

He escorts us to a barn behind the house, rolls open a huge door, and reveals an enormous private railway car.

"Goodness gracious, that's beautiful."

"Yes, ma'am, it is. It's an original Pullman. Eighty-three feet of the finest construction in the United States. I just got in these velvet draperies, and each piece of furniture is restored Venetian Renaissance baroque."

Even though I'm not versed on the décor of the time period he's referenced, I nod at the stunningly beautiful piece of history. It's over-wrought by my standards, but I'm intrigued as the older gentleman shows me different aspects of his work with no hint whatsoever of his supposedly difficult nature. For a moment, I'm swept back in time, trying to imagine traveling in this opulent luxury compared to today's sardine-can airplanes.

Lem leads the way out of the far end onto a small platform I can easily picture hosting politicians waving to crowds or families bidding their loved ones hello or goodbye. He strokes the polished handrail, and his eyes go a little long. "I've tried to find the railcar the Whitsons owned way back when, but I think it might have been destroyed in the Great Storm of 1900. They were from Galveston, you know."

The Whitsons are a huge part of my ancestry, of course, from Evajean's side of the family, so I do know the origins of the love story that started this dynasty. I'm happy, though, to let him tell me all about the thing of beauty Mr. Pullman made for Cameron and Lisette. It's not the details that fascinate me as much as how animated Lem is while sharing pieces of history he knows so well. By the time he's done, Lem's laughing and flirting with me, clearing loving having an opportunity to show off his toys to someone new.

"You have to come back next week." He gallantly tucks my hand into the crook of his arm as we make our way back to the house. "It does this old heart good to have a pretty lady to entertain."

I don't want to make false promises, but I make the mistake of glancing in Jake's direction and catch the pained hopefulness in his dark eyes. "I'd love to." I leave it at that, and don't commit to actual days or times.

When we're back in the truck, Jake's quiet for a long moment. "I don't get it. Lem was normal as could be today, but he was biting Doc's head off last week. You must think I'm crazy."

I'm not a touchy-feely kind of doctor, but I reach over and put a hand on his forearm and give him what I hope is a comforting squeeze.

"I don't think that at all. Early-onset dementia's erratic and frustrating, especially for long-term caregivers. It's also confusing and exhausting. I'd like to send you some literature on supplementation from a continuing-education seminar I attended. There's a lot of good work being done on diet and vitamins and some really fascinating information on peptides. I can't prescribe them, but I can get you to some folks who are really trailblazing outside of pharmaceuticals."

"That would be great. I can't thank you enough."

"I'm glad I could help." And I'm stunned to realize I'm not uttering a trite phrase. I mean it, and it breaks my heart to think of Lem starting down the dementia road, as my short time with him was lovely.

"Can I take you to breakfast?" He stops me as I raise a hand to decline. "Please accept. It's the least I can do."

His expression is so hopeful and sincere, I can't make myself say no. "Sure, that sounds lovely."

And I can tell Lila I'm doing exactly what I said I'd do. I'll leave out the home visit, but assure her I'm fulfilling my promise to smother pancakes and biscuits in butter and then drown them in syrup. Something homemade and heartwarming.

Jake's handsome face lights up as he starts the truck and puts it in gear. "Great. There's a new breakfast place called Bloomin' Waffles that just opened up. Want to give it a try?"

"Sounds perfect."

As we pull away from Lem's, I realize it really does.

CHAPTER NINE

CAMMIE

I'M NOT surprised to find Ally gone from the suite when I wake up. It was a fight to get her to stay the night at all, but I'm sure she was at Brian's place before the sun peeked over the horizon this morning. Of all of us, Ally may be the quietest, but she's definitely the most stubborn.

And there's a whole lot of stubborn claimed by the MacInneses as a whole, and the Terrible Trio in particular.

A quick shower and two ibuprofen take care of the hangover trying to take hold. Even though there are plenty of groceries in both suites, thanks to the quick run Boo and I did to the market yesterday, I throw on some clean sweatpants and a Dallas Cowboys tank and head down to the big kitchen.

As I hoped, Eunice is at the enormous BlueStar Heritage Classic Series stove, stirring something. Sometimes I think it's just water she keeps on the burner so she'll have something to mess with while she's dispensing her well-earned wisdom. If it's a prop, I don't really care.

I pause in the doorway because I don't want to startle her. "Good morning."

She turns, and her smile's as comforting as her chicken soup. "Good morning to you, sweetie. Sleep well?"

"Wine dreams aren't always the most restful, but I'm good." I gladly let her pull me into a lung-squeezing hug. She steps back, and I can't help tugging at the hem of her racerback top and nod at her stylish yoga pants. "What's up here, Miss Fitness? Athleta? Lululemon?"

"Better. When I started working out, Mina made me my own line. I call it Grannie Gear." She does a slow twirl and pats her thigh. "Full of pockets and sass."

She's got that right. In this town, nothing gets past a Grannie.

"I heartily approve."

"I'm going to make over all my recipes. Gonna put Paula Deen and Bree Drummond out of business."

Lord above, I love this woman. "Are you now?"

"Yes, ma'am. You can bank on it. And CT's daughter Bethanie is my secret weapon. Do you know her?"

I go to the cabinet to grab a mug and look around for the forty-cup urn that's usually ready and waiting this time of the morning. "I know her vaguely. I heard she was headed down a bad road, but our Kiki helped her do a U-turn."

"Kiki and Traycee, who owns the Emporium. All three of them are wonderful testaments to love and perseverance, but Bethanie's become a marketing guru. She's working on a fancy degree now, but she's already got a thousand cookbook and workout ideas."

"Trey mentioned it."

"God love that boy. I sure do. Anyway, Mina's gonna expand the Grannie Gear from athletic to streetwear."

If anyone can take the internet by storm, it's Eunice.

"I want to hear all about your plan to be the next world-champion octogenarian weightlifter, but first, I need coffee."

"Sit right down, and I'll make you a French press."

"Oooh, aren't we fancy this morning?"

"Just for my favorite girls. Where are the other two hooligans?"

"Ally left at oh dark thirty, so she's probably already painted three sides of Brian's place. I left Bailey alone, hoping against hope she's sleeping in. I take it you haven't seen her?"

"Not yet. I was hoping all three of you would come down for breakfast."

"Just coffee for me, thanks."

She gives me the stink eye as only Eunice Greene can. "That'll be decided in a minute. While this coffee is makin', tell me what this nonsense is about you being so broke the church mice are bringing *you* crumbs."

Oh, here we go.

I knew full well before I came down that I wouldn't escape the second-in-command of the Grannies of Magnolia Bloom, but I'd had a sliver of hope I'd get a whole five minutes before getting *Euniced*. It's a shame, really, that her grandson is the lawyer of the family. Not that Trey isn't a great attorney, but no witness would get off the stand without confessing to every sin committed, whether related to the case in question or not, if Eunice were on cross-examination.

"Let's just say I stopped by the bank and realized I should case the joint."

"I've got the bail fund ready, but let's not jump straight into a felony. Start at the beginning."

She pours us both a cup of exquisitely brewed Arabica heaven, and I tell her. All of it. Eight years of a pretty wonderful marriage. How being with Johnnie made all the snide remarks disappear. Yes, he was twenty years older than me. Yes, I started out as an intern in his firm, but we didn't sleep together until I'd graduated and was a junior associate. Yes, I get it. He was my boss, but he was soon my husband, and somehow neither of us gave a flying fig what anyone thought. We loved each other, and I earned, not slept my way, into my tiny cubicle office that was no different than any of the other associates'.

I get to the part about his heart attack and finding out the extent of his debt—and, by extension, mine—and the tears start their jailbreak.

Eunice goes to the stove and stirs for a moment, then returns with a fierce frown. "Wait a minute. Texas is a community-property state.

Why were you responsible for what he did before you two got married?"

"Technically, I wasn't, but without rehashing a sixteen-month-long probate, I did what was right even if I could have gotten away with shorting a lot of people."

"So you gave every last nickel you had to his daughter by his first wife who probably wouldn't spit on you if you were on fire?"

I stop my paper napkin shredathon and force myself to relax. "I still have five or six shekels, and we're not that unfriendly with one another. We just never had a relationship." I can't hide my smile as I think of a few magnificent catfights Eunice broke up between the three of us. "It's not some episode of *Knots Landing* where we're pulling hair and throwing wine on each other. Her folks were divorced long before I came along, and she's actually a nice woman. Understandably, though, she never had any great desire to become best buds with me."

Nor I with her, truth be told. Not out of animosity, but simply because our worlds intersected only once a year at Johnnie's birthday parties.

"Still, I don't think—"

I put my hand on the veined wrist attached to an arm with biceps bigger than mine. "You're sweet to want to defend me, but I promise you, my attorney has already hauled me over the coals several times. I didn't want Johnnie's reputation tarnished, and truthfully? I left the marriage with exactly what I came in with. I have no regrets."

Eunice harrumphs. "I did like him, even though he could pontificate better than a revival preacher."

I grab a fresh napkin to stop my nose from running along with my new tears. "He certainly could, but beneath all his gusto, he had the biggest heart." My throat closes, and I have to take a long sip of hot coffee to loosen it up. "I'd give it all up and live with him in a single-wide trailer, if I could have him back."

Just like that, I'm crushed again against the soft chest that comforted me after the breakup with my first boyfriend. The same hand strokes my head that pushed back my hair while I puked my guts up after mixing beer with cheap wine at the bonfire Sheriff Lancaster had broken up by the lake when I was sixteen. The same hands that shook me by the shoulders when I sobered up while she assured me she'd find her old wooden spoon and take it to my hide if I ever did that again.

"Aw, honey, the hurt'll fade a bit. When I lost my Neville, Mina and Fina weren't even in kindergarten. I thought I'd never be happy again. But I was. And you will be."

I pull back and wipe my nose on a napkin. "But you never married again."

She gives me a wicked wiggle of her eyebrow. "Who says you have to be married to be happy? I took a lesson out of Violet's playbook. Do you remember her?"

"I do. She was always crazy nice to me. To all of us."

"That she was. She was an inspiration to me in many ways."

This time, it's my turn to issue a side-eye. "Do you have a Brian Steele hidden away we don't know about?"

I should have known better than to try to outwit Eunice. "No Brian, but I had a Michael and a Joseph, though not at the same time, mind you."

It's no hardship seeing where Mina and Fina get their spunk.

"Good for you, girlfriend. Not that I didn't already know, but the women of this estate, whether MacInneses or not, were and are badasses."

She sends me an eye roll for the ages. "Your generation thinks you're the first for everything, especially sex."

"Not this girl."

"You're a rare one, then." Her pat on my arm's almost as good as a hug. "But you always were special."

My heart squeezes. I know I'm only one of dozens of MacInneses who grew up with Eunice as our surrogate mom and wrangler. If the estate had a dime for every cookie or chicken salad sandwich or glass of lemonade dispensed in this kitchen, we'd all be billionaires. Instead, we're just beneficiaries of a bottomless well of love.

"So, what are you going to do now?" She moves to the stove for another whirl of her spoon, and I realize just how many times I've seen this dance of hers.

"First, I'm going to try and not think for a week. Then I'm going to polish my résumé and hit the state bar want ads. My counsel might have thought he had a fool for a client, but I got a stellar letter of recommendation as the partners kicked me to the curb."

"Bastards."

I'm touched. Eunice reserves her curses for extreme circumstances and her favorite people. It does my heart good to know she's a hair from rounding up the rest of the Grannies and a passel of pitchforks to go after my old firm and the hypocritical jerks benefitting from Johnnie's name and reputation, thanks to me. It still stings that my tiny office has already been reassigned and my nameplate tossed in the trash.

The three partners with mistresses younger than me were the most pleased to see me go, but they'd better look over their shoulders, as one day, karma's going to bite their butts.

"The business piece is over. Johnnie and I thought we had plenty of time left together, but life had other plans. It's done, and I'm free to move on."

Uh-oh. I recognize that mischievous sparkle.

"You should talk to Trey. He's—"

"Thank you, but I need to do this myself." In fact, the last thing I need is a Grannie suiting up to play Cupid. Knowing Eunice, she'll have Mina designing activewear with wings on it before I can blink.

"You girls put the mule in obstinate."

No, we just give the Grannies a run for their money.

"We are MacInneses."

"Lord love a duck, that's the truth. Through and through." She pats my cheek and moves back to her stove. "But I still wish you'd talk to Trey."

I appreciate her concern and love, but part of my issue is I've had time to take a hard look at myself over these last months. One thing I have to own is it's past time for me to stand on my own two feet.

And that scares the hell out of me.

CHAPTER TEN

ALLY

I GRAB a rag from the box on the workbench and wipe the oil from my fingers before dropping Beauty's hood back in place. I didn't think she needed a change yet, but I'd just driven her hundreds of miles without checking first, so I'm feeling a little guilty. She's been a trouper, and I promise her full synthetic when it's time. She doesn't respond, but I'm used to that. While I enjoyed the late-night gab session with my sisters, the peace and quiet of Brian's property is welcome.

When I parked outside an hour ago, the sky was still dark, and I approached the huge rolling doors with equal parts anticipation, reverence, and dread. The creak of the hinges stabbed my heart, the surest proof that Brian is no longer here.

The house and outbuildings are officially owned by the estate, but it was Brian's place since long before I was born and would always be to me. With him gone, it doesn't seem right to call it anything else. All that matters is the spic-and-span house dwarfed by two equally chaos-free barns hidden from view by massive magnolias. It's an Eden and has always been the place I could come to when I'm overwhelmed by too many people or too much noise or too much... too much.

Brian understood without saying a word. I'd find him in one enormous, cool cavern or the other, and he'd hand me a tool. Then, in as few words as humanly possible, he'd tell me what needed fixing on the unending list of to-dos. He understood that claiming a creeper and sliding under a vehicle was darn near as good as hiding in the woods. Heck, sometimes I had to fight Kiki for a crescent wrench or spanner or needle-nose pliers, as she, too, found solace in the church of Brian Steele's barn. My cousin and I have hardly seen each other in our grownup years, but we had much in common in our teenage ones.

The empty space feels wrong, out of sync, and my breath hitches at the stab of sadness cutting me in half. It's logical that whatever tasks he'd been involved in have been cleared out, but grief bears down on my heart at the stains on the bare concrete. Many of his tools are still on the corkboard, the spot neat and clean and orderly, as if only yesterday Brian stowed each one away at the end of the workday. I'm so lost in my gloom, I'm nearly sent sprawling when something butts against my leg.

Baaa.

A beautiful black face looks up at me, and I swear the dark eyes almost hidden behind the shock of kinky wool are saying, *Everything will be okay. I'm here now.*

"Well, hello there." I stroke the soft head pressed against my thigh. The silken-fleeced sheep shifts, and I can see he or she isn't alone, as two smaller versions bound in, begging for equal adoration.

"Mon dieu, Lulu. I'm going to put you on a leash, I swear."

The breathless, French-accented voice comes from behind me, and I turn toward the surprise addition to our clan. Juliette is every bit as stunning now as she was at Brian's funeral, with her fair skin and sassy hair so black it shines blue in places. She puts her hands on her hips and glares at my tiny flock of ovine friends.

"Hello there. It's so nice to see you again." I approach Juliette with my hand out, and my four-footed buddy, who I now know is Lulu, stays right beside me.

"Bonjour, Alyssa." She takes my hands and gives me a kiss-on-each-cheek greeting. "I did not know you were coming, although that is ridiculous, as I cannot keep up with all the comings and goings here. It is like living near the Gare du Nord, although I should say Grand Central Station since I'm trying to be more American."

I'm delighted at my new cousin's dry humor. "I get it, which is why I'm staying here." I wave my hand around the barn, but encompass the tiny house and the general quiet alcove all around us.

"Bien sûr, it is lovely. I did not mean to intrude, but this little hellion took off when she saw you drive by, and I nearly killed myself trying to follow."

"It's Lulu, right?"

A bump into my leg confirms my assumption.

"Oui, she is my escape champion who brought me together with Rory, so I cannot stay angry with her, except when she runs away, and I'm scared to death something is going to happen to her. I lost track for a moment, so I assume that is when she rounded up her partners in crime."

Juliette directs the last sentence with pretend harshness at Lulu, who just *bleps* her tongue at her French companion and nudges her head under my fingers for another rub. Lulu's cohorts dance around me, letting me identify them as boys, as they don't have the spot on their hind ends that females do. They appear equally immune to censure as their ringleader.

"I can see you don't need a membership at the gym if you have to run after this miscreant, and now she has a crew." I sink to one knee and wrap my arms around her silky neck, resting my nose in the little space between her eyes. Lulu leans in, nudging her head up as if telling me, *I like you.*

"I have a small flock on my farm in Kentucky, all from our original MacInnes line. I love them so much."

"Mais oui, I have heard of your small enterprise making cheeses and toiletries. I am anxious to get my hands on some."

"I'll send some to you the next time I get there."

"Maybe you could teach me what you do? Share your recipes?"

"I'd be happy to, but from what I hear, you have plenty of paintings waiting for your magic touch without adding any new hobbies."

"I think my poor skin would be most grateful for the assistance. Solvents are not kind to the skin."

"I can imagine." I gesture toward the door. "Do you have a moment for a cup of tea? I think the kitchen is still intact, and I have supplies from the store."

"That sounds wonderful. I accept, but you should know we will be unable to escape our attendants. Lulu will make it quite impossible to talk unless she can be part of the conversation. As to the other two, I assume she has already influenced them into bad behavior, although I will check with Rory as soon as I am able."

I lead the way, including the entire group with a wave of my hand. "The more the merrier.

Juliette helps me bring in the bags I left on Beauty's passenger side, and I appreciate her kindness as she starts unloading the groceries in companionable quiet. When we're both stirring tea in oversize mugs, I look at my four-footed guests lying on the cool linoleum at our feet.

"I want to name them. It seems wrong that Lulu has one, and the boys don't."

Lulu lifts her head and all but nods.

Juliette scratches one of the boys behind the ear and earns a nuzzle into her palm. "I would urge you to not become attached, but alas, I think that would be a lost cause, as you say."

"They do have a way of insinuating themselves into your heart, don't they?"

Juliette stirs a dollop of honey into her cup and looks at me, her head cocked. "Will you be staying long?"

The lack of concern in her expression leads me to believe she hasn't heard the sordid news. "I take it you haven't been watching the news today."

"Pardonne?"

I fill her in on the broad strokes, and her expression goes soft, conveying the depth of her concern.

"Ça me rend triste, Ally."

"Don't be sad, but I appreciate the sentiment. I'm a bit shell-shocked, but with my two new friends, my world is brighter. Maybe I should name them Willie and Waylon."

"I'm sorry?"

"Nelson and Jennings?"

Juliette lights up. "Ah, bien sûr! Rory taught me to dance with these gentlemen." She taps a paint-stained fingernail on the tabletop. "As well as a certain lovely lady singer who is amazing."

I'm afraid the sound coming out of my throat is a little garbled. "Well, she's a little bruised right now, so I'd rather just be one of the innumerable MacInneses around here."

"Would you like to talk about it? I have been told I'm a good listener."

"I guess you don't watch much television? That would explain why you've been spared the gory details of my marriage going up in flames on every so-called entertainment show."

"I find the silence more companionable as I work." After blowing into her cup, Juliette takes a careful sip. "And I'm very sorry."

I add another tick mark in the column of things I like about my elegant, European cousin. "I had a good vent with my sisters last night, ending with too much wine on the balcony, but you're a sweetheart to offer."

We go through another cup of tea getting to know each other. I know the raw basics about her, including her renowned talent as an art restorationist, and she's delightfully animated as she tells me about our many-greats-aunt Gavina's paintings.

"My sister and I are working with Sotheby's Paris on an exhibit of her work along with other female artists ignored through time. Gavina's mother, Evajean, of course, has French ancestry both through her natural maman and her stepmaman. We are in the early stages of planning, but I am excited about bringing the exhibit here after it runs in Europe."

Her excitement is palpable and infectious. "That's incredible. I can't wait to see it."

"I am hoping to include Emmett Everson from the gallery in town as well. He is a charming man and has become a dear friend."

"I know the Eversons, but not Emmett in particular. Just more of the interconnectedness of all of us that makes Magnolia Bloom special."

"Indeed. It feels strange to be part of such an extended family, coming from the tiny community in France as I do, but each day I grow to love it more." She gives her head a little side-to-side wobble. "Even if the Grannies did take a moment for me to get used to."

I laugh as I make a quick trip to the sink with our empty cups and return, feeling my ribs loosen a notch. "They are special. It's like having our own geriatric CIA."

"Mais oui. One is well-advised not to cross them. Beware them most when their smiles are the sweetest."

"You've got that right."

Juliette rises and offers me her slender hand. "It has been so nice to talk with you, but I have overstayed my welcome for today. Are you coming to the lake for the big picnic this afternoon?"

I start to say no, but my certainty that I wanted to be alone is short-circuited, much to my surprise. "I hadn't planned on it, but yes, I think I will."

"Wonderful. I will see you later, then, and I will let Rory know about your visitors."

Lulu jumps to her feet and follows Juliette out the door, but I notice the boys don't move an inch.

"Think you're pretty smart, huh, guys?"

If sheep can grin, Willie and Waylon give looks conveying they're exceedingly pleased with themselves. I shoo them into the backyard, set out a big pot of water, and let them meander on the lush grass as I get my things set up in the guest room. Nothing's been moved or cleaned out yet, and the house exudes the empty energy of abandonment. I didn't intend to use Brian's room, but once I discovered his clothes still hang neatly in the closet and his drawers are still filled with items folded with military precision, I felt both comforted and distressed. I still chose the second bedroom without hesitation.

I grab a bottle of tea from the fridge. I've never been a soda girl, which my dentist assures me is why I've never needed to give in to the pressure of veneers or tooth-destroying whiteners.

I head to the back porch and watch the sheep graze. It strikes me, hard, that there's no point in turning on my phone, as there's no one for me to call. The more well-known A to Z became, the less I trusted anyone, and as the years went on, I convinced myself I like the isolation, as I'm an introvert at heart, despite what people think of my public image. And always, always, my thoughts ended with some version of, *But I have Zane, and he's all I need.*

Today, though, it hits deep. And it hurts.

I'm not asking for pity. I've had a golden life, all in all.

But the tears come when I have to face that since I was twenty years old, it was Zane and me against the world. We defied the odds, and I thought, believed, that we were different.

Now, I wonder if I ever knew him at all. That's what has shredded my heart the most, although I'm smart enough to know that I'm in shock, and the pain really hasn't started yet. We were more than husband and wife, musical partners, lovers.

We were best friends.

Were.

The world I built around us is gone. In the snap of a finger.

Or, more accurately, in the blink of a camera flash.

CHAPTER ELEVEN

BAILEY

ALLY'S awfully quiet as we stroll downtown. The Terrible Trio has made quite a dent in the local shops, or rather, Ally and I have. Cammie's been understandably cautious with her wallet, so big sis and I pulled the older-sibling card several times to splurge on her without eviscerating her pride. We all have new swimsuits, flip-flops, and sun hats, just in time to head back to change for the big shindig on the lake.

We all troop down to the biggest of the three family docks. The shore is a mass of bodies in everything from itty-bitty bikinis to caftans to cutoffs and board shorts. Juliette sees us first and waves us over to the picnic tables where she's helping Eunice set out massive platters of sandwiches, bowls of potato salad and chips, and gallons of tea. Predictably, there's a tower of red Solo cups with a stash of Sharpies waiting close by in the always-futile hope that it will cut down on the pile that will end up in the recycling.

The lake is alive with boats, and it's impossible not to feel revitalized by the youthful exuberance coming from the skiers and wakeboarders talking trash at each other at the tops of their lungs.

A gorgeous MasterCraft pulls up to the dock with almost wakeless precision, earning nods of approval from several watchers. Jake agilely jumps out and ties off to the pylon with obvious skill, and I can't help but take in the whole picture—from his mirrored aviators, to his muscled chest revealed by his unbuttoned shirt, down to the strip of white skin where his wet trunks have slipped from the weight of the lake water. My rapt regard is held way past proper, and I can't recall the last time a man's so thoroughly captured my notice.

"His eyes are up there," a voice mutters beside me.

I look at Cammie crossly. "Very funny. Like I don't already feel like a cougar as it is."

She pulls down the bridge of her sunglasses so I'm hit with the full force of her glare. "There's maybe, what, seven years' difference in your ages? Eight at the most? Jeez Louise, Boo, we've fully entered the twenty-first century."

"Doesn't matter. I still feel like I should go to confession or something."

"Good thing we're not Catholic, then, ain't it?"

I'm saved from tussling with her on a subject I really don't want to get into by the arrival of more family. The hugs commence with Kiki and her new cute-as-all-get-out hubby. Mina and CT. Shrieks can be heard a mile away as Fina comes down the hill with her fiancé, who introduces himself as Anders. Then we slip into the free-for-all of food, Frisbee, and football, like I'm twelve again. I'm related to half of this madding crowd by blood, the other half by love or history. With magnolia blossoms the size of dinner plates releasing their exquisite perfume, this just might be heaven.

I'm contentedly stretched out on one of many blankets covering the grass when a shadow falls over me, and a tall, dark, and Ray-Ban'd man slips down beside me. I haven't been self-conscious in my new bright red maillot all afternoon, but I find myself pulling my cover-up together. Then I feel even more awkward, but thankfully, Jake doesn't seem to notice.

"Man, I love this. You ready to hit the skis? I haven't seen you up yet."

Oh, but I witnessed his hotdogging on a slalom, arms bulging and thigh muscles evident even from shore, throwing rooster tails the likes I haven't seen in years.

"Thanks, but I haven't been on the water in forever. I'd probably end up swallowing half the lake and be sick for a week."

"Come on, I know better than that. It's like riding a bike. You never forget."

"No, but muscles go soft, and I'm afraid I'm one slice shy of being a loaf of Wonder Bread."

I hadn't meant for that to be a provocative statement, but my breath catches at his slow pan from my mirrored lenses to my red-painted toenails and back again. I have no doubt the red of the flush from my chest to my forehead matches my bathing suit.

If he's about to make an inappropriate remark about sandwiches, I'm saved by a teenager coming to a screeching halt on the grass beside us. "Come on, Uncle Jake. You said we'd go out after we waited thirty minutes."

A brow hikes over the rim of his aviators, which should be cliché but instead is cute as hell. "Come on, Bailey. It'll be fun. Right, David?"

David clearly couldn't care less what my involvement is in this conversation, but he nods gamely. "Yeah, sure. Come on!"

Which is how I find myself in the back of the boat Jake expertly pilots, letting David whoop and holler as he performs an array of tricks on the disc I've never mastered. David's sisters taunt him, egging him on to ever greater feats until finally he tosses up the rope and signals he's done.

"You're up, Bailey." Jake has hauled in and stowed the disc, and he's pulling out the ski he so expertly maneuvered a short while ago.

"No, I—"

"Come on, chicken." This, to my surprise, comes from David, clearly light-headed from his impressive and youth-fueled exertions.

It's not that I'm prone to being heckled into action, but the pure happiness on everyone's faces reminds me how much I loved this once. I accept the life jacket Jake holds out, trying not to blush when I take off my wrap and slip into the vest, and he helps adjust the straps so it fits correctly. Then I'm in the water, handle in hand, feet steady, wondering what the hell I'm doing, but I shout, "Ready."

Jake may have had fun with David, but he's a pure gentleman with me. I delight myself by getting up the first time and, after a minute of acclimating, give him the thumbs-up to increase the speed.

Skiing feels like flying when it's all going right. It takes a little bit, but then I'm doing my own rooster tails and cutting across the wake, yelling my head off. Was I really an undergraduate the last time I did this? Jake hauls me down the lake until my muscles start to quiver. I give him the throat-chop-I'm-done, toss up the rope, and slowly lose speed, then sink into the water to wait until the boat loops around and pulls close enough for me to reboard.

"See? Told you you never forget."

"I'm happy to inform you that you are annoyingly right. That was amazing." I know I have a goofy grin on my face as I wring my hair out and flip it over my shoulder, but I can't help it. I was terrified the exertion would kick off my stomach issues, but just the opposite has happened. From a medical standpoint, maybe endorphins suppress cortisol, but whatever the reason, I'm sitting in the sunshine, relaxed, without my gut being on fire for the first time in far too long.

Jake hands me my sunglasses, and our fingers meet. It's seems straight out of a ridiculous rom-com, but I jerk back like I've been shocked. To keep from embarrassing myself even further, I hide my face by becoming engrossed in unclipping the life jacket.

David's sister is demanding her turn, so I'm saved from trying to form a coherent sentence, instead taking up the observer position in the back of the boat as yet another beautiful, youthful Broder shows off on Lake Maggie.

I tuck my legs underneath me and studiously avoid looking at the older, definitely beautiful Broder pushing the throttle forward, unable to ignore that my racing heartbeat might just be matching the pulse of the powerful engine underneath me.

CHAPTER TWELVE

CAMMIE

"Well, that's not something I expected to see." Ally slips her arm around my waist so quietly, I'm startled.

"Me, neither, but I like it." I watch the antics on the lake with a twinge of jealousy. Bailey is clearly relaxed for the first time in heaven knows when, and even Ally seems strung a little less tightly.

I cut her a glance. "There's someone else I haven't heard laugh in a long time."

"There does seem to be a dearth of that amongst the three of us lately."

"Sucks."

"Indeed." She gestures toward the water. "You going out?"

"You and Boo are the skiers, not me. You know that."

"Never too late to learn."

Ally glances behind my shoulder and gets a devious glint in her eyes. "Hey, Trey. You just get here?"

"Yeah, had a closing run late, but no office talk. It's party time."

There must be something in Magnolia Bloom's water, because we do tend to grow 'em tall around here, and Trey has much more than height in his arsenal of gorgeous. His dark brown hair catches hints of red as the hot sun shoots through the tree branches, and he's built an impressive array of muscles from Quinton Everson's coaching... or trying to stay ahead of his Grannie. Either way, he certainly could make a side hustle posing for romance covers.

And dang if I don't have an immediate image of me in a half-unlaced kirtle while a huge fan blows my hair over my shoulders. Trey's authentic kilt shows off his mouth-wateringly muscled thigh as he bends me backward over his arm—

What the absolute hell is wrong with me?

I feel guilty for the insane directions my thoughts went. I've been processing losing Johnnie for almost two years now, so while I don't feel I'm betraying him per se, it still feels awkward to notice that I'm noticing another man.

"I think Jake's coming back in." Ally steps forward. "If you're game, you could teach Cammie here how to ski. She's been putting it off for ages."

My meddling sister better watch it, as I'm quite good at stirring the pot, too.

A horrified frown only serves to sharpen the angles on his masculine face. "You don't know how to ski? A MacInnes? Isn't that against the law?"

"No, I don't know how, and I will not be taunted into it." I glare at both of them. "I was a tan-on-the-dock kind of girl until the sun police took that away from us."

"I'd be happy to show you."

"Go on, Cam. Do something fun." Ally's voice is gentle and, yes, a bit teasing, but I know what she really wants is for me to let go, even if only for a minute. I don't tell her she has no room to throw stones, not in front of Trey, or anyone else for that matter. We sisters might rag each other mercilessly at times, but we have each other's backs all the time.

Jake is super patient, sending away his nieces and nephew and totally willing to give me a shot. I'm glad Bailey stays on board in case I make a total space cadet of myself. Tooling over to a quiet cove, he and Bailey chat while Trey fits my vest and explains all the basics. Who knew getting ready to launch oneself onto two little slivers of wood could be so intimate? Even though he's a complete gentleman as he helps me, of course.

I'm a bundle of nerves by the time he climbs aboard the boat and positions himself where he can see me. I'm not surprised I feel better knowing he's going to eagle eye me the entire time, because there's something about Trey that is just… soothing.

"Okay, Cameron, remember. Let the boat do the work. Arms straight, knees bent, head up. Ready?"

I give the signal, and to my utter shock, I get up on my first try. Maybe it's the MacInnes genes at work, I don't know, and really, I don't care. Every cell I have is singing.

Jake slowly takes me around the cove, and I'm just about to get cocky when I tip my ski and face-plant right into the wake I was so sure I could cross. No one teases me, though, as the boat pulls around, and I get back aboard.

"Excellent!" Trey holds up a hand, and my embarrassment flees as I high-five him, Bailey, and Jake in turn. "Want to go again?"

"No, thanks. That was fun, but I'd rather not press my luck. I can't believe I got up, though."

"I never doubted you." Trey's voice has an undercurrent that I have to be imagining.

Instead of trying to figure it out, they're stowing the kiddy skis, and Trey takes his turn. Needless to say, he's a thousand times more impressive than I was, but I don't care. I'm the most competitive of the Terrible Trio, but for once it's not the end of the world that I'm not the best, most accomplished, and top of the list.

By the time we tie back up to the dock, everyone's ready for ice cream and watermelon, and as I wipe away the sticky juice dribbling down my chin, I think I take my first real, deep breath in twenty-three months, two weeks, and four days. A glance around makes it easy to see why. Bailey's actually laughing at something Jake's saying, Ally's smiling at something Kiki's telling her, and I'm surrounded by sunshine and warmth and laughter.

Family.

My huge, crazy, mixed-up family.

I feel it, for an instant. A few pure seconds of joy, then my brain reminds me that the F words are better fits.

Fraud.

Failure.

Fiasco. Fake. Forgery. Flop.

I interrupt my inner thesaurus before it ramps up to full speed, trying to tell myself I can put aside the disaster that's my life for now. Unfortunately, I didn't get a slice of whatever joy my sisters have swallowed. The momentary lightness I felt is gone, and I want to run, escape the reminders all around me that happiness is just an illusion. My rose-colored glasses have not only been knocked off my nose, they've been crushed under the brutal boot heels of disappointment.

Instead of feigning a headache or some other lie, I tell Trey the truth. "Thanks for the ski lesson, but I'm a little overwhelmed right now. I'm going to go lie down. Tell Ally and Bailey I'm okay, if they ask."

He agrees, not bothering to hide his disappointment, but not arguing, either. I appreciate both.

When I make it to the suite and turn the shower taps wide open, I own up that I did, indeed, lie. I said I was okay.

Thing is, I'm afraid I never will be.

CHAPTER THIRTEEN

ALLY

WITH THE SUN setting and the boats all secured to the different docks, inevitably someone pulls out a guitar as another group lights off the bonfire already laid in the pit. It's the true magic of the lake, but I slip back into the shadows of the magnolias.

Please, please don't let anyone ask me to sing.

Thankfully, I'm just one of the family around here, and either no one thinks about it, or everyone has heard my silent plea, because I'm left alone.

"Hey, you okay?" To my surprise, it's Pastor Harville, or just plain Harville, as he insists since we're family now and all.

Can I lie to a preacher? He's one I like and respect, but I'm resisting the urge to throat-punch the next person who asks if I'm okay. I mean, I'd never hit anyone, especially my cousin's husband, but come on. How "okay" can anyone be when they've had their hot mess of a marriage splashed across the media?

"I'm just trying to put it all together. Today, I just want a beer, a pile of potato salad, and for not another person to ask me if I'm all right."

"Understood."

Great. I didn't lie to a pastor, but he doesn't deserve my snark. "I'm sorry. I don't mean to be snippy."

His smile is gentle, but teasing so I feel like less of a heel. "No apology necessary. Nosiness is an occupational hazard." He nods toward the fire. "You going to join in?"

"Not a chance, but you should. I happen to know you've got a pretty good tenor thing going on."

I know this because I was at Brian's funeral, and Harville sang along with the rest of us as we bade goodbye to one of the kindest men I've ever known.

"I'm happy to hang back here with you, if that's all right."

Kiki, do you know what a gem you have here? Dumb question. Of course she does. I've seen these two looking all gooey-eyed at each other across the picnic table.

The crowd quiets as a voice becomes more noticeable, and I find myself frozen in place. I can't see who's singing, but the woman is doing a stunning job covering "Bridge Over Troubled Water." It's been a long time since music has taken my breath away.

The song's difficult for a trained vocalist, but the pure, unpolished sound drifting over to me is enough to make me tear up.

I used to sing like that. Carefree and easy and just for fun. I'd hang with my friends and play a slightly out-of-tune guitar and not care, everything twining together, flowing. A symbiosis with instruments both manmade and natural. No auto-tuners. No retakes.

I want to not care again.

I want to be unpolished again.

I want to sing just because again.

"Who is that?" My voice cracks against the raw emotion I'm feeling.

"That's Suzanne Steele. Brian's great-niece."

The image of her from the funeral springs to mind. Taller than me, but then, most people are, with long, strawberry-blond hair held back with simple combs from a delicate, heart-shaped face. So sweet and gracious, speaking to everyone who'd come to the service. We saw each other often growing up, usually at Brian's place, but I don't remember her being a singer. As we didn't run in the same crowd, it's not a surprise.

"She's amazing."

"She's got a YouTube channel that's really getting traction, but I'm worried about her. She gets so nervous performing in front of people, and I'm afraid she leans on Bud Light courage a little too often. I can't figure out how to help."

I look at the handsome man my cousin married, and not for the first time, I'm struck by his genuine kindness. Although not particularly observant in the faith, our family has known him since he accepted the calling to the pulpit. I liked him then. I like him more now.

"You can't fix everyone, Harville."

He nods, but I'm sure he's not agreeing with me so much as arguing in his particular way. He watches the crowd around the pit, our position allowing us to see the light flickering over Suzanne's face.

"You know how there are just some people you meet, and they have this spark, and you're both captivated and afraid at the same time? You know they're an old soul."

"Are you sure you're not part Buddhist?" I can't help teasing him, even though I know exactly what he means.

"It's my secret superpower."

My respect for the pastor tips over into full-fledged admiration. "I promise to help you hide your cape."

"I appreciate that." He takes a drink from his soda, his attention glued to Suzanne. "Someone's going to discover her, and if she doesn't get a handle on her confidence, she's going to be destroyed. I've seen what addiction can do to people. Adding success only makes it worse."

I make no claims to knowing everything about fame, but one thing I know absolutely is he's correct. I've seen people in this business spectacularly crash and burn. I've lost friends and watched acquaintances lose everything. I'm not sure which is worse – the slow suicide by addiction, or the brutal dives off of actual bridges. Harville has seen this from his perspective as a counselor, so he doesn't need my two cents so I go silent to breathe in the rest of the song. The crowd claps and whoops when she's done, and the next song is a rousing country hit, *my* hit, in fact. The one I hated the most that raced up the charts and seems determined to stay there. For me, the moment is broken.

Harville gives a small cough. "I want to clarify what I said. I don't think Suzanne has an alcohol problem, but it's something I'm familiar with, and I don't like where the signs are pointing. I hope I'm wrong."

"You're a good man, Harville Crowder. You know that?"

"I try. Fail a lot, but I keep chuggin' along doing my best. Luckily, I surround myself with people a whole lot smarter than me and get to sound cool when I'm just repeating what the Buddha and many like him said."

I don't try to argue. I know from many sources that he's not falsely modest, but deeply averse to adulation.

Zane used to be that way. In the early days, although he's always been the focal point onstage with his irresistible good looks and spellbinding voice. He shared the glory, and not just with me. He'd call out each band member by name during our performances, making sure they had a second in the spotlight. Some of our early backups have gone on to launch their own impressive careers, and I have a secret soft spot hoping we had a little to do with it.

Over time, he changed, getting giddy at venues in the round or with runways so he could immerse himself in the crowd. I'll never forget the day he headed out from the wings for an encore without realizing he left me behind, remembering only at the last second to reach back with an open hand.

I can't help but wonder now if that's when we broke.

After a bit more chitchat, Harville joins the throng, but I stay in the background, which becomes easier as twilight falls, leaving me pockets of inky shadows to slip through, gliding from one to the other with no one paying me any mind. I make it back to the big table, grabbing a beer from the cooler and a chocolate chip cookie as big as my face. I don't plan on wearing sequins and Spandex again for the rest of my life, so I pretend I don't give a flyin' fig about the fats, carbs, or any other macro.

A hand reaches past me and snags a cookie just like mine. A quick glance reveals the cookie nabber as Suzanne, the very person who won't get out of my thoughts.

Her chuckle has the same husky-whiskey-breathy tone that captured me while she sang. "I think I'm gonna kidnap Eunice and hold her hostage until she gives me this recipe, but then, I'm too afraid of the Grannies' retribution to ever go through with it."

I take a bite and savor every buttery calorie. "It might be worth it, though."

"Amen to that."

We're both enjoying the noise and the softening energy of the evening when I risk what's on my mind. "You were amazing. I haven't heard a rendition of that song done with that much heart in... well, forever."

She coughs on a cookie crumb, and I thrust my beer at her.

"Here. I haven't taken a drink yet."

She throws back a mouthful, and her coughing subsides. "Thanks for saying that. From you, it means the world."

I sigh. "Please, tonight I'm nobody special. Just another Magnolia Bloomian forgetting to put on a second coat of zinc oxide."

"With this red hair, I have to bathe in it. Gives me a super-sexy vibe."

I laugh and grab another beer. "Ah, the joys of being one shade shy of see-through."

We clink longnecks, and she gestures to the thinning crowd. Those with the youngest kids have already left, dads carrying exhausted toddlers, moms hauling folding chairs, wet towels, and sand buckets with little plastic shovels. "This is the best thing about springtime. The magnolias blooming, the lake warming up, and everyone hauling out the water toys."

Just a year ago, Zane and I spent a week in the Ozarks not too far from here. Things were strained, so we got away to reconnect, and it was one of the best weeks of our marriage. Or so I thought. We had a play food fight in the kitchen while loading up a cooler, hauled everything down to the dock, rigged out an amazing boat waiting at the pylons. I impressed Zane with my driving skills, and the only nod we gave to the possibility that there might be a telephoto lens out there somewhere was to go below to a well-appointed stateroom to make love. It was some of the best sex of our marriage.

Turns out it was also some of the last.

But those few days were bliss. No security. No roadies. No staff. Just the two of us doing it all ourselves, like the tired but contented families around me.

Just... normal.

Then we went back to Nashville, and it was as if someone flipped a light switch, the strain returning. And worsening.

"Springtime's my favorite, too." My voice is as soft as Suzanne's. "Maybe it's so special around here because it's so short before summer pummels us."

"You should write a song about it." She claps a hand to her mouth, horrified. "I'm sorry. I didn't mean to tell you, of all people, what to do."

"There's nothing to apologize for, and honestly, the last thing I want to talk about is me. I'd like to go back to you. You really are talented." Even in the dimming light, I can see her blush, but I press a bit further. "Harville says you have a YouTube channel."

"I do. My brother's the king of all things digital, so it's more correct that *he* has a channel."

She drains her beer and goes after another. I don't judge. I've had many nights of my own bolstered by false courage, but Harville's voice echoes in my head. I want to say something brilliant, but the truth is, whatever pithy line I should offer won't pop into my head until I'm in the shower later tonight. I decide to leave before things get awkward.

"I'm going to head back to Brian's. I'm staying there for a while, and I'd really like you to come over and chat."

"Oh, dang it. I was supposed to clear out the place. I just haven't been able to face it."

"I understand. Don't worry about it."

"I've been chicken, is all."

"I'm happy to help you clean, but that's not why I'd like you to stop by. I'd like to talk about you. You are super talented, and if you're going to pursue your art, I'd like to give you a few tips. Maybe a couple of warnings, too."

She looks at me like I'm trying to hand her a bar of gold bullion. "Really?"

I squeeze her wrist. "Really."

"O-okay. Thank you so much. I can't believe—"

I add the tiniest bit of pressure in my grip to stop her. "Just come by whenever you'd like."

"I will.

"Good."

I head for Beauty, now seeming a little lonely in the field that was packed when I arrived, but at least I don't have to fight a crowd as I drive to my little hideaway. Willie and Waylon act like puppies when I check on them, and I duly note a barrel of food and a small trough that's been erected in the few hours I've been gone.

I throw my wet things in the washer and my body into a cool shower. I love swimming in the lake, but I love being clean and in dry yoga pants topped with a baggy T-shirt even more. The fun, the food, and sunshine all combine to make me relaxed for the first time in a long time.

As I curl into a recliner and pull the paperback I nabbed this morning into my lap, I have to face that it's been years since I've had peace. I've had quiet. A lot, actually, but those evenings were fraught with worry about Zane and what was happening between us. Now I have a glimpse of release, even though it's wrapped up in a blanket of fear and anger and worry. I have a lot to work through, but at least the amorphous miasma and dread that have been my constant companions have morphed into something identifiable, something I can deal with and work through.

I'm still numb, no doubt, but for tonight I'm going to read about dragons and sorcerers and spells.

I'll battle my real demons tomorrow.

CHAPTER FOURTEEN

BAILEY

At least I greet Sunday morning without a headache. A carb hangover and a little dehydration from a mild sunburn, maybe, but nothing alcohol related.

Even though the unit has all the essential appliances for me to fix my own breakfast, I head downstairs to the big kitchen for a dose of memories as much as a fresh bagel. I'm fully through the door and unable to back away unnoticed before I realize the room's full of people obviously involved in a meeting.

Several voices call out "good morning" as I hold up a hand. "I'm sorry to interrupt."

The person who stands at the far end of the table, to my distinct surprise, is Jake Broder. "Please, come join us. We're having a planning meeting for the new hospital, and a second opinion from a professional is always welcome."

Doc stands, as if it's a foregone conclusion, and waves to his seat.

A round of agreement circles the table, and I find myself in Doc's chair with a fresh cup of coffee in front of me before I can figure out how to extricate myself.

I nod to Kiki, then Mina and CT, then Fina introduces me to her fiancé, who was the CEO of a pharmaceutical company in Denmark before he stepped down from that position. He'll be a huge partner in this venture. *This* being the first full-fledged hospital in Magnolia Bloom.

Ideas fly full and fast. Kiki passes out reams of data on other regional hospitals, both close by and around the country.

"I'm not sure why y'all want me in on this meeting, although I'm flattered."

"Because you have perspective." Kiki's voice draws me to her end of the table. "We didn't know you'd be here, but it's wonderful that you are."

"But I don't know small hospitals. I've been at Memorial Hermann since residency, and the last thing you can call that beast is small."

"So tell us what you'd do differently, if you had a magic wand."

"That's easy, but completely unrealistic. I'd have double the doctors and triple the nurses. The health issues of Americans aren't getting better, so to ask for less patients is a pipe dream, though it'd be the miracle I'd love to see. Since that's not going to happen, I'd love a way to ease the burden on the staff. There's never enough of us, at any level, and what I see every day is exhaustion and burnout. But no one can run a hospital at a profit and make my vision real."

"What if we aren't trying to create a profit-driven model?"

My head pivots toward Jake, as I'm sure I didn't hear him correctly. "I'm not sure I follow."

Folding his hands on the table in front of him, Jake leans forward, his face earnest. "We want to use a nonprofit model and actually serve the area. Care centers are closing left and right as people move away from city centers. Still, Texas has five or six of the top regional and community hospitals in the country, so we have some good examples to draw from."

Doc, who's been standing behind Jake, shifts on his feet. "I'll go to my grave beating myself up for not being here when Brian collapsed. I'll always wonder if we could have saved him if we'd gotten him care sooner."

I wish I had words to reassure him, but I know too well the torture of wondering what I could have done differently with patients I've lost. *If only* is a brutal game with no winners. "It's incredibly hard to keep small hospitals going. I applaud your vision, but I've seen this before. I was invited to a planning session at a small facility that wanted to expand its specialty in pulmonary hypertension. It started out highly idealistic and devolved in no time into the C-suite making millions and millions in their golden-parachute contracts, a few doctors raking in plump salaries, and the rank and file struggling."

Jake's face is serious. Earnest even. "We plan to be mindful of the heart and soul of the hospital."

I hear him, but reality is a harsh taskmaster. "I'm required to attend rah-rah speeches much too frequently, then go back to the floor and watch nurses wet themselves because they literally, I mean literally, have not had a chance to pee because they can't leave their patient, and there's no one to cover for them. All while I can tell you the brands of the cars and yachts of the people who wouldn't know which end of a stethoscope to put in their ears."

The room has gone silent, and I feel like an asshole. I didn't mean to say so much, but once the spout was opened, I couldn't stop myself.

I look down and take a deep breath. "I'm sorry. I came in here and rained all over your parade."

Jake palms the table, meeting my eyes. "Don't apologize. Kiki printed out a dozen articles and stories about the nonprofit system, but you didn't know that. Couldn't know that. So let me reassure you that we're going to bring in folks who know the side of the business that we don't and doctors who know what they're doing, and no one is going to have a salary with seven or eight digits. We're not going to pay people in chickens and dried beans, but we are going to find people who want to do the right thing. They're out there. We just have to look."

I push back and stand, my nerves on fire and my stomach a sea of acid. I remember being idealistic oh-so-many years ago. "I hope you're right. I want you to be right. I'm just not sure even the combined MacInnes-Broder forces are enough to beat this Godzilla."

There aren't enough words to describe how awful I feel as I head back to my suite, and I nearly start crying when a deep voice comes from behind me before I can reach the back stairs.

"Bailey, hold up."

I stop but don't turn. "Jake, I apologize. I love your ideas, but—"

He walks until he's in my line of sight. "That's just it. They're ideas right now. Just because you're coming from a cautious side doesn't mean we don't want to hear you. All of us have different pieces of business experience, and it's all good, but you have inside information we could really use."

I can't stop myself from taking another step back and putting more space between us. "I appreciate what you're saying, and I hope I don't sound like a total downer, but I'm supposed to be taking time off this week. I desperately need to get away from work, and I don't want to get dragged into anything more complicated than choosing between a Dos Equis and a shot of Herradura. I'm sorry."

"I'm the one who's sorry. I'm really excited about this project, and I get out over my skis more than I should. I didn't mean to press."

Great. Now I feel like an exponential jerk. I meet Jake's lovely, deep, dark eyes and find a smile somewhere in my Grinch heart. "I do think it's a great idea, especially if your operating system fairly compensates the employees and will roll profits back into equipment and patient care. I'm just a little jaded, and I let that color everything I said."

"Voices of reason are a good thing, but how about I promise not to talk business if you'll agree to go with me to the Magnolia Moon for a little no-work-allowed dancing?"

I can't tell if the unease inside me is a warning or something waking up.

"I'm not quite clear on how those two options go together."

To his credit, Jake's expression is mischievous and charming. "Let's just say I want to make up for starting your morning off with a headache by promising you an evening of nothing but fun. Vacation, remember?"

Him mentioning dancing brings memories flooding back of Sunday afternoons of teen-only dances at the Magnolia Moon, which then became family-filled events those nights. The atmosphere was far different than the crowds on Fridays and Saturdays. Not that those were bad, simply that the Sunday folks had a mind-set less about drinkin' and more about dancin'. And they were always a blast.

"Please say yes. Make me feel like a little less of an ogre."

I'm sure I surprise him by not arguing. "I haven't been to a Sunday dance in so long I can hardly remember. That sounds like fun."

"Really? That's fantastic. Can I pick you up around seven?"

"Thanks, but I'll meet you there."

"Spoilsport."

I give him an arch look. "I've agreed to go. Count your blessings."

He steps back and gives me a salute. "Yes, ma'am. See you there."

He honest-to-goodness whistles as he returns to the kitchen and I to my rooms, and I think I need a quick run to Traycee's Emporium for some fancy jeans and a cute top. I have boots, of course, because I might not have been dancing in a long time, but I am a born-and-bred Texan. I'd never break the code and come home without my best Luccheses in my bag.

I'm just surprised I'm going to get to use them... and how much I'm looking forward to it.

CHAPTER FIFTEEN

ALLY

THE THREE OF us get out of the estate's Escalade we've borrowed for the evening. We could have come in Beauty, but the old-style bench seat doesn't have three seat belts, so we erred on the side of caution. As the door shuts behind me, I'm transfixed by the billboard attached to the roof proclaiming we've reached the Magnolia Moon. The building is showing a bit of wear, but the sign has clearly seen a fresh coat of paint.

"Boo, I think you should've been the attorney, because I still can't figure out how you conned me into coming tonight."

Cammie doesn't join in my teasing, instead linking arms to make us the Terrible Trio once more before heaving a sigh. "Wouldn't have been a trip home without a Sunday at the Moon. And besides, where else're we gonna wear rhinestoned jeans?"

"You're not wrong," I have to admit. "But we sure never looked this good at any of the teen dances we came to like George Strait was our religion."

Cammie obviously found hot rollers, because her blond locks are an envy-producing waterfall of waves. Her cobalt-blue keyhole top makes her eyes look even more gorgeous than usual, and the hue sets off the spray of sapphire stones on her left leg. Bailey tied a plain white button-down over a black tank, and I would bet she doesn't realize her simple look is sexier than any shirt cut down to her belly button. Her ebony jeans sport swirls of crystal and pearl Swarovski trailing down the impressively long outseam I've envied since her and Cammie's marks on the bedroom doorjamb steadily marched above mine starting at seven. Her hair is French-braided in a beautiful long plait, but I know my middle sister. It's to keep it out of her face, not for fashion, no matter how ridiculously put together she looks with such little effort.

As for me, I'm wearing dark indigo jeans with my bling concentrated on the calf. Not too much, just a sprinkling so I'm not completely a plain Jane. My top, from Traycee's rack of new arrivals, is sunburst yellow. I didn't want a color quite so look-at-me, but she refused to sell me the gray plaid I tossed onto the counter. At least I got out of there with nary a bit of lace or anything that sparkles on the shirt.

Bailey gives a little gasp and reaches with a slightly frantic hand toward her back pocket, then she releases a relieved sigh. "Everyone have their licenses?"

Cammie and I do identical checks of our back ends, because every person walking through the door of the Magnolia Moon gets carded. Doesn't matter if you haven't got a hair on your head and use a walker —no ID, no entry.

"As an adult and a lawyer, I appreciate the policy. As a kid, it annoyed the heck out of me."

It's amazing my rebel sister became a lawyer since she was once fully committed to skirting the rules. "Only because you couldn't use a fake one to get beer."

Her eye roll is impressive. "Like a fake ID would have done me any good within fifty miles of here."

"A hundred," Bailey chimes in, "but that didn't stop you from chasing trouble at any opportunity. While Ally and I were inside learning how to two-step, you were usually off with Jolene Meyerson and whichever guys you were calling your boyfriends that week."

Cammie acts like she's chagrined, but no one's fooled. "I was always back by the time Mom and Dad got here for the family dance."

I mock-frown. "Only because you wanted to be able to claim with a straight face that you obeyed the rule that we had to all come together."

"We did," she insists hotly. Then the unrepentant twitch of her lip gives her away. "We came together, we just didn't stay together." She yanks me and Bailey closer to her and squeezes. "And you never once ratted me out."

We set off at a sedate pace toward the front door where a bouncer sits on a high stool, religiously checking each person waiting in the short line.

We unhook arms to get out our identification, and Bailey nudges Cammie. "You ever talk to Jolene? You two were inseparable back in the day."

"We... lost touch, but not before Ally made Jo and her mom's millennium by introducing them to Dolly. Jo hated her mother for years before, but from that day forward, she made sure no one shortened Jolene to Jo ever again."

"That's our big sis. Best friends with the greatest country diva of all time."

"Hardly," I mutter, overly absorbed in checking my own driver's license, knowing it's nothing short of silly, but I don't do well with compliments. Never have. And it was merely Dolly's unbelievably kind heart that made the moment happen. It's not like we have each other on speed dial. Still, it's stunning how everyone expects me to know every single person in the industry. While I know a few and have worked with a few more, it's hardly the case that I can pick up the phone and chat with the greatest legends in country music.

Which is where Cammie and I are spectrum opposites. Cammie doesn't know a stranger, or didn't back in the day, whereas I have been bricked by life too many times to risk getting close to people. I don't talk about it much, even to my sisters, but no one knows how lonely stardom can be, and they wouldn't believe me if I told them.

I strive for something in the general and profound realm rather than the personal and exposing. "I can look back now and see just how sweet those times were. It was all very Norman Rockwell, and I don't think most people get to experience such innocence. Life in a small town isn't perfect, but there are some benefits you can't explain to someone who hasn't lived it."

Bailey steps up to the dude, who sitting down is as tall as I am standing. He nods us all in, and the change from the brilliant evening sun in the parking lot to the dark interior of the Moon takes a second to acclimate to. Then someone shrieks, and my heart falls. I can't get away for a godforsaken second, but then my ego is given a rolled newspaper to the nose when a gorgeous brunette swoops in and pulls Bailey and Cammie in for a hug that has a blast of White Diamonds hitting me a second later. I don't know her name, but clearly she's one of B's and C's friends from high school. A bout of meningitis held Bailey back in junior high, so she and Cammie were in the same class from then on, putting two years between our graduating classes. While it drew them closer than their almost-twins looks already did, I felt even further afield from the orbit of their charm and energy.

Deciding I'm being a ridiculous, maudlin mess, I head to the bar to rectify the missing ingredient. If I'm going to wallow, I might as well have a Dos Equis since I don't have any cheese to go with my whine.

The house lights are only half down, and I can see there's already a MacInnes contingent at one of the big tables, so I step up to buy a couple of buckets to cover the first round. The man to whom Kiki said Tidy sold the Moon is on the phone and gives me a silent *I'm sorry* and holds up a just-a-second finger. I remember his name is Buddy and recall Kiki's super-fast recap of how she met him last year. I give him props for helping her get her head together so she didn't blow her future with Harville, who, by the way, is going to be a daddy and might as well be holding the real moon up all by himself.

Buddy gives a low, "Damn it all," before he ends the call and tosses his cell phone to the side. He hides the strain well as he moves in front of me, although I can see it in the bunch of his shoulders.

He plants both palms on the bar in a gesture I call *long-term bartender pose.*

"What can I get you?"

"A bucket of Dos Equis and one of Lone Star."

The Lone Star is a nod to my dad, who is as unpretentious in his beer as he is in his life.

As Buddy takes my cash, the barest scent of magnolia reaches me before a female shoulder settles next to mine with a tiny bump. A quick look makes me happy in a way totally out of sync with the moment. "Hey, Suzanne."

"Hey. Thanks again for what you said yesterday."

"You're welcome. I'm glad you're here.

She gives Buddy a "hey" before her face turns puzzled. "That didn't sound good."

He gives a spot on the bar only he can see a vigorous rub with his towel. "Turns out Ryan isn't as good with a chain saw as he thinks he is, and the idjit just about took his own thumb off. He won't be playing a guitar again before summer's end. If ever."

A glance at the small stage already prepped with a stool, amp, and mic fills in the story.

Suzanne reaches across the bar and puts a comforting hand on Buddy's, a gesture so easy and kind it makes me like her even more. "I'm so sorry. Half the fun of Sundays are the small sets, and Ryan might be a goofball, but he's always a favorite."

"Maybe this is providence." He takes my cash, but keeps his gaze on her.

She tenses, pulling her hand back, her energy withdrawing just as deliberately. "Don't even think it."

I glance between the two, telling myself to keep my mouth shut. This isn't my business. Not my monkey, not my circus. Not my—

"I'll do a set for you." My mouth, clearly, is haunted because it keeps moving independently of my brain. "But only if Suzanne will sit in with me."

Buddy and Suzanne both whip their faces in my direction, but it's too late to withdraw the words.

"You're kidding, right?" He turns around, counts bills from the register, and returns to me with my change.

I put a five in the tip jar and stuff the remaining dollars into my pocket. "I love small venues, always have. I haven't had a chance to indulge in a long time, and besides, this is the home crowd. Most folks here know me from when I had braces and should've owned stock in Clearasil, so why not? It'd be fun." I turn to Suzanne and put a hand on her arm. "I'd love to do this with you, but my only terms are you wait until we're done to have a beer."

"I can't. I—"

"Look, I'm going to be straight up here. You've got something special, but you have to see it comes from your soul, not a bottle."

There's some fidgeting in the line, reminding us we're not the only customers getting drinks. I'm not sure what gets the credit, but Suzanne takes a deep breath and nods, which has us both turning to Buddy.

I lift both hands in a what-now? gesture. "Any chance you've got a guitar or two around here?"

It doesn't take but a few seconds to establish that Suzanne will get her trusty six-string from her car, and I can borrow the Yamaha, Martin, or Córdoba from Buddy's collection in his office.

Which is how I, Ally King, country music icon, end up having the time of my life on a tiny side stage in the Magnolia Moon dance hall on a Sunday night. Even as we set up, I'm afraid it'll turn awkward and spoiled, but I wait out the buzz circling the room like electricity making a circuit. Then the real joy of being in a small town settles in, and everyone agrees to be complicit in the mirage that I'm just any one of the innumerable folks who've shared the tiny spotlight. Even if I am *that* Ally King, tonight they're going to let me be plain ol' Alyssa MacInnes.

For the first time in a decade, I tune my own guitar. It's insane how giddy it makes me.

Suzanne has adjusted a stand, and I flip through the sheet music in her binder. I'm flattered at how many pages have my byline, but my heart skips an actual beat when I get to the bottom and find an original copy of my first long-form ballad. It's in my handwriting on a piece of paper from a spiral notebook, with notes from my almost-failed chemistry class on the back. In a snap, I'm back in the sciences building, wondering why the heck I chose chemistry to fulfill my science component and kicking myself for going general studies the first year when I knew I wanted to major in music... All to culminate in me tuning out the TA and letting the words that filled my head flow over the blank lines instead of chemical compounds.

"No Shadows at Noon" had burst from me without warning, almost perfect from the first scratch of my pen. I distinctly remember losing that notebook and wondering what happened to this piece of paper, but I always assumed I just dropped it, and it was thrown away.

"Where'd you get this?" I ask as Suzanne puts her strap over her shoulder, shrugging to settle her gorgeous classic Fender against her.

She looks over to see what I'm gesturing to. "I bought that at an auction ages ago. I couldn't believe it when I won and have always wondered if it was real. I decided it didn't matter in the end."

I brush my finger over the words indenting the page, as if relearning them by Braille. "It's real. It's the first draft of the song."

Her pupils, already open from the dim light, go even darker. "Wow. That song means more than you can ever know."

I've sung this piece in public only a handful of times. I was perversely glad when it didn't chart, because somehow that kept it mine, not something strangers everywhere could decide was written about them. I get that it's a universal condition that somedays everyone feels so small they don't think they even cast a shadow, but these words have a special place in my soul, and I'm good with it staying if not private, at least intimate.

"Want to do it?" Once again, my mouth has spoken without permission from my brain, but the expression on Suzanne's face makes it as impossible to take back as the original impulse that landed me on this stage the size of a few sheets of plywood.

"Can we save it for last?"

I nod and think she's wise. Our voices will be warmed up by then, even if we keep the set short.

Buddy gives us a warm intro, and as if she and I have been playing together for ages instead of never, we find a rhythm starting with "Dime Store Cowgirl." I pick up the harmony and let Suzanne shine, thinking that I might have to carve off some of my love for Kacey Musgraves for this new star. There will only ever be one Kacey, but there just might be only one Suzanne Steele, as well.

The strangely magical moment is made easier with no crowd pressing the stage. Instead, the floor is full of folks who don't seem to care a whit who I am, or Suzanne for that matter. They're here to show off their two-step and West Coast Swing moves, and we're good enough to keep toes tapping and feet gliding across the well-worn boards.

We keep to tall glasses of soda, but by the time we get through some Emmylou, a bit of Dolly, a couple of mine, and finally get to "The Chair," we know it's time for a break. We nod at each other, and I flip to where we started and take over on guitar. It doesn't matter that it's been literal years since I've played this song. It's as if my fingers can't wait to get to the first C-G7-C. Not the most original opening as far as chords go, but one that has a special place for me.

This time, I take melody, and as we both hold the final note, I know we've hit it out of the park.

The rousing applause as we leave our little stage isn't the same as the thunder from the Ryman Auditorium or the Hollywood Bowl, but it feels so much nicer, so much more real, than anything I've heard in a long time.

With no help from anything synthetic, Suzanne and I are a little high when we join our extended families around the tables near the cutout of the railing around the dance floor. We catch our breath and enjoy folks executing an energetic polka to the canned music Buddy has started from his playlist.

I'm surprised when I'm the one who initiates a hug, but her return embrace nearly knocks the breath out of me.

"That was incredible. Oh my God, this is the best night of my life."

"I told you you're amazing. Now you just need to believe me." I don't want to take anything away from her, but this has been wonderful for me, too. It's only one set, but I've been transported back, not just because the Moon was where I learned to dance and did a heck of a lot of early sets as a teenager, but because I'd forgotten what it's like to just be in the music, in the moment, with people who, for the most part, are related to me in some way. Not necessarily by blood, but by history and shared small-town upbringing. Shared history. Shared roots.

No one wondering about the take at the door. No one guessing what label or agent might be in the crowd. No one worried about a scratched note or missed cue.

Just a guitar and a mic and the music. That was all. No expectations. No judgments. Nothing riding on it.

And I haven't felt this happy or this relaxed since before I signed... Zane and I signed... the first contract with a major label, and everything changed.

A deep, gravelly voice that could've belonged to Sam Elliott speaks behind me. "Girl, that was some good singing."

I turn in to my father's embrace, almost melting as his strong arms wrap around me, and for one second, I'm safe. His starched shirt is the perfect crisp and scratchy texture under my cheek, his woody cologne an instant time machine back to every important moment in my life. Daddy has always been there, spruced up, as he'd call it, and quietly waiting in the wings, his presence telling me I'm going to be all right.

Another voice comes from behind him, this one not nearly as welcome. "That was fabulous."

The crowd parts like the waters before Moses in the way I despise as Zane steps closer. I'm surprised I didn't heard the rise in the crowd noise, but I was too protected by the bubble of what just happened, which Zane bursts by his mere presence. The ring of *nobody special* that was extended to me has been shredded, and I can see fingers frantically typing on cell phones all around me.

Zane thrusts his hand out. "Howdy, ma'am. I'm Zane King."

My eye roll nearly detaches my optic nerve. Suzanne goes ramrod stiff with an I'm-in-the-presence-of-God reaction.

"Zane." I let the one word stand as merely an acknowledgment, not an invitation.

"If I'd known you were going to do an impromptu, I'd'a gotten here earlier."

"Hence it being called impromptu." I know my voice is edged, and I couldn't care less. The only thing concerning me is getting him out of here before what has been a wonderful couple of hours turns into a nightmare, or more of a nightmare. Even in the dimness, I can see he's brought two from the security team, one staged by the door and the other a few feet behind him.

He's in full thank-God-I'm-a-country-boy mode. Stock Wrangler jeans, pearl-snap Western shirt, perfectly creased black Stetson. He loves his reputation as this tough cowboy, cultivated for years, but I know just how much of it's staged. I know the carefully arranged camera angles to make me look fat have worked to make him look like some kind of modern Marlboro Man. My current level of cynicism makes me smile internally at the comparison—tough and rugged on the outside, a waiting cancer on the inside.

If I were in any condition to be fair, I'd chide myself at my hyperbole, knowing full well it's my hurt and anger painting such a horrible picture of my soon-to-be ex-husband, but today I'm just not that interested in playing nice.

I'm touched and humbled when Harville steps up beside my father, and Trey flanks me on my other side. Zane's bodyguards might be six-five and two-fifty, but mine are a hundred percent goodness and love. It would make an interesting shot on the tabloid pages—me between a sixty-five-year-old man, a preacher, and the string-bean-no-longer giving one of the biggest moneymakers in Nashville a combined stink eye that has Zane backing up a step.

"I'd forgotten what it's like here. It's been too long. I'd love to—"

I cut him off, turning to my father. "Daddy, would you mind taking me back to the estate? The room's getting a little crowded." I reach out to Suzanne, clasping her hand. "Thanks for the set. I hope you'll take me up on that offer."

"I'd love to, but if you'd like me to come with you now, I can. Buddy will take care of the stage."

She hasn't let go of my hand yet, so I give hers a quick squeeze, certain she can't know how deeply touched I am by her support.

"I appreciate it, but I think I'll just go have some downtime." I find a smile and a wink for her. "It was a great set, though. We'll deconstruct it when we get together."

I turn away, my smile fading, and go as quickly as my short legs will carry me. I give a quick nod to Bailey and Cammie, who've stepped closer, both of them reading the scene without requiring a cheat sheet. It's not that I need Daddy to be a papa bear, but I do need a ride as I can't leave Bailey and Cammie stranded. Mostly, I have to get Zane out of the Moon before it becomes pure pandemonium.

He loves it.

I hate it.

I stop when we're all outside the venue, spotting Daddy's Suburban at the edge of the parking lot. Sad how the Moon has gone from my hometown honky-tonk to a *venue* in minutes flat.

"Ally, hold up."

I stop, not so much for Zane's sake as for Daddy's. It's not that he can't keep up with me, but I know his nerves have gone on high alert, and I feel bad for being the tangential cause of his blood pressure rising when it's something I worry about far too often.

If I'm the reason Daddy has a stroke, I'll—

"Can we talk? Please."

I gesture to the tricked-out Jeep in the fire zone, blatantly ignoring the Do Not Park sign. At least he wasn't so pretentious as to bring the stretch limo.

"Is Paris in there?"

Paris. For the love of Pete, her name alone should've warned me two years ago when she joined the team.

"Jesus, Ally, what do you think I—"

The look I give him should have melted him like that scene in *Raiders of the Lost Ark*, but I don't get that satisfying result. At least he bites off the retort about to come out of his beautiful mouth.

And it is beautiful. He is gorgeous in all the stereotypical ways. Tall, dark, handsome, broad shoulders, narrow waist. Pure sexy with his just slightly crooked teeth that have become part of his trademark aw-shucks smile.

The smile I loved with every atom of my being since I was nineteen years old.

The smile that is tentative, with just enough sadness in the corners to start ripping my heart out and shredding it like he tossed it into the maw of a wood chipper and walked away.

"We need to talk, Ally. Even if you don't believe me right now, I'm worried about you."

I take a step closer, but he's smart enough to know it's not a softening on my part. "So here's the deal. I haven't had a chance to get my head around all this except for one thing."

"Ally, if you'll just listen for one second—"

I hold up my hand, palm out. "I'm talking. You're the one who's going to listen. I'll dig into this, and I'll own the pieces that are mine, but I'm done letting you take the lead. You've gotten too comfortable in the driver's seat, but you better buckle up, buttercup, because I'm done riding shotgun."

I have no idea where all my gumption came from. I suppose I can credit a year of being mostly alone with it brewing in the recesses of my brain, just waiting to come out while I was worrying, wondering, and wavering between certainty that everything would turn out for the best and knowing something was terribly wrong.

I know the crunching sound on the gravel behind me is my dad. I know he wants to fix everything. I know I darn sure wish he could.

But I am certain he can't.

I'm not asking him to, but he's a frayed thread of sanity weaving through a braid loosely forming thanks to Bailey and Cammie, holding me together and convincing me I'm not alone.

I've got a lake full of tears ahead of me.

But I've got family behind me.

CHAPTER SIXTEEN

BAILEY

I WATCH my sister leave the bar, and my heart sinks. Even though we've had a couple of long talks between the balcony and shopping, we've kept it surface level, letting Ally reveal what she felt comfortable with.

Which, with Ally being Ally, wasn't a lot.

My Lila ringtone comes from the table. I grab my phone and head for the far corner of the bar where the music is muted, and I can see and hear my girl.

"Hey, baby. I miss you."

"Miss you, too, Mom. So what the heck with Aunt Ally?"

I feel my mouth open and shut, but no sound comes out. I try again. "Sorry?"

"You know Ruth Everson? Taylor's daughter? She and I stay in touch, and she livestreamed Aunt Ally singing with a lady I don't know, and then Uncle Zane showed up. The video gets really muddled, but Aunt Ally is clearly pissed, and then she walks out, and Ruth said she'd call me back when she got more deets."

"Deets?"

Lila sighs. Deeply. "Details, Mom."

"Sorry. Once again, I'm horribly deficient in youthspeak."

"Yeah, well, when you make Plato feel young, I guess…"

"Hey!"

"Aristotle?"

"Not funny, you."

"Seriously, what just happened?"

Not for the first time, I'm incredibly grateful cell phones were barely a thing when I was a teenager.

"Short version is Aunt Ally played a set on the fly, and then things got awkward when Uncle Zane showed up."

"Uh, yeah, didn't I just say all that?"

I refrain from a mom sigh. "Not sure what you want from me, hon."

"I was hoping you'd say Uncle Zane went down on one knee and confessed to being a gigantic jerk and begged for Aunt Ally's forgiveness in front of everyone because he's an asshole, and I don't like him right now."

"Hard to argue with your assessment, but no, he did no groveling I'm aware of, although I'm not sure it would have made any difference."

"Makes me hope he doesn't come to graduation. It's so weird."

"Uncle Zane knows he's in deep doo-doo right now."

"Really, Mom? Doo-doo?"

"Poop?"

"Please stop. Call me the instant you know any more news?"

"I promise. You'll get the deets the instant I do."

"Mom."

"The 411."

"Goodbye, Mom."

"The—"

"I love you, Mom."

The line goes dead.

I'm still chuckling when I get back to the table. Gods above, I love my girl.

A text comes in before I can sit down.

Forgot some deets. Smiley emoji. Staying with Dad next weekend. Can't make the ceremony. Back in Guatemala.

Jake, who was as captivated as the rest of us during Ally's set but has been quiet all evening, sets a fresh beer in front of me and perches on the stool to my right. "You good?"

"Hmmm? Oh, yes. I was chatting with my daughter, and she's letting me know she's going to her dad's unexpectedly."

I tap out a quick acknowledgment and put my phone away.

"I don't mean to ask a rude question, but it's unusual for her to go to her dad's?"

I take a long draw on my beer, enjoying the coldest, most refreshing sip in the entire bottle. "Short version is she doesn't know, and will never, that the cool dude who now thinks she hung the moon and gives tons of time to Doctors Without Borders was once a gnat's hair from being thrown out of college for partying so hard even his frat brothers were like, 'Dude, slow your roll.' I somehow pinged his radar at a party, and the punch line from that night is such a cliché I'm ashamed, except for Lila. She's the best thing that ever happened to me."

"How old is she?"

"Seventeen, graduating from high school in two weeks. I'm still in shock about that."

"You sound incredibly proud."

"There aren't enough words to express it."

I spare him the longer story, that Lila knows her Dad only as the incredible guy who's decent and kind and one hell of a hard worker. Unless he chooses to tell her, she'll never know the frat boy who refused to admit he fathered a child back in the day. I didn't pursue Ted to take responsibility for our unbearably immature partying and inevitable night of drunken sex. He shocked the heck out of me when he contacted me when Lila was eight. He had some come-to-Jesus moment without any evidence of cult influence and wanted to be part of her life.

I admit I was initially reluctant to give him access to her at all. I put him through the wringer to prove this wasn't some bizarre or cruel stunt. In the end, Ted clearly had some life-changing event, and while he wasn't an every-other-weekend-and-Wednesday kind of dad, he was good about keeping in touch and getting together with Lila each time he landed in Houston. In some ways, he was a Disney dad, flying her out to stay with him in San Diego two or three times a year and taking her to exotic locations every birthday, but he's wound up being a far bigger part of her life than I ever imagined.

Jake's phone buzzes. He lifts it to his ear, plugging his other one with his finger. "Doc? What's up?"

My stomach clenches because I know more than most about what's happening in Jake's extended family.

"I'll head over right now. Thanks for calling."

I realize I'm clutching my beer much too tightly and force my hand to relax. I, of course, have to ask. "I'm going out on a limb here. Uncle Lem?"

"The housekeeper texted Doc. Lem was sitting on the floor in the kitchen, apparently having fallen, but he couldn't remember how it happened. Any details, really, and he's angry again."

Jake puts his phone in his pocket and grabs his keys from the tabletop.

"Would you like me to come with you?" I wouldn't be much use diagnostically, but I feel I have to offer moral support.

"Yes, I do, but I don't want you to feel pressured. I know Doc pretty much arm-wrestled you into going yesterday."

"He's good at that, but if your uncle did take a fall, and he won't let Doc come over, maybe I can give him a quick exam. I don't have any instruments—"

"I still have Doc's bag in my truck. I was going to take it by his office in the morning but ran out of time."

"I guess the Fates have stepped in, then. Let me tell Cammie what's going on, and I'll be right with you."

"I'll get the truck and meet you outside."

We move in opposite directions, and by the time I explain things to Cammie, Jake's already at the front door. I slip in the passenger side and wish I could think of something brilliant to say to ease the tension from his handsome face. Instead, I just reach across the distance, hoping my squeeze on his forearm conveys my concern. To my shock, he takes his hand off the wheel and covers mine, keeping them clasped the short drive to Lem's. The spring moon is so bright I can see the worry in his clenched jaw.

I get an even bigger shock when we arrive. He parks, hurries around to my side of the truck, and reaches out to thread his long fingers into my hair and gently pulls me to him, his face closing to mine in slow motion. His lips brush mine in a kiss so soft and sweet, I'm lost. It's not that it's been a long time since I've let a man this close. I mean, that's true, but it's more that Jake has blindsided me, slipping past my guard, and I didn't see it coming.

I know I should stop him.

It would be the wise thing to do.

And there's not a cell in my body that agrees.

People do the strangest things under pressure, especially in medical situations, so I'll chalk this up to skyrocketing cortisol.

He presses closer, his mouth firm and searching, and I kiss him back. My brain's been disconnected, and all I can do is clutch his shirt with both hands to keep my knees from giving way. Or maybe to pull him closer. This is so unlike me, I'm not sure it is me, but I don't have the excuse of being worried out of my mind for a relative.

I don't have any excuse at all.

Especially for the fact that I like kissing Jake Broder, and—

He stops, and there we are, wide-eyed and winded, and I'm going to take the kissing lead if I don't do something to stop myself from giving in to the urge to be utterly wild and reckless.

"Jake, I—"

"I'm not sorry."

I'm not, either.

"I didn't mean to do that quite so soon, but it's all I've thought about since yesterday, and I'm not sure what's up with Uncle Lem, and I'm worried about him, and you look so beautiful in this moonlight."

I like flustered on this man. He was so sure and steady at the lake, but he's clearly a little undone by me, and... I like it.

"Breathe, Jake." I smile at him because I can't do anything else. "I don't need two Broders with head injuries to treat."

"Aren't you Miss Bossy? You must be the one who put the terror in the Terror Trio." The mischief on his handsome face nearly does me in.

"It's the Terrible Trio, thank you very much, not terror." Who put this flirty woman in my normally boring body?

He clearly likes me a little out of sorts, and I can't ignore the flutter in my chest.

"I like terror better." He winks and retrieves the medical bag from the rear floorboard, escorting me to the sidewalk with a warm, gentle pressure on my lower back.

We climb the steps to the porch I send out an internal page for Dr. MacInnes to please return to her brain, stat.

The door opens, and Lem's face is furrowed and cranky until he spots me.

"Well, well, hello again." He waves a hand to usher me inside, not giving Jake so much as another glance. "Did you come to see my new Lionel 1927 Brute? It's a Buddy L size and has three Build-a-Loco motors. It's heavy, though."

"I'd be delighted to see it." I want to look him over first, hoping his mood will hold. "Before we do that, though, would you mind letting me check you out? Then you can give me the grand tour."

"Who told you?" His eyes narrow as he faces Jake. "You need to stop bothering the pretty doctor about me."

I cut in before Jake feels the need to explain. "I don't mind at all, Lem. It's a pleasure to get to come see you again, and after the Pullman car, I'm thrilled to get a look at the Brute."

He levels his I'm-on-to-you-lady gaze on me, but his sweet smile returns. "Well, all right, then. I suppose it wouldn't hurt."

He's quiet and cooperative as I do a quick assessment. No visible bruising or subcutaneous hematomas I can discern. Pulse and blood pressure are slightly elevated but not dangerously high. Pupils are responsive. I have Lem lead the way to see his new toy, and his gate is slow but gives no appearance of pain or muscular impediment.

With Lem's back turned, I give a thumbs-up to Jake, and his shoulders sag in relief.

"Uncle Lem? I'll go fix us all a cup of tea while you show off for Bailey. Is that all right?"

"Sure, sure. Thank you, boy."

Jake stops and clears his throat, adding gently, "Would you like me to ask Doc to come join us? It's been a while."

Lem's steps become shorter and quicker, and his answer's obvious when he doesn't turn to look at Jake. "No. I don't ever want to talk to him again. He let Hannah die."

The distress on Jake's face makes my heart ache. "Uncle Lem, she had cancer. You told me a hundred times how Doc came by every single day to check on her. He got her into that drug trial on compassionate use. He tried."

Lem grows more agitated, his back going rigid and his jaw working like he's chewing something hard. "He should have tried harder."

I signal to Jake to stop. I know he's trying to reconnect Lem to a more realistic version of events, but even without having the details, I know enough about dementia that arguing is only going to agitate his uncle more.

I get Lem calmed down again by letting him expound on his beloved trains. His pure joy as he talks is all I need, because I wouldn't know a G gauge from an S gauge to save my life, much less the multiple choices in scale related to the gauges. It's enough that Lem does, in exacting detail, and it's clear his brain is vibrant and firing when he can talk about his passion.

I'm happy to stay until he winds down and seems content for us to leave. I've texted Doc all his vitals and even snuck a short video while Lem was holding court. I ease my conscience about recording someone without permission by knowing Doc will treat the information as privileged and will protect both the data and his friend with ferocity.

Back in the truck, Jake looks at the house for a long moment and then turns those molten-chocolate eyes on me. "You are really something, you know that?"

"That's sweet, but I haven't done anything, other than having to break your heart by telling you that you're going to have to either get your uncle in assisted living pretty soon, or be prepared to hire full-time nursing."

His arms tense but he drops his hands from the wheel with an obvious effort. "I don't want to take him away from here. It's where he's lived for most of his life."

"I don't think you have to, yet, but this is a big house, and he's losing the ability to track space and time. Elder care isn't my specialty, so I'm hopeful you can get him to a specialist to see what symptoms we can mitigate."

His gaze goes warmer. "We. I like that."

I don't want to clarify that I meant the term as the universal and not the specific *we*, but fatigue is forming frown lines on his forehead.

"You're clearly not sleeping, either."

"So you're a psychic as well as an amazing doctor?"

"Just observant. Which is kinda my job."

"I'm mostly worried about Uncle Lem, but the job I'm doing over in Atlanta has hit some snags. Ridiculous red-tape issues with permitting. I swear cities make ordinances so ridiculous so you either spend most of your time jumping through hoops and filling out paperwork, or you go bankrupt with all the fees."

"You're not the quitting type." Another thing I find I like about handsome Jake.

"They've succeeded in making me more pissed off and determined to win just to spite the bureaucracy."

"Then you're gonna love what you have to do to get zoning for a medical building and the equipment you're going to need for Broder Memorial."

"I don't mind a fight, especially when I've got people by my side who want to be part of the solution, not the problem."

He cuts me a sideways glance, and I give him a you're-silly shake of my head. "Smooth, Jake."

"Hey, my grandfather's the best when it comes to talking his way into getting what he wants. I've learned from a master."

"Nice try, but I'm here for vacation, and then it's back to Houston for not only my daughter's graduation, but my job. That thing I keep mentioning? Where I have a contract and do doctor stuff, and they give me a paycheck?"

"Broder Memorial, although I don't know that that's actually the name yet, could let you do doctor stuff and pay you."

The man will not quit.

"You don't even have the land yet, and you're already hiring staff?" I'm teasing, but my nerves have returned, this time focused on what one kiss has done.

"We do have the land. We just don't have those pesky permits mentioned a second ago."

"Then I think we're putting the cart before the horse. But you're sweet to be so enthusiastic."

And I have a life to go back to.

"Sweet? If you tell me next I have a great personality, I'm going to start day drinking."

"Which tangentially leads me to say I'm not sure what happened a few minutes ago, but you need to get any ideas about me out of your head."

"Too late."

"Jake, I'm serious." Arguing with this man is impossible. "I'm way too old for you."

"Define *way*. My math calculation is I'm seven years younger. That's nothing."

"How would you know?"

"My grandmother Sarah is—"

"One of the Grannies."

"Correct. And Grandma Sarah says you have always been the most determined of you three."

If he's enlisted Grannie help, I will need reinforcements, although I'm not sure, in this situation, my sisters would have my back, other than to shove me toward Jake.

"Your grandmother isn't wrong. Ally's the quietest but most obdurate. Cammie uses humor to deflect. The nice word for me is 'unstoppable,' although lots of folks would pick something much less flattering. Which should tell you to stop arguing with me."

His smile is downright devilish. "In college, I was a master debater, so I like a challenge."

"I'm not a challenge, and even if I were, I'll be gone in a few days, and your life will resume to what passes for normal for you, and I'll return to Houston and what passes for normal for me."

He leans in a bit closer, getting inside my personal space all too easily, and more disconcertingly, not uncomfortably. All the atoms between us heat up, and instead of wanting to pull away, I feel a shiver ripple down my back, and I have to force myself not to close the gap between us.

"You, Dr. MacInnes, definitely need to take that stubborn crown from Ally."

I wish I could see him for a wild night or weekend, but Jake's not a one-off or a friends-with-benefits guy, and when I look into those brown eyes a little too long, I see something I can't have. A wrong-time, wrong-place, wrong-life man I can't get close to because I probably wouldn't want to let him go.

"I have a daughter to get through college, and if Princeton does send her that coveted letter, I'm gonna be paying off another passel of student loans besides mine. I don't think Broder Memorial can afford me."

"Let's cross that bridge when we come to it."

"There's no bridge, Jake." No man, either. "I'm a mother first and then a doctor. I've worked my butt off to get where I am, and my time's divided between my daughter and the hospital."

He drives around to the back kitchen entrance with ease, telling me he's more than familiar with what's unofficially the family entrance. As smoothly as he did outside Lem's house, he slips his hand around the back of my head. My I-don't-have-time monologue melts against the heat of his body as he leans over and kisses me softly, slowly. Deliciously.

He pulls back, and my eyes open slowly. Stern. I must be firm with this man.

"You don't fight fair." If my voice was any more breathy, it would have ruffled his hair.

"Nope."

Another kiss makes me forget my argument against him. Against this. I'm grateful I'm sitting, because he's made me weak and wanting something I haven't had in a long, long time.

"Sleep well, Bailey. I'll call you tomorrow."

I get out and wave him away, making my way inside with the thought that if my dreams are filled with kissing him, and my imagination kicks in and continues the story, I'm not going to get any sleep at all...

CHAPTER SEVENTEEN

CAMMIE

I LOOK around the bar as the crowd descends into a mixture of excited chittering and deathly silence. At the family table, everyone is quiet, the laughter and hugs and excitement of seeing Ally practically glowing under the simple spotlight interrupted by Zane's record-scratch arrival.

I want to yank that Stetson off Zane and stomp it into an unrecognizable pulp. For a precious few minutes, she played like the old Ally, our Ally. The Ally who became one with her music, the kind of transcendence I haven't seen in years, the artist lost in the spell of her music.

And then Zippity Zane had to show up.

I crumple my bar napkin, and Trey rejoins me. "Have we lowered the DEFCON level yet?"

"I think so. Ally had a few choice words for Zane, but he left without causing a bigger scene." He takes a spare napkin of his own, precision-folds it into a little star, places it on my head as though it's the Spencer tiara, and leans back.

My insides go a bit mushy. I know this man so well. All calm and cool on the outside, but he wants to launch Zane into outer space just like I do.

"I'm worried about her, but I'm so glad our dad showed up. She was always super close to him."

"You're not?"

"I'm sure a psychologist would have a field day deconstructing it, but here's another long story short: After the divorce, Ally stayed with Dad, Bailey and I stayed with Mom, and we had a few years where the three of us didn't spend much time together."

Trey gives a low "humph" before draining his bottle in a long gulp that has my attention raptly transfixed on his throat.

"Sometimes my family is its own episode of *Dr. Phil*, yet it's all proof that people are the same everywhere, even when you think your drama's unique. You know I was an only kid with a single mom, but you probably have no idea my football coach kept me from completely ruining my life. Believe me, I get family trouble."

It's impossible to grow up on the estate, with Mina and Fina Greene being a huge part of my youth, to not know that Trey's bio dad had been the grossest epitome of a broken and evil man. And sweet Trey, this man returning peace to my soul, is the only human alive to know exactly how his dad died. We don't have the details, but the hunting accident traumatized a boy barely into his double digits. That Trey turned into such a good guy after such a horrific event is yet another testament to the amount of love flowing around our quirky, though not without flaws, family and town.

"Isn't it strange how singular events have so much power? A bout of meningitis put Bailey back a year in junior high, and that put two years between me and Bailey against Ally. We all were so busy with sports and extracurricular stuff, and somehow, it became Dad chauffeuring Ally around and Mom hauling me and Bailey. I don't think it was anything intentional, just consequential."

"It's my theory most parents are trying to get through as best they can and not ruin their kids entirely."

I give my own quiet "humph" this time. That he can be so positive considering his paternal nightmare speaks volumes about this intense man who has managed to keep an amazing sense of humor despite it all. "I'm not a parent, so all I can offer is that feels right."

"Living in a small town can be a blessing and a curse, but in my case, I'm glad for it."

"Ally and Bailey and I were talking about that when we got here this evening."

A woman clears her throat behind me. It's an automatic response to turn, but I'm frozen before I'm completely facing her.

"Jolene." I'm not sure if I thought it or said it aloud.

"I heard you were in town."

I stiffen. "Come to gloat?"

I wouldn't blame her. She's standing there in curve-hugging jeans, perfect makeup, and red hair that used to be corkscrew-curly lying in silky waves from, I assume, an amazing Brazilian blowout. I know because we used to spend hours doing each other's hair and makeup before going to the skating rink, trying so desperately to be cool around whichever particular jock we had crushes on that week. We shared our dreams, our hopes, our diaries.

We pinkie-swore we'd be best friends forever.

Until I met Johnnie Arthur Dallas.

She winces. "You should remember I've never been much of a grudgeholder."

Trey touches my arm and nods toward the busy bar. "I'm going to get a fresh round. You want anything?"

"Just water for me this time." I put my hand on the one that's sliding off my wrist, like I'm lightning, and he's my grounding rod. "Thanks."

Those few seconds are enough for me to take a deep breath and fully face the person I haven't seen since she agreed to be in my wedding, despite her reservations. I've missed her dearly.

Ever the well-trained MacInnes, I gesture to the empty stools around the table. "Take your pick."

She hesitates, her expression as uncertain as her posture. "You sure?"

The sound coming from my throat could never be called a laugh, but it does contain irony. "I'm holding the barest scintilla of pride by my fingernails, but sure, why not? It gives you a chance to go all 'I told you so' and tell me you think I'm an idiot."

"What I was thinking was how much I've missed you."

Well, butter my butt and call me a biscuit...

I'm crying, and she's crying, and we've smeared our makeup, and then we start laughing, and I accidentally snort, and she cries harder, but this time from laughter, and just like that, we're hanging on to each other for dear life, and the years slide away.

Then we're talking about how we were both maniacs when we rushed the fanciest sorority on campus as a lark, and then we both got in. Jolene's mother was over the moon, wanting Jolene to be a Tri Delt more than life itself. My mother cared only because she thought I'd get good postgrad contacts out of it.

We both grab napkins and wipe our noses, but she starts first. "Don't think I don't know that the only reason they let me in was because you said you wouldn't pledge if I couldn't."

This time, my snort is deliberate. "And don't think I don't know the only reason they let me in was because Ally just won a Grammy, a CMA, and a CMT, and the music world was abuzz."

"Maybe, but you couldn't care less if you got in, and it made LeighAnn furious you never showed proper reverence for the honor bestowed upon you."

"Yeah, bitch never forgave me."

We exit off memory lane, college edition, and spend a little time in a traffic circle around law school. Of course, that's where we get a little awkward again, because our estrangement started when she got mad at me for even considering going out with Johnnie. She told me I was certifiably braindead, in exactly so many words, but I'd already fallen in love with him, and then we didn't speak for the last half of our third year. It made finals brutal, not having her to study with and talk to, but Johnnie coached me through exams and the bar. He was an ace no one else in my class had. Still, it hurt that Jolene and I didn't get drunk together to celebrate our success.

I realized down the road that she was right. I got sucked into Johnnie's world and gave up all my friends from college and law school by telling myself it was just a facet of starting my career.

Yeah, I didn't really believe me, but as time went on, I stuffed more cotton into my little inner voice's mouth.

Jolene pushes her hair behind her shoulder and seems to find the collection of bottles on the table fascinating. "So, um, you want to maybe get together for a burger before you leave town?"

"I'd like that, especially since I might be staying for a hot minute." I do the laugh-cough combo that seems to be a permanent part of my vocabulary these days. "I don't exactly have law firms lining up to offer me jobs."

"They will. You've always been a force of nature, Cam. Someone will snap to and realize they'd better grab you fast. In fact, send me your résumé, and I'll give it to my HR department."

Old Cammie would have laughed and said, "Hell yeah!" But new Cammie's a little gun-shy, a little too afraid to tempt the Fates or the universe or whatever the hell is out there that's decided to see just how much I can endure before I break.

We exchange numbers and promise we'll make a date soon, and I swallow against more threatening tears. There's the part of me that wants to put on my happy face and brush away the past and another part that's simply exhausted and beyond the ability to pretend. At least today. Maybe by the time we meet at Vivann's, or some other gastronomical gem on the square, I'll be back to my old self.

Trey clearly has superb timing, because just after we hug again, he returns with drinks, and I slug down the ice water. It fortifies me enough to say yes when he asks me to dance, and I learn something new about my old friend.

He's an amazing lead.

Knowing how to dance in a small town is almost a law. Going out dancing is one of the limited entertainment possibilities, but back in the day, Trey was a hang-with-the-dudes kind of guy when the teens took over the Moon on Sundays. His drink of choice was root beer, and while he wasn't the laugh-and-jeer kind, he was the stay-out-of-the-line-of-fire type.

First thing I notice, Trey and I are almost the same height. It usually bothers me, and it definitely bothered a few dudes I dated before I met Johnnie, but with Trey, it doesn't seem to even be a blip on his radar.

Second, Trey has clearly fixed the hole in his social-skills base, because he is smooth and confident and makes me feel like I'm skating. Every turn gives me that stomach whoop like I'm on a merry-go-round, every spin is led that perfect fraction of a second before the beat so the move is effortless, and I feel like I should be on *Dancing With the Stars*.

I'm the right kind of breathless when, after a two-step, a West Coast Swing, and a very energetic Viennese waltz, we make it back to the table. "Dang, you got some skill while I was gone."

"Dancing in a Texas town is like having to know how to golf in a big city. You'd be amazed at how many wives of prospective clients make it clear it's their getting-to-know-you venue of choice. I think it's because it's the only way they can get their husbands on the floor."

"Whatever the reason, I'm grateful. You're amazing."

Trey goes into that quiet space, and I swear a cone of silence drops around us because I feel like we've suddenly become the only two people in the building.

"No, Cameron, you're amazing. And I've missed you."

Aw, crap. There it is. That clenching in my stomach and instant surge of acid eating up the back of my throat. Johnnie wanted me to go on. He told me one night after he'd had a little too much Scotch and was being uncharacteristically maudlin. Johnnie was a lot of things, but he was rarely sad or depressed. He had a love of life that was infectious. If I were being truthful, sometimes it was frustrating, which was born out when I was faced with the consequences of his often blithe, *Everything will work out.*

That's true, in one sense. Everything worked out, but it came with a huge cost, both in real dollars and emotional ones.

"Hey, you... pretty lady with the sad face. What's up?"

I smile at him, wondering for a split second what my life would have been like if I let him kiss me under the bleachers. Somehow, even then, I knew it would lock me in Magnolia Bloom, and nothing and no one was going to do that. Not back then.

Now?

Now it's too soon to be having these crazy thoughts.

"Nothing's up in particular. Just a little overwhelmed to be back and learning all that's going on with my sisters. But hey, that's life, right? Just one big ride."

Trey reaches over and tucks a strand of hair behind my ear, then glides his finger down my jawline. My entire central nervous system lights up. I'd probably short out an EKG machine if I were hooked up.

"Don't," he whispers.

"Don't wh—"

"I mean it. Don't. Don't pretend everything's all right. Don't pretend you can joke your way out of what's happening."

I know he's being Trey, trying to help.

And I just can't. Not right now. Not yet.

"Hey, my system has worked fine, and truth be told, I've been taking care of me for a long time, so you can take yourself off guard duty. I need a friend, not a therapist."

I put enough bite behind my words that he moves back, his nod slow and his smile sad.

"Then, as a friend who knows you need a job, can I offer you some work until you decide what you're going to do?"

"I don't need chari—"

"It's not charity," he cuts me off with a frown. "Damn it, Cameron, can you lighten up for one second? Not your pretend lighten up, where you crack some joke."

I stare at the floor because he's right, of course, and he's zinged me right in my soft spot.

I take a deep breath before looking up again. "So, what's the offer?"

"Jake Broder just closed a huge deal in Tarrant County, and they're going to be doing a high-end subdivision. Gated, golf course, whole shebang. My office is going to do all the contracts, title work, and closings. I've reached out to a few colleagues who I thought might be interested in joining forces, but so far none of the folks I'd really like to work with have the bandwidth to come on board, and here sits an eminently qualified lawyer who knows Texas title and closing laws like the back of her hand. Must be fate."

"I started in real estate, that's true, but I've done more probate these last few years."

"It's not like the laws have changed that much. You'd be up to speed in about twelve seconds."

I have to admit the offer is intriguing on several levels. I enjoy real estate work more than probate because, generally, in real estate transactions, everyone's happy. Doing title work is meticulous and sometimes boring, but those were exactly the aspects of it that I loved. I get a lot of grief about my personality, called *quirky* when people are being generous and *annoying* when I go too far, but the truth is, getting lost in my work saves my sanity. It forces my brain to shut up and stay focused.

And in the end, if I'm completely truthful, beggars can't be choosers and all that.

Dropping my cover is hard, but I swallow and find my voice. "Tell me more."

The financial details are fair, and I appreciate that he's not patronizing me by offering a ridiculous deal, nor trying to take advantage of someone with my level of experience. The offer means I don't have to max out credit cards to stay alive, nor beg my cousin for family charity on the estate.

Before we finish a fresh round of beers, we've hammered out a tentative plan, and as Trey excuses himself to go to the restroom, I'm left at the table with my pulse rising again.

I remind myself this is only temporary. It doesn't cement me into Magnolia Bloom.

But it does expose my heart to memories and might-have-beens, and that is probably much more dangerous.

CHAPTER EIGHTEEN

ALLY

PASSING through the front gates in my dad's Suburban means I can release the breath I've been holding, because while they are thankfully few, the lens rats have to stop there. This is private, posted property, and I'd have the sheriff on their picture-taking asses faster than heat lightning. The additional mile to Brian's place will add even more padding to my comfort zone.

I'm hoping the reduced media presence means I'm becoming old or uninteresting news, but it's probably just an indication of what a pain in the butt driving to and hanging out in East Texas can be. Regardless, I'm glad for the diminishing fascination with my smallest move. Like many others before me, the scandalmongers will set their sights on another victim, and the intermittent bits on television and short articles in the press will keep fading, unless the divorce gets really ugly. I hope that doesn't happen, but it's not entirely within my power.

When we reach Brian's, I jump out of the truck like my boots are on fire, but look over at my father, who's clutching the wheel like he's personally responsible for it staying in place. Daddy is a man of few words, but his body language is shouting that he's upset, though the concern radiating from him head-to-toe lets me know it's not at me.

"Want to come in for a bit?" The last thing I want is for him to track Zane down when his protective mode is dialed up.

Unhinging his death grip on the steering wheel, he gets out and shuts the door with such softness it tells me he'd rather slam it off the hinges. "Of course. Got any coffee?"

Daddy puts his arm around my back as we walk up the steps to the porch. I unlock the door and see the simple white curtains flutter in the evening breeze. I left the windows open, so the illusion of safety isn't lost on me, but the estate is a little island of incongruity in an insane world. It's not that the odd theft doesn't happen, but it's rare. We've always thought the estate is like a military base without armed guards and razor wire. Its size and tight-knit community make it, in its own way, a self-policing entity. My fiction-loving brain thinks how easily we could be some cult compound, but for the most part, it's a little piece of heaven, and I'm incredibly lucky to be a part of it.

I start the kettle and rinse the French press while the water heats. Hand to God, I'm a coffee snob, but thankfully CT and Mina have started carrying a small line of unique brands at the Magnolia Market. I make a mental note to kiss both their cheeks in gratitude the next time I see them.

My father, the poster child of patience, picks up a tattered copy of *Lonesome Dove* from the coffee table and sits down in the kitchen with me, takes his hat off, and lays it on the crown, the perfect curve of the classic Stetson preserved from years of careful handling. This is his dress hat, one of the first I bought him once I made some real money and the one he swears he'll be buried with. I always remind him that event is unequivocally forbidden. He casually reads the back-cover copy like he hasn't memorized the dang thing over the years or worn out at least one DVD. I sent Daddy a condolence bouquet when Larry McMurtry died, and he got a chuckle out it.

After four minutes pass in comfortable silence, I pour him a mug of the dark, rich elixir of life, this one a single origin from a small farm in

Nicaragua. I'd still find a can of Folgers in Daddy's kitchen, but I'm determined to bring him over to the decadent side of coffee that actually deserves the title.

It's one of our favorite arguments. Daddy takes the side that if the red plastic canister was good enough for his dad, it's good enough for him. I counter and threaten to come to his house in the dead of night and throw out anything with blend on the label. Hey, I deserve a few perks from the years I've spent two hundred days on the road, missing holidays and staying three nights in the hospital from exhaustion and dehydration.

Not that Daddy knows about that particularly bad week.

I take my first sip, even though I'll regret it in a few hours when I can't go to sleep. "Thank you for always being my knight in shining armor, Daddy. I love you, you know."

"Of course I know, pumpkin. I just wasn't expecting a high-noon showdown within five minutes of you getting home."

"I'm not sure this rises quite to that level, but I was hoping I'd have more than forty-eight hours before Zane figured out I was here. I was pretty sure he'd go to the farm first."

"You may have a lot of names for him right now, but stupid isn't one."

"I don't know, I rather like it."

My dad's lips twitch, but he just gives me his classic one-brow acknowledgment. "I'd be the first to admit he's done something monumentally asinine, but not that he's congenitally an idiot."

My frown contains no teasing whatsoever. "Whose side are you on?"

"Don't ask silly questions. Of course I'm mad enough to chew nails and spit barbed wire, but I'm gonna do my best to get you off full boil, because we both know that won't end well."

"Surely I have a right to, as you say, spit enough barbed wire to refence the whole estate."

"You do, but I'm fair to certain you'll just stuff it all inside and give yourself an ulcer that'll make Bailey's look like child's play." He gives me a warning look. "Don't get mad at me, but while you're stewing, you need to put in the mix that Zane has always been the one to come to you, and even though emotions are high, he came here, to you. I know why you sent him packing tonight, but you keep the moat around your castle pretty wide, and I'm not sure the chains work anymore on your drawbridge."

"Hell of an analogy, Daddy."

"I may be a hick from Fort Worth, but you're the one who got me started reading fantasy novels."

"First of all, getting you to read something besides treatises on World War II, or that book in your hand for the tenth time, is one of my greatest achievements, and second, you own one of the biggest Kubota dealerships in the United States, so I don't think you can play the hick card ever again."

"Thanks to you, my big-hearted girl."

"I didn't—"

"Dang it, girl, can't you just once take a compliment? You bought a dealership because that bass player's uncle in your band way back was going bankrupt. You pay more than it's worth to keep him from losing everything, then sign the paper over to me like you're payin' off an IOU for a candy bar. I'd still be selling used cars in Atlanta if it wasn't for you."

What's up with my agent, now Daddy, trying to make me out to be some kind of angel? It's ludicrous, and I tell him what I told her. "Don't paint a halo on me just yet."

"Oh, I won't. I may be your daddy, but I ain't blind to any of my three girls." He takes another long sip and sits back. "Now, you know I love you, but you can be awful pigheaded sometimes."

"It appears I take after my father."

"That may be, but there's times when digging in your heels is a good thing and times when it's not."

"I'm gonna go way out on a limb here and guess you're about to tell me this situation's a *not*."

"Well, it's kinda like when you wanted to pay off all of Bailey's medical school loans, and she wouldn't let you."

"Yeah, and now Cammie can't buy a bagel at the day-old store, but I knew nothing about it until a day ago." I slap my thigh and then clench a fist to keep from beating on the table like an overwrought child. "I have more money than God has little green apples. I can help them."

Daddy reaches over and cups my chin before tracing a callused thumb down my jawline. "But maybe they don't want to be beholdin' to you. Maybe they'd rather have a sister than a banker."

"I'd never ask them to pay me back."

"Debts ain't always on a balance sheet, baby girl."

"Daddy—" I cut myself off and rake my fingers through my hair. "I feel like we're in a *Twilight Zone* episode. Half this conversation is quite esoteric, and the other half you're telling me stuff about me like I don't know."

"Sometimes I don't think you do. Did you call either one of your sisters over these last couple of years other than to say, 'Hi, how's the weather?'"

"That's silly. Bailey's been a wreck getting Lila through high school, and while I didn't know about the financial stuff, Cammie lost her husband. I couldn't put more on their shoulders."

"You just said they shoulda put more on yours."

"That's different. I don't have children, and the love of my life didn't drop dead from a heart attack."

"No, but you're mighty lonely in that turret you've built around yourself."

"The only turrets in my life are right over there." I point a thumb in the general direction of the castle and swallow the urge to snap. It's not his fault I'm stretched to breaking, and I know he's trying.

"Listen, honey, I'm probably the last person qualified to be a marriage counselor, but don't make any decisions while you're hurt and angry."

"You're telling me to forgive him."

"Nope, not even close. I'm suggesting you might refrain from drawin' and quarterin' him just yet. It's not about forgiveness, but right now you only see the bad, and that's a poor board to dive off of."

"I'm not ready to be calm and logical, and it's not fair to ask me to be."

"I know it's not, but life's never fair. Still, the universe gives you what you need, not what you want."

"That's very Zen of you."

"I hired this floor manager who's real quiet. Makes me think of you. He's the best man I've ever had on the job. Anyway, you know how I always eat lunch in the breakroom late so folks don't feel awkward with me being there, but I want 'em to know they can come talk to me casual-like if they want to? So once a week or so, he joins me, and he gave me this book called *Mindful Self-Compassion*."

I'm not sure how Daddy moved from *Lonesome Dove* to mindfulness, but at the moment, I'm not too sure about life in general.

"Did you read it? You're not exactly known to be a self-help kinda guy."

"I might surprise you these days, baby girl. When a man's looking at the other side of the hill, you start to think."

I don't like any references to my father aging. His silver hair's distinguished and a sign of wisdom, not that he's topped life's roller coaster and is gaining speed on the downslope.

I swallow around my dry throat. "What did this guru impart?"

"Basically, do you want to be right, or do you want to be happy?"

"Right now, I just want to be mad."

"Fair enough, but it's easier to be mad than it is to be hurt. Still, you've got your sisters to help you make voodoo dolls to stick pins in, and I'm here to keep you from cutting out your own heart."

I play with the handle of my mug, wanting to ask a question I've withheld for a long time and needing to do something, anything, to stop talking about Zane. "Speaking of cutting out your own heart, do you regret having me? I made you give up baseball."

The man who's been my rock since I was old enough to call him Daddy doesn't hesitate. "Not for one second. Getting the call from the majors was a dream come true, sure, but your mom was so sick that first pregnancy. I wasn't going to run off and be gone most of the year."

"But—"

"Baby girl, the second that nurse put you in my arms, I knew what God meant for me to do. I could probably have tried again, or gone into coaching, but I couldn't do it. Once Boo and Cam came along, well, things worked out the way they were supposed to."

"But then you and Mom divorced, and you were stuck with me."

"Stuck? Good gracious, don't you ever say that. Your momma's a... different kind of woman. I thought I knew her when we met, but whether I was blind or she changed, it doesn't really matter. She was a woman of the eighties, and I had to support her decision to share both the burden and the joy of being a parent. She wasn't going to metaphorically let me drive off into the sunset while she raised three babies and tried to finish her degrees, and she was damn right to do so."

He's got my mother pegged. Perhaps he's been mindful a lot longer than I realized.

"Nothing's more important to her than those blasted letters after her name."

"Don't think that. She loves you three more than you'll ever know. She's just... wired different than me, ya know? Doesn't make her bad. And, honey?"

He reaches over and takes my chin, making me look at him with no filter, no hemming, no hawing.

"Nothing, and I mean nothing, has been more important than being a daddy to my three girls."

I lean forward and rest my cheek on his chest, listening to his heart beating strong and powerfully under my ear as he wraps his love and his arms around me like the warmest of blankets.

"Your mom and I made mistakes, but we tried our best, and you need to take that away with what you're going through. You and Zane had some good years, and now you're moving on. Remember the good. Don't hang on to the anger and the hate, baby girl. It'll eat you up."

I sit back and wipe my face, nodding. I did tend to put him on a pedestal and make Mom the villain, but the truth is, my mother's drive was just as responsible for me seeking my dreams as Dad's love and support. "Thank you, Daddy. For everything."

"It's why God put me on this old ball of mud, pumpkin. Now, you got any sweets around here?"

CHAPTER NINETEEN

BAILEY

I NAB the last bite of ice box pie and sit back with a groan. Ally and Cam got their fair share of Vivann's signature dessert, but I'm no fool. My sisters are determined to fatten me up, and if that means I get more chocolate, who am I to argue?

"And Jake just did as you asked? Stayed away?" Ally sets down her fork like she's waiting for me to retract what I said.

I shouldn't expect Ally to be anything but skeptical. Our lives are radically different. I'm a doctor. People generally listen when I make requests. In my big sister's case, people tend to be more disingenuous, say yes to her face but mean no. I know she's been hurt, burned, and that makes me sad, but it's not something I can fix.

"Jake's one heck of a guy." I take another sip of iced tea and wish I had Ally's way with words. I sound weak, even to myself.

Cammie snorts, and I realize it's one of the few things I don't miss about her when we're apart. "Apparently, he's one heck of a kisser, too."

I check near our table, wondering how many other diners just learned the news of my intimate moment with Jake Broder.

Why did I open my mouth at our wine finale on the balcony yesterday? Right. Because I forgot alcohol tends to free all my secrets. Thanks goodness we're finishing lunch on the square and are about to go our separate ways. It's been a glorious twelve days of time spent together and exploring on my own, but I'm antsy to return to Houston. I checked on Lem for Doc a couple more times, but otherwise, I did a lot of walking, shopping our local venues, and generally obeying my teenage taskmaster's requirement of relaxing before I explode all over everything.

"That would be gross, Mom, and I'm not cleaning it up, 'kay?"

I assured Lila she didn't need to search the internet for a hazmat suit anytime soon.

I firmly cut off all teasing about Jake and enjoy my last hour with my sisters. Besides, they're both staying at my house for Lila's graduation, so this time it'll be days, instead of months on end, before we get back together.

We finish our goodbyes and see-you-in-a-fews, and before I can blink, I'm back in The Woodlands. After hugging my girl, I take her for ice cream and then send her off to her best friend's house for more graduation festivity planning. Not having her hovering lets me sneak into town and through the back door of my office building, intending to give my desk a once-over before a full day tomorrow.

Unfortunately, I'm spotted by a fellow in the group. Fortunately, I really like Miles. Unfortunately, Miles has been pushing to do dinner more than once a week. Fortunately, he's got a great sense of humor and seems to accept my repeated refusals to do more than our Mondays at Magee's. Unfortunately, my recent trip home seems to have awakened a long-dormant part of me that wonders what it would be like to change the pattern, make our dinner as friends an actual date, and whew, what if it went further? Because I know darn well he'd like it to. Until recently, I thought that a bad idea. Now?

"Hey, Miles." I make the first move, gesturing him to hurry and shutting the door behind us after I glance up and down the hall like I'm a cat burglar casing the joint.

He smiles at me in his I'm-sexy-and-I-know-it way. "I think I like this."

I shake my head in mock despair and move around to my chair, leaving him on the other side of my desk to perch on the arm of one of the Queen Annes.

"Not that I'm not glad, but I thought you weren't back until tomorrow."

I hike an eyebrow at him. "You're that familiar with my schedule?"

"I am when we're short-staffed, and I've done extra appointments and rounds."

Guilt slides over me like melted cheese on a Whataburger double-double. "I'm sorry. I shouldn't have taken so much time."

"No one deserved some R&R more than you, but before you start arguing with me, I'm glad you're here under the radar, because I want to talk to you."

"Isn't that what we're doing?"

"Jeez, get a little rest, and you come back all smart-aleck-on-steroids?"

I pick up my favorite pen, given to me by my dad at my white-coat ceremony, and pop the cap on and off the classic, old-school fountain pen. "Are we getting to a point?"

"Yes, *we* are—"

The door opens, and the secretary who keeps our group mostly in line pokes her head in. "Oh! Sorry, Bailey. I thought you were out, so when I heard voices, I wondered who was in your office."

"No apologies necessary. Thanks for checking."

The older woman who takes no guff from any of us gives Miles a sharp nod and leaves, but I'm pointedly reminded that my illusion of having twenty seconds by myself is now dust in the Houston wind.

Miles pretends to shudder. As the most recent member of our squad, he gets the least slack of anyone. "She scares me."

"She should. Take my advice and don't get on her bad side. Now, you were saying?"

"I was saying I wanted to talk to you about this at dinner, but you keep managing to avoid my innumerable charms, so I guess I'll have to get to the point. Come with me to the new group. I know you like almost everyone, so it'd be the same home team, just with much better benefits. I've been assigned to sweet-talk you into taking head of PH/PAH, and it'd be—"

"Whoa, whoa there, Dr. Motormouth."

"Come on, Bailey. You know none of us are truly valuable to the giant machine. We're all cogs here. Nobody's irreplaceable."

"I never implied I'm irreplaceable, but I am someone who values commitment."

"Your contract's almost up. I know they've been leaning on you to re-sign."

"And how would you know that?"

"Anyone with half a brain can see it from a mile away. You think Johnson or Nelson come over here to talk to any of the rest of us lowly staffers, yet dog your heels like a Bluetick Coonhound? Gossip's the fastest spreading virus we have around here."

I cough a mock laugh. "Hunting dogs? Really? I know darn well you're from Paducah, so don't try to Texan me."

He gives me his best hurt-puppy, look but my warning glare's extra firm. "All right, all right, got it." He raises his hands but shifts to the actual seat of the chair, leaning forward with his elbows on his knees. "No more games, although I'm destroyed my affable warmth and devastating good looks didn't sway you."

I'm not about to tell him he indeed has an impressive arsenal of talents that warm up my lady parts. Those are not, however, valid arguments to the issue at hand.

"I'm flattered, but let's not kid ourselves. Starting a new group in this town where you can throw a rock in any direction and hit either a doctor or a lawyer makes this new endeavor a small fish in an overcrowded pond."

"Maybe, but we've got some great talent, so it's not like we're all fresh out of residency and exhausted, with our main goal being not killing our patients."

Oof. That hits too close to home, but I've not had any wine today, so my secret nightmare's safe.

I cap my pen before I dry out the nib and ask the question I should have led with. "If you're going with the others, why are you here? They've all given their notices and exited stage left."

He has the grace to look chagrined. "Um, well, if I'm forced to continue my honesty streak, I'm the ringer hanging around charged with getting you to come along. And—"

There's a quick two-pop knock, the door opens, and my favorite cardiologist comes in, looking harried. "Hey, Bailey, heard you were back. Do you have a sec—oh, Miles. Sorry, didn't see you."

"Hey, Rich, good to see you. Could you come back in a few?"

Rich looks between me and Miles, and I find my back going stiff. Rich is a great guy, a fabulous heart specialist, but I'm not comfortable with the things I imagine are pinging in his brain.

"I'm sorry, Rich. Can I come see you in five?" I fight for a smile that doesn't read *I have nothing to be flustered about. Ignore the pulse pounding in my neck.*

Tucking the file under his arm, he turns to leave. "Sure, sure. Thanks."

Rich leaves with one questioning backward glance, which Miles evidently takes as a signal to get up and put the brakes on our conversation. "I'll leave you alone, but think about it."

The door snicks shut again, and I wonder why I don't just take the thing off the hinges and leave a gaping maw so anyone who feels like it can come into my space and demand my attention.

Forcing a long breath, I push aside my frustration and the harsh truth that I'm the one who trained everyone from the receptionist to the chief of surgery that I'll always make time for them.

I pull a pad of paper over and free my pen again, drawing concentric circles in my favorite violet ink, trying to do a quick pro/con list. Cons are easy. Starting in a new position, even one where I'd be a little higher in the pecking order, still means a lot of work, to say the least. The pro slot has a pretty enticing entry, though. Lila will be off to college, leaving a hole in my life and a lot of free time, time I'll need to fill so I don't go crazy worrying about her. And, if I'm being honest, a new job would keep me too busy to worry about a certain builder in

Magnolia Bloom with his own enticing offer I'm trying desperately to forget.

I rake my hands through my hair and put my doodling pen away, reaching for a plain old rollerball and pulling a stack of folders toward me to put something productive in motion. If I can't get my thoughts in order, at least I can get some of these charts off my desk. Then I remember Rich.

"Days need to be thirty-six hours." I push my chair back to head down to his office, wondering what emergency I can help alleviate on a day when I'm not supposed to even be here.

Four people call my name, but I wave and keep walking. I'm sure they'll catch me when I come back this direction.

So much for time off.

A pain slices through my stomach. I round the corner and pause, putting a hand on the wall to steady myself. Acid climbs up my throat, forcing me to the closest cooler for a cup of water, gulping it down and wondering why the hell I didn't put a roll of antacids in my pocket.

Oh, yeah. I'm not supposed to be here. I'm supposed to be enjoying my last few hours of vacation.

I have no one but myself to blame for my stomach's sad situation, but what's done is done. It's not like I can just up and change who I am or how I operate.

Straightening after the spasm passes, I head on down the hall, ready, as always, to fight the good fight.

CHAPTER TWENTY

CAMMIE

A LOT CAN HAPPEN in two weeks. I've gone from unemployed and
fighting hopelessness to having a contract opportunity that I didn't
imagine in the many hours I've agonized over what my future holds.
Trey's offer was nothing short of heaven sent to tide me over until I
figure out what the heck I'm going to do with my life.

Nice thing is, I'm sitting in a for-real office with a for-real door and
a for-real window in a for-real Victorian mansion turned office
building in the budding business district of Magnolia Bloom. We
cleaned out the space in the turret at the opposite end of the hall from
his and repurposed various pieces of furniture from a carriage house
out back that was long ago turned into a storage unit. The end result is
a lovely, if eclectic, space where I can help him with his fortuitous
overflow work.

I could get used to coming into work every day in this beautiful
piece of restored architecture surrounded by a manicured lawn and a
small but intricately tended garden. It's perfect, down to the stereotypical wraparound porches, gables, and intricate trim galore. I'm just glad
I'm not the one who has to pay to maintain such an intricate façade.

Still, it bears repeating there are turrets on each end, and now I can trade stories with Kiki about having an office in such an idyllic space.

A quick knock precedes Jocelynn's entry. "I'm about to head home. Need anything?"

The woman looks at me with eyes far older than her thirty-five years. I quickly learned that she was one of Trey's original clients when he took any work that would come through the door and did more divorces than he ever wanted. Jocelynn liked to be call Joss now, which I can understand from someone who escaped a brutal marriage and clawed her way through junior college to get a paralegal certificate. She's changed her look, her name, and her spine's now solid steel.

I'm not surprised Trey hired her and let her work her hours around her classes, and I'm equally unsurprised Joss is more fiercely protective of him than any Rottweiler ever dreamed of being.

I still haven't passed muster yet, but she seems to be giving me a little more opportunity to prove myself worthy of my own second chances. "I'm good, thanks. Enjoy your day."

I don't get a "you, too," but at least the left corner of her mouth lifts before she retreats.

I don't have time to get reabsorbed in the files I'm familiarizing myself with when a much deeper voice interrupts.

"What are you still doing here?"

I give Trey a mock frown. "I'm kissing up to the boss to show him he hasn't made a horrible mistake."

With a laugh, he comes in and settles himself in an overstuffed chair with outdated upholstery that's going to have to do for now.

I fold my hands on my desk and don my calm, professional attorney expression. "How can I help you, sir?"

"For starters, you can have dinner with me. I'm flying to Houston tonight and staying with a friend from law school, then spending tomorrow in the bowels of the Harris County Courthouse to do some old-school records work. I need sustenance." He gives me his perfect Trey grin. "And scintillating company."

Something pings in my gut, vibrating at a *holy flirtation, Batman* frequency that nearly has me racing for the bathroom. Praying none of it shows on my face, I up the wattage on my smile in the hopes of hiding the blind panic doing an F1 speed trial around my spleen.

"That's sounds lovely, and you're really sweet, but—"

"But it's too soon, and I'm a doofus."

"No, well, yes, you're a doofus, and that's what I lo—um, appreciate most about you, but it's not too soon in the strictest sense. Besides, having dinner doesn't mean it has to be a date."

He looks at me for a long moment in his unique Trey way. "That's true, but what if it were?"

"Then it'd be a bad idea."

"Because we're working together?"

"Obviously, yes, but also because I'm only now able to think about what I want for my future. I'm not rushing into anything."

"I don't think dinner is rushing, but I respect your decision."

Of course he does. There's a part of me that thinks my guardian angel, if I have one, is holding her head in despair for once again missing a chance with Trey, who surely, if there's a list of the ten most genuinely good guys on the planet, sits in first place. A little voice warns me we're far from hormone-ridden teenagers, and if I mess things up this time, I might not get another chance.

I tell the voice to shut it. Even if it's correct, I'm not ready, and I know it. For once in my life, I'm going to take things slowly.

I shut my electronics down and pick up my satchel. "We'll do dinner another time, but if a certain longtime family friend is already in Houston on Saturday, I might offer an invitation to join me at Lila's graduation. The after party is going to be off the chain."

Trey imitates my signature snort. "I don't think people say that anymore."

"They should."

"I'll have you know I've got my very own invitation, along with Mom and Gran. They've already sent gifts, and I'd planned to drop by for a quick hello and to give her mine in person. So, I don't need your stinky old pity invite."

I should have known he'd be on the guest list. "What was I thinking? Eunice is Lila's favorite Grannie. Bailey wouldn't have it any other way."

"I'm glad we've got that settled, so to answer the question, I'd love to join you. I'll meet you at the PAC. Save me a seat?"

"Of course."

Slapping his knees, he stands and heads for the hallway. "Are y'all flying or driving?"

"Since Ally wants to drive, I can say both."

"All these years, and she hasn't changed." He gives me a long look. "Tell her to be careful. I just got you—I mean, you just got back to town, so we don't want to lose you." He double taps the doorframe. "Come on. I'll walk you to your car."

"Dude, this is Magnolia Bloom. Not exactly a hotbed of crime, so I think I can make it all the way to the parking lot by myself."

Parking lot might be a little grandiose for the asphalt square behind the grand dame now having a second life as a business.

"Maybe, but you're home now, so you have to toss your big-city ways and reacclimatize to small-town rules. So hurry up. I need to get to the gym."

I quit arguing as we shut off lights and lock the doors. I pull out first, since I know he'll wait until I do. It's good I'm alone, because Trey's statement of the obvious hits me.

Home.

But is it? In the strictest sense, of course it is, but on a deeper level?

I distract myself by imagining Trey in shorts and a tank top, or better yet, no shirt at all, and tell myself to focus on the road. I don't need my mental meanderings to go there, although it's pretty difficult to stop that train now that it's left the station. Two years of grief left me shut down in every area, but my libido has apparently reawakened from its long nap and wants to get back in action.

I wag a stern librarian finger at myself to shush. Even though my desire's fine in an it's-time kind of way, the rest of my brain not attached to my lady bits isn't ready. Under other circumstances, I might be jumping up and down and waving my hand in demented fervor, shouting, *Pick me, pick me!* But I'm no longer the impulsive wild child I used to be. Getting kicked in the teeth can do that to a person.

Why whatever powers-that-be decided I needed a universe-sized ice bucket challenge poured over my heart and soul, I'll never know. But it was an efficient, if ruthless, way to get the girl who was rather lax in the seriousness department to change directions. Waking up to find the person you've loved madly for seven years dead will brutally shut a person down.

With my brain going numb, I make the exhausting fifteen-minute commute to the estate. I pull up to Brian's, and Ally's got one of the Escalades gassed up and ready to go. It takes a nanosecond to put my travel case in the back, and we're off, the A/C jacked up and cold enough to cure meat. Ally turns off music barely loud enough to be background noise, and we head due south in church-worthy silence.

"Haven't seen you much this week."

Hmm. She waited a whole five minutes to begin the inquisition.

My siblings think I'm somehow unaware of my defense mechanisms, although I've assured them both to the contrary. On a snippy day, I'd remind Ally that she goes mummy quiet when upset, and Bailey makes copious lists of things to fix the situation. They know, and I know, I'm more likely to channel my inner Robin Williams because I learned young to make people laugh to deflect or diffuse. Up to now, that skill's been a winner for me.

Today, I put a gentle finger on ghost-Robin's lips. My heart broke when he took his own life because I always saw the pain behind his incredible eyes and smile. I always wanted to meet him, sure that if we ever shook hands, I'd feel as though I'd met someone who would truly get me. I didn't have the honor, but I look over at my big sister and realize I've had another kindred soul right beside me all my life.

I just haven't truly seen her until now.

I missed that Ally's way of coping is every bit as powerful as mine, both in distraction and in compounding a wound that never quite heals.

I reach over and take her hand, threading my fingers with hers, and after the initial shock, she returns my grip fiercely. "To answer your question, lest you think I'm ignoring you, I'm okay. Getting okay-er every day. I'm just trying to process Trey asking me to dinner before I left the office."

"What's there to process? You've been friends since you were both potty-trained. He's hella cute, and you're so gorgeous it should be illegal. And most importantly, you're both smart and caring and generally wonderful."

"Aw, shucks, ma'am. You're gonna make me blush."

"Doesn't take much for those of us whose base shade is Casper the Friendly Ghost, but be serious with me for once. Why not go to dinner with him? It's not like you haven't been processing for a long time."

"There's no timetable on grief. I wish there was, 'cause a rule book that would make Bailey giddy would be kinda handy." I hold up my free hand. "Don't snap. I'm dead serious. For once, I wish I had someone to tell me exactly how all this is supposed to roll out. People with the best intentions tell me about losing their brother or sister or mom or dad, and many have tried to tell me how losing their pet is every bit as painful as what I'm going through. To be honest, each well-intentioned story is useless. I appreciate their intention, but when someone starts, I just want to run away."

"No one can tell you how to do this. I get it. I swear I'm not equating losing my marriage to what you're going through, but everyone and their dog has an opinion on what I should do. Maybe it gives me a tiny glimpse of what you've been through."

I release my bone-bruising grip and smooth my ragged cuticles in desperate need of a manicurist. "I may be the baby, but this time I can play the wise one. You're still in shock, but what you're feeling is betrayed and bereft and lost."

"Johnnie didn't betray you." She cuts me a quick glance. "Did he?"

"Not in a sexual sense, but when I got over the initial tsunami of emotions, I got so angry because he didn't tell me about our financial situation. I guess I should say *his* financial situation, but that's semantics. I mean, I was Vesuvius-level pissed off, and then I felt ten-to-the-millionth-power guilty for being mad at him, then I'd get even madder at him for leaving me... Oh, hell, let's just say trying to get my head around all this has been, to state the obvious, brutally difficult."

"Which makes me teasing you about Trey a little insensitive."

"Nah, you're not. Truth be told, if I made a list of qualities I appreciate, not only in men, but in humans in general, Trey would tick off most of them. I guess I'm saddle shy and not sure I have the energy or the courage to get back on the horse."

"Understood. No judgments from this side of the car."

We fly by miles of row crops I recognize. Wheat, sorghum, and smile-inducing sunflowers, but the view along the endless miles of highway is also broken up by pecan orchards, olive farms, and lots of drought-tolerant and acid-loving muscadine vines taking in the already-intense sun and destined to be one of the Texas varietals gaining popularity. Which sends my attention span of a gnat to seasons, planting and reaping, and the unstoppable nature of time.

I corral my thoughts scampering in ten different directions, look over at Ally, and brush her hair back from her shoulder. "Do you ever wonder how it would have been if we'd all stayed together, instead of me and Boo going with Mom after the divorce, and you staying with Dad?"

Ally perks up. "Funny you should mention it. I asked Daddy almost exactly that. I feel like I got the good end of the deal, since you two got stuck being under Mom's relentless drive, and I got Dad, but then, I cost him his dream."

"He said that?"

"No, the opposite, but come on. Dad was in the farm league for years and just got his big break. The Texas Rangers, for heaven's sake, then *wham*. We came along like three dominoes—bam, bam, bam. He swears he has no regrets, but I still wonder."

"You're chasing your tail, Al. We can't change the past."

"I know. I've just been nostalgic lately."

"I get, it though. Being with you and Boo more in the last couple of weeks than the last couple of years has made me weepy."

Ally gives me the do-tell sideways look. "Something turned Cameron MacInnes weepy? Dang, girl, maybe you should be the songwriter."

I appreciate her teasing, because despite all the processing I've been doing, staying in this space is hard for me. I've had as much as I can take under an emotional klieg light. "Yeah, yeah. Shut up and drive, granny."

She does, and I'm left to play Bailey and start a mental spreadsheet of all the reasons I should go out to dinner with Trey...

And I come up with ten more for why that would be a really bad idea.

CHAPTER TWENTY-ONE

ALLY

I'M glad Cammie needs some quiet time, because I'm confident she'd have turned the conversation to me and how I'm doing, which is reasonable in a turnabout-is-fair-play kind of way, but I've stewed for two solid weeks over my conversation with Daddy, and I'm still not ready to discuss any of it. I watched Willie and Waylon trying their best to distract me, acting much like I imagine prepubescent human boys do, tussling with each other, racing around the yard, coming over and butting against me, and pushing each other away to get more attention.

I showed them my appreciation with head scratches and scoops of Rory's secret-formula feed. I've yet to meet up with him. The bin gets refilled regularly, but apparently he's got stealth ninja skills. Just the other day, I found the boys under the shade of a newly erected lean-to, despite the fact the back porch is completely covered, and the ancient pecan trees provide more than enough shade.

But even the antics of my two new companions and worrying about both my sisters aren't enough to get my mind off what Daddy said. His words invaded my sleep with the strangest dream of me chasing Bailey and Cammie with wads of cash in my hands, screaming at them to wait as they run from me as fast as their legs can carry them. In the real world, the one single thing Bailey allowed me to do was pay a portion of the ungodly tuition to Lila's private high school, but that was because it was for Lila, not for herself. As for Cammie, she's refused any help ever, giving in only to take the high-powered laptop I sent her in law school as a birthday present.

Apparently, I'm not the only mulish one in this family, Daddy.

I probably shocked Zane when I answered his call a few days ago, the short conversation still stuck in my head.

"Ally? Wow, thank you for answering."

His voice was sincere, no hint of sarcasm. If I have to be honest, and I really don't want to be, being bite-y is my go-to, not Zane's. It's one of the things I always liked about him. Even with his buddies, he doesn't do the insult-as-affection thing.

"What's up?" I chose to nix chitchat and get to the point.

"I wanted to check with you about coming to Lila's graduation."

My stomach decided to see if it's actually possible to turn itself inside out.

"You're coming?" I couldn't hide the shock in my voice.

"That's what I'm asking about. Lila called and said she hoped I would, after letting me know she's really mad at me, but she doesn't want me to think she doesn't love me anymore. Ending, of course, with I have to ask you first."

"That's our Lila, or should we say Bailey 2.0?"

"Exactly. She's certainly carrying on your family tradition in conflict avoidance."

I couldn't deny that glaring truth. I stayed silent for a few breaths, then let go of the need to say something barb-ridden and mean. "Tomorrow's about Lila, not you and me. If you want to come, we'll just pretend it's Vegas 2019."

I don't think he expected me to say something teasing, not yet, so it took a long second before he laughed. That show was excruciating. We had a big fight right before we went on, and the 2019 tour was ironically named Lovin' Country A to Z. The whole tour was a showcase of all our hits about love being enough to make it through anything.

Ouch.

When we did "Holding on in the Rain," one of our bestselling songs, I dug my nails into his palm so hard they broke the skin. Not my finest hour by any stretch, and I apologized profusely.

Eventually.

"I promise not to draw blood."

His laugh was louder that time. "Thanks." He paused, and a soft sadness replaced his humor. "I'm pretty sure, though, you're not gonna let me hold your hand."

"That's true."

"I think I'll bring my oyster-shucking gloves, just in case."

I hit the mute button to hide my chuckle, glad we weren't on video, because I smiled. I'm not saying I'm not still crushed, but I've never been someone who can maintain rage for days on end. I was that mad one time for a week and ended up in the ER from a case of hives so bad I thought I had the measles. But like I told Daddy, I may need to be angry for a while, but that doesn't mean I want to be evil. My urge to go scorched earth has passed.

That doesn't mean I was feeling all kumbaya during our phone call, either.

Zane cleared his throat. "I guess I'll see you tomorrow. With no icky love songs in the set, we should be fine, but I'm sure she'd understand if you want to go solo."

"No, I'm fine with what we planned. Would you mind bringing Patsy?"

I left Nashville lightning fast, and I missed my favorite guitar.

"Happy to. Anything else?"

Could you bring my heart back? Or some magical superglue? Or the secret of how to fall asleep without staring at the ceiling for five solid hours until exhaustion finally won?

"That's it."

"Okey-doke. And, Al?"

Don't say you're sorry. Sorry wouldn't fix anything.

"Yeah?" The hesitancy in my voice was Guinness World Records-worthy.

"Thank you. For letting me come. I don't deserve it, and I really appreciate you."

No, he didn't deserve it. My gut didn't deserve having to face him so soon, but guess what? Life wasn't fair, and I wasn't going to blow my niece's graduation to assuage my own ego.

All this replays in my mind as the miles fly by. Cammie's the perfect traveling companion, content to ride shotgun and open snack bags and offer napkins as necessary. We've been using my phone to stream music, so when Sarah calls, her name comes up on the dash display.

I glance over at Cam. "My agent. Do you mind?"

"Of course not, silly."

"Hey, Sarah. S'up?"

Sarah's used to me and launches right in. "The label wants that last cut and pronto. They weren't pushing it before, but now they're working under the guise that no press is bad press, and they want that single out now while you're front-page news."

"Screw them and the herd of horses they rode in on."

"Unfortunately, the one they're going to screw is you. I'm sorry, sweetie, but you letting Zane be the smiling front of A to Z means sympathy's on his side right now, and they want to wring every cent out of this they can. You know that douche canoe who just took over at the label has never liked you, but you were making them too much money to do anything against you. Well, now he's cackling like a hook-nosed witch stirring a boiling cauldron, thinking he's really going to show you who's boss."

"I admit we're late, but not beyond reason. The point is, I don't think contracts mean squat to this guy."

Sarah's invisible nod comes through loud and clear all the way from Nashville. "A contract's only as good as your tolerance for litigation and your willingness to spend a metric crapton of money on blood-sucking lawyers."

I look over at Cammie and wince. She controls a silent laugh and acts like she's going to come across the seat at me with fangs and teeth. It's incredible, despite the conversation happening, that a spear of happiness moves through me.

"Good news is I have at least half a metric crapton of money still available, but even if I'm pissed off, I'm not the vindictive type."

Besides that, I'm not ready to fight tooth and nail about something I am bound to produce anyway, but this is more than that, deeper. This is setting the stage to fight for a career I'm desperately afraid has been destroyed, and not because of current circumstances. I've tried to write four times now over these last weeks, but even a cathartic revenge song won't come to me. The music's gone. The words are gone.

"I appreciate the heads-up, Sarah, but the big issue is what song we're going to do. With modern technology, we can go to the studio separately to record, and we have the best mixer in the industry."

Our sound engineers are phenomenal, but the truth is, this won't be our best song. The magic that was Zane and me is now shattered at my feet like a busted snow globe. Part of the ineffable quality that makes our music unique is how we improvise while recording. I'm arrogant enough to know my writing has always given us a solid platform, but every time we start playing around when we get with the band in the studio, even with session musicians and not *our* folks, the result is almost always different than I imagined, and better for it.

"That's a pretty big 'but.'"

Anger's crept into my jaw, so I force myself to unclench. "Yeah, I know."

"I don't want to push, God knows, but we're gonna have to address this sooner rather than later."

"I'm not making any promises, and if it costs me some fines, then I'll consider it therapy money. I'll call you soon. I promise."

"Let me know if I can help."

"Thanks, Sarah. You're the best."

The interior of the car goes silent as I don't restart the playlist. I need a moment to think.

"Is Sarah also Zane's agent?"

Cammie snatches me from the dark well of my thoughts. "Yeah, she's been with us almost from the start."

"That could be a problem."

I give my sister a quick look, and then the obvious hits me. I've always been the one who does the heavy lifting with Sarah. She and I work out terms and conditions and offers, and most of the time, Zane wants to know only the percentage increase in our favor from any previous negotiations, and he happily signs on the dotted line.

My fingers clench on the steering wheel. "Conflict of interest."

How could I have overlooked something so glaringly obvious? But thankfully, I have Cam to keep me from being a complete fol.

"Yup. She sounds super nice, but in the end, this is business, and she's gonna make decisions from that viewpoint. Besides the in-your-face danger of her knowing too much about both of you, you realize you're in the bargaining stage, right?"

"Huh?"

"Stages of grief. They don't necessarily happen in exact order. You're a hair past shock and denial. You're probably sitting in anger right now. You're tilting into bargaining, and it'll sneak into everything."

"I don't want to think the years-long friendship Sarah and I have is false."

"It probably isn't, but in the end, are you sure she'll choose being your friend over making a lot of money?"

I consider the answer for two alfalfa fields and another vineyard. "No. I don't know. She's been great to work with, but she's savvy and shrewd."

Cammie gets a hay crop and two huge swaths of tilled and fallow earth. "I'm sorry. I don't mean to be a wet blanket."

I give her the best smile I can manage. "You're being an awesome sister and a great attorney. I may not know about Sarah, but I know with my whole heart there's no conflict here."

She offers me her pinkie, and I hook mine without hesitating. "Always, baby. Always."

We're hitting the outskirts of Houston and the traffic from hell that exists regardless of time of day or day of week, so I'm saved from further conversation by having to concentrate so we end up at Bailey's gorgeous house in The Woodlands in time for dinner.

A stranglehold hug from Lila takes a bit of the edge off my nerves and saves me from my navel-gazing. I don't have to say more than four or five words, as our job is to nod and smile as Lila rattles off everything she's planned and organized and scheduled. She has no idea how much I appreciate her youthful exuberance.

It makes the black hole growing in my heart close up the tiniest bit.

But I know it won't last.

CHAPTER TWENTY-TWO

BAILEY

I DON'T THINK about Lila's father much. I'm mostly grateful he turned out to be a good guy who enjoys his daughter, even if he'll never get a Father of the Year Award. Considering he's redeemed himself from being a mere sperm donor, I don't complain.

Still, as I watch Lila delivering her speech as salutatorian, I'm sorry he's missing this.

She's so incredible. So intelligent. So funny. So beautiful. And she's mine. Although she looks a little tired, she practically glows as she pays tribute to her teachers, mentors, and fellow students.

"And last, but as the cliché goes, certainly not least, I have to thank my mom. Not everyone's as lucky as I am to have someone in their corner 24/7. A cheerleader who never quits." She looks at me and winks. "But don't give her pompons and ask her to do the splits. She'd end up in traction."

I don't mind the laughter floating across the floor as both of us have to blink back tears. I hear Cammie on my right sniff and Ally on my left. I have to work at staying mad at Zane when I see him hand them each a tissue. I need him to not be nice, because I've always really liked him, and I can't have him going around being sweet while I'm obligated to continue plotting how to kill him and hide the body.

"Stop it," Ally whispers to me out of the corner of her mouth.

"Stop what?" I whisper back.

"Stop thinking. Stop making lists. Just enjoy the moment."

I give the smallest *blep* of my tongue at my big sister I can get away with and not lose all my dignity in this room full of people, many of whom are at least as equally famous or notorious as Ally and Zane. To the point, there was a little buzz when Zane walked in, but right behind him was Matthew McConaughey, who's uncle or cousin or something to one of the graduates. I should know, but honestly? Lila has a cadre of friends I adore, and I don't have time to worry about the rest of the school roster. Her gang has a reasonable handle on the extent of their privilege without being mean girls in training, but they're still young and don't truly grasp how much prestige is in this room. Still, my girl has a solid head on her shoulders and cares about more than herself.

Lila finishes up with an expected but heartfelt plea to her fellow graduates to reach for the stars and all that. The choir takes the stage, and then the valedictorian gives her speech, but I've tuned out by then, too busy staring at the back of Lila's head and wondering how time goes by so quickly. It takes a concerted effort to push down the panic turning my pancreas into a paperweight as I try to figure out how I'll manage the hours with her gone.

I decide to take Ally's advice and watch in awe as my girl glides across the stage, takes the commemorative holder that will soon house the final diploma from the principal, hugs her favorite teacher, and smiles for the photographer. The class isn't large, so the big moment's done in another few blinks. Then it's a mass of moving bodies.

"Hey, proud momma." Jake's voice makes me smile before I turn and accept his hug. He sat with my mom and dad in the row behind me. Trey, last in the line emptying the row, gives me a thumbs-up.

"Hey, yourself. Thank you again for coming."

"She's amazing. Like her mom."

"I can't take the credit. She did all that awesome herself."

My mom moves in, and I realize I'm holding my breath, waiting for her opinion of the day. I'm seeing sparkles when she finally says, "I'm proud of Lila and, of course, am delighted she's accepted the offer from Princeton. She'll do well."

A covert deep breath keeps me from blacking out. I accepted a long time ago that education means everything to Dr. Marianne MacInnes, and she's got her sights on Lila being the second PhD in the family. Knowing Mom won't make any sideways remarks to Lila today takes a weight off my shoulders. I've been a constant and determined referee between Lila and her grandmother, but sometimes Mom sneaks past my job as goalie and lands a barb or two.

Dad pops in for his turn, which is all hugs and smiles, but short and sweet, as the group ebbs and flows while everyone jockeys for a moment with both Lila and me. I don't mind, but in the oddest way, it reminds me that this is a marker, a moment where lives change. Not just Lila's.

Mine, too.

Maybe I will take Miles up on that offer and join the new group. I'll have time to fill and could certainly stay busy.

Yet another touch to my back has me turning left. I get it. Texans are a hugging lot, but seriously, once everyone is milling about in the atrium, the faculty should have charged by the embrace, and in the next hour, they could have paid the tuition for every kid in this school.

I don't mind, even if my cheek probably looks like a sample palette at the Mac counter, and I'll be bruised by the time I get home.

Lila, who's not overly prone to squealing—well, not more than the average seventeen-year-old girl who's just graduated at the top of her class—hits a wince-drawing decibel. I can forgive her, seeing the joy on her face as she races across the room to throw herself at one of the biggest stars in country music who also happens to be her uncle. He was hanging back in an unobtrusive, un-Zane-like fashion. He catches her, because one, he's a big dude and can easily manage my sprite of a child, and two, this has been their deal her whole life. He swings her around, and she giggles, then he kisses the top of her head and calls her *short stuff*, thankfully considering the crowd and altering it from the usual *short shit*. She might look like a mini-me, but she's tiny like Ally, and Lila pretends to be angry, claiming on cue that I kept the tall genes from her on purpose.

I'm about to start laughing when I notice my baby going from grinning and rosy-cheeked to ghost white. Her eyes roll back in her head. Thank God Zane has her as she starts to drop, and he eases her to the floor.

I force myself not to scream and scramble to her side.

"Lila! Lila, baby, open your eyes."

I have my hand behind her head, but even though I know she didn't strike anything on the way down, I'm careful not to move her neck.

"Move back. Move back, please."

I hear Zane's deep voice, but I'm glued to my girl. She's breathing, thank God, but I take her wrist to find her pulse.

"Excuse me, please let me through."

Someone kneels beside me, and I look left quickly enough to establish that it's Dr. Wagner, head of the ER at Houston Methodist. He puts a hand on my arm.

"Bailey, let me do this. You need to step back."

I snarl so hard spit flies from my mouth. "Don't tell me what to do, James. I'm a doc—"

"Mom? Mom, I'm okay."

We look down, and Lila's lids are open, fluttering a bit, and her face is still nearly transparent.

"Hey there, Lila." James's jovial baritone is light but his expression serious as he takes her wrist from me and casually measures her pulse. "Didn't have enough excitement yet today or what?"

She tries to sit up, but I put a restraining hand on her shoulder. James pulls out his phone and uses the flashlight to do a quick check of her pupils. Mentally telling James he can go to hell for all I care, I lean close enough to see for myself that they're even and responsive.

"I'm fine, Dr. Wagner. I don't know what happened. It's silly, and I'm embarrassed. Let me get up."

"In just a second. Do you hurt anywhere? Any numbness, tingling, sharp pain?"

"No, I'm fine. Really."

"Can you wiggle your toes and fingers for me? Move your legs."

She obeys, and as she has on sandals, I can see the ten little piggies I kissed a thousand times when she was a baby move as instructed. James tells her to let us help her and to move slowly, but we get her to her feet with only a tiny wobble after she lifts her head. She seems recovered, and pink returns to her cheeks with a vengeance when she sees how many people are looking at her.

James pats her shoulder and looks at me. "My best guess is dehydration and exhaustion, if I can go by what my Janie's been putting herself through this last semester. I'd take her to her PCP and have her checked out, though."

I'm as aware of the audience as Lila, so I bite my cheek and make myself smile. As if I need to be told to take my child to her primary care physician after an incident like this. James is a good guy, if full of himself, but now's not the time for a who's-the-better-doctor pissing match.

We move to a table in the far corner as the crowd still mills about. Some folks have left for the big shindig on the roof. A stage has been set up, a portable dance floor laid, food deserving of a royal wedding arranged, and enough sodas for the kids and beer and wine for the adults to float a cruise ship.

I push a lock of hair behind Lila's ear and make myself smile. "Hey, kiddo. You okay?"

"I'm fine, Mom." Lila's frown is impressive. "Dr. Wagner's right. I haven't been drinking enough water is all."

We both know it's not all, but I force myself to let it go. Her pulse is regular, her color is acceptable, her speech has no hint of a slur.

"I'll do my best to up so you can have your day."

My daughter has the audacity to open her mouth in an exaggerated O and turns to Ally. "Did you hear that? I need witnesses."

Ally gives her a high five. "You got 'em, kiddo. We'll never let her live it down."

"Good, because Mom couldn't shut up if you slapped an entire roll of duct tape over her mouth."

"Ouch!" Even if true, it hurts to hear it blurted out quite so bluntly.

Maybe it's because her blood sugar is low, or her electrolytes are out of whack, but apparently my Lila has decided right now is the time to pick a fight.

"Mom, I'm not saying this is your fault, because I'm a big girl, and I wasn't watching what I was doing, but for realz, can you just chill? I know you said you would, but you won't, and you'll pull out one of your lists and make sure I've responded to Princeton, which I have, and requested dorm and cafeteria plans, which I have, and bus schedules, which I can get online, and—"

"Okay, okay! I'm sorry."

"No, you're not, but I get it, understand it even, but sometimes you're just too much. You've converted your experiences into my requirements."

I'm speechless. My child has felt this way, obviously for a long time, and I didn't see it. Worse, I feel drawn and quartered in front of half my family.

"Honey—"

"You did your undergrad at SMU, med school at Cornell. You interned at Johns Hopkins. You freakin' went into labor with me during your final exams and didn't even go to the hospital until you filled in the last bubble. I think you knew what you wanted to be the instant you popped out of Grandma."

"That's not—"

"You love me, but you don't listen. I don't know what I want for dinner, much less the rest of my life. I'm seventeen! Not everyone knows what they want to be yet. I want to slow down and figure it out for myself. I love you, but I'm not you. I know you're just trying to be a good mom, but you're trying to make me you. You want to keep me from making mistakes. You can't. You shouldn't. Your job isn't to make sure I never stumble. It's to be there so I know I'm not alone as I pick myself up and try again."

I can't breathe. I can't form words. I know I should be saying something, but instead I'm mute with the knowledge I've made my child a wreck. I try to draw in enough oxygen to figure this out. To fix—

"Just stop it!"

I rear back, her words having a pH of battery acid and hitting me like a prizefighter's best kidney shot.

"I really need you to stop. Right now, you're pulling up a mental spreadsheet, and you're already filling in columns and rows with how you can fix this."

When I can speak, my voice is pathetic, barely audible. "Dear God, Lila. I'm so sorry."

"Please, if you love me, don't apologize. Just quit thinking that if you can come up with enough A/B testing, you can fix everything. I'm just a kid." Tears begin streaming down her face. "I just want to be a kid for a while, and I don't want to go to Princeton."

Her voice rises, loud and unfiltered and utterly raw.

"You don't mean that."

"Yes, I do. It's all you've ever wanted for me, but you won't listen. It's not what *I* want for me."

Ally and Cammie, who've been watching this exchange with horrified love and concern etched on their faces, move closer, creating a little conclave.

Ally speaks first. "Hey, how about we all agree there's a pretty big conversation that needs to happen, but today's supposed to be your day. We can talk about it tomorrow. After you've had your big party."

Cammie chimes in, "Or we can duke it out right here, right now. Question is, what do you want, Lila bunny?"

Lila buries her head in her hands, and her body trembles for a long minute with Ally gently rubbing her back. When she looks up, she sucks back tears and takes the tissue that appears over her shoulder. She doesn't even look, just says, "Thanks, Uncle Z. You're a jerk, but I love you."

Clearly, today is Lila's day for saying exactly what she's feeling, but Zane chuckles. "I love you, too, short stuff."

Lila studies the table for another long second. "Aunt Ally's right. Now's really not the time, but Aunt Cammie's a badass for letting me know we'd do this in front of God and everyone if I needed to. What I want is to press pause. It feels so good to just say out loud that I don't want to go to New Jersey, and I don't know if I want to go to law school or medical school or basket-weaving school. But I do know I just want to have five minutes where I don't have to think about it. So let's go to the party and dance and have fun."

I rub the smudge of mascara off her cheek with all the love I have for her bursting from my fingertip. "How'd you get to be so smart?"

"I have a great mom who loves me. She's just a little pain in the ass sometimes."

"Or a big pain. Giant pain," Cammie offers, sotto voce.

"Hey!" I pretend affront as I pour my gratitude on my sisters with my eyes.

"Come on," Ally orders, gesturing at the crowd moving toward the stairs and elevators. "Let's get this party started."

Lila launches herself at me, and I hold her against me so hard my arms nearly seize.

"I'm begging you, Mom. Don't beat yourself up. I've been wanting to tell you this for the whole dang year, and while I didn't plan for all this to happen today, I'm really glad it's out. Just enjoy this with me, all right? I'm not mad. I love you."

"I love you—"

"—to the moon and back," she says with me.

I deserve one of my own Tony Awards for the smile I give my girl. I love her more than the entire galaxy, and I'll make tonight special for her.

And I'll figure out how to fix this mess I made.

We start walking toward the PAC, and I wish I could pull out my phone, but since I don't dare, I start a mental list...

CHAPTER TWENTY-THREE

CAMMIE

"Would you look at that?"

My question's rhetorical as, of course, Bailey, Jake, and Trey are watching the stage as raptly as I am. "I don't know how she does it."

Ally and Zane went on minutes ago, and the rest of the room's as glued to the raised platform as we are, but for different reasons. They're either seeing superstars performing or superstars in crisis, but Bailey and I see our big sister earning her Tony Award all over again. You'd never know she's internally alternating between incandescent fury and soul-sucking sadness.

I understand, being recently and intimately familiar with the stages of grief. I hope she sticks around long enough for me to help her. The big *if* being if she'll let me.

To his credit, after duly enthralling Lila's table full of teenagers, Zane leaves with as little fanfare as he came in with. Ally returns to the big-people table, giving me and Boo the stink eye before we can speak.

"Don't you dare ask me if I'm okay."

I raise my arms in the surrender position. "I won't, I promise. I have a fair to middling idea of how fast your pulse is racing, and I'm neither a performer nor a doctor. You know, though, that middle sis here is biting her tongue to stop herself."

"She can keep biting, then."

Trey does the lip-zip motion, Jake puts his hands in the air, and Ally gives them both damn-right nod.

I don't recognize the small band taking the stage next. I don't keep up with country music besides Ally's, but my familiarity with the guy is irrelevant, because he's got a great voice, and the dance floor's filling up.

"Two-step with me?"

Trey's standing, offering me his hand. I happily say yes because it's a spritely number, therefore safe.

He was a good leader back in the day, but time has created a master. The dances we had at the Moon were a treat, but this is a decadent dessert. The problem arises when the song ends but flows effortlessly into a nice waltz. Which means instead of heading back to the table, I'm gliding over the floor in the arms of a man who's been a part of my life since we shared a blanket at nap time and held hands during buddy walks. His leads are a perfect example of everything about him —considerate, well-planned, and all intended to make me look skilled and graceful despite the fact that it's been years since I've done more than the rumba box at an occasional wedding reception.

I forgot how much fun it is, but more, I forgot how intimate dancing is… or can be. Pre-Johnnie, I cut a rug with a lot of guys, but none ever had my breath catching, and not in an I'm-out-of-shape way. More in a he's-cute way.

Actually, it's a why-does-he-have-to-be-so-dang-cute? way.

Maybe taking this contract work from him is a bad idea. Maybe I need to go wait tables at the Waffle Wagon and get rid of any impediments.

And maybe my brain needs to shut up and enjoy the dance.

I'm so caught up in the moment, in Trey, I don't realize he's led me away from the crowd and that we're half hidden behind the ficuses staged in one corner. We lean against the railing and let the wind cool the sweat on our necks with the lights of Houston spread out before us like a Texas version of the Vegas Strip, but instead of the Bellagio and the MGM, we see the JPMorgan Chase Tower and the Wells Fargo Bank Plaza, both lit up enough to make the ERCOT grid groan.

Trey raises my hand to his lips and kisses my knuckles. "Thanks for the dances. You're still as electric now as you were when you sent my teenage hormones into overdrive."

Oh, how I want to pop off something pithy, steer the conversation away from dangerous shores.

"Wasn't it a mere thirty-six or so hours ago that we had a discussion that this isn't a good idea?" Nope, nothing funny there at all.

Trey whispers the pad of his thumb down my jaw. "I think it's a fantastic idea."

In truth, a lot of me agrees with him. Quite a bit, actually. I mean, what harm could one tiny kiss—

Trey's front pocket buzzes, and he winces. "Sorry about that. I forgot to turn it off."

My humor decides to spring back into play. "But you left it in pleasure mode, I see."

"Ha-ha." He pulls the device out and glances at the screen.

To stop anything more ridiculous escaping, I say, "You can take it."

"It's just Stephen Kline checking in with me. He's a little too obsessed with our new project, and while I appreciate his fervor, he can be a pain."

I go cold, from the top of my head to my newly painted purple toenails. "Did you just say Stephen Kline? Five-nine, bad-combover Stephen Kline from the firm of Johnathan Arthur Dallas?"

I step back, and Trey is looking at me like he's accidentally kicked a snake and warning rattles have been fired off.

"Yes." His voice says *yes*, but his tone says *uh-oh*.

"The firm that couldn't wait until Johnnie was cold in the ground before showing me the door and giving my office, small though it might have been, to one Stephen Kline, who just made partner?"

"Okay, Cameron, I've clearly done something wrong. Nuclear-reactor-overload wrong. But I don't know what it is, so just spell it out for me."

"You didn't tell me you're working with my old firm."

His mouth opens, then closes. His brow furrows in confusion, then eases back. "I wasn't aware I was supposed to go over my client roster and connections with you that aren't related to the subdivision project."

"Trey, he works for the firm that treated me like dried cow patties."

He starts to reach for me but stops himself. "I knew you'd had a tough couple of years, but I wasn't exactly read in on the details by Stephen or, more importantly, you." He sees my expression and changes lanes. "I just started working with him a year ago. I didn't know I was supposed to be boycotting the firm on your behalf, since we hadn't exchanged more than a 'hey, how's your momma and 'em?' in a decade."

I know I'm being ridiculous and unreasonable, but I just can't stop the avalanche of memories of everything that firm did to me the second I lost Johnnie. Then the unresolved anger I thought I ignored to extinction that Johnnie didn't fight harder to make me partner sooner resurrects in all its thorned glory. I'm the coyote getting pummeled by a falling anvil, only to have insult added to injury when a boulder follows a few seconds behind.

None of it's Trey's fault. Logically, I know that, just as I know why Johnnie hesitated. The other partners still cashing in on my dead husband's name hated me from day one and were happy to block my entry into the upper strata, junior though I would've been. I also realize there's no way Trey could know any of what transpired. Some gossip, sure, but then, Trey wasn't a gossip kind of guy, so he probably had zero idea of the political maneuverings behind the debacle of my departure.

My humiliation stings like alcohol in the thousand cuts I endured on my way out of Dallas and my old life. What's worse is he's right. I haven't see him in nearly ten years. Yet his opinion of me now feels ten times as weighty.

He needs to see the fun-loving me, not Private Cammie. Private Cammie, who's losing her marbles and wants to find a speed bag to pound so hard I tear it off the swivel. Private Cammie, who wants to dig Johnnie up and wallop his big barrel chest and ask him *why*. Why didn't he tell me the truth?

Why was I good enough to earn his love but not his trust?

I've tried and tried and can't get past the *but*. Johnnie respected me, but not enough to challenge the others in the corner offices and make me a partner. He believed in me, but not enough to give me high-profile clients. He loved me, but not enough to confess we were hocked to the heavens.

Ally's voice slices through the silence. "What're you two doing over here, or should I ask?" Her teasing tone drops as she sees my face.

"Just trying to cool off and not stink up the dance floor. What's up?"

Ally and Trey both give me looks telling me I haven't tricked either one of them, but I'm not digging out of any more emotional quicksand. Not tonight.

"We're about to move the shenanigans to Bailey's house for a pool party. The uncool adults have to stay inside, but it's the only way Bailey will let Lila out of her sight." Ally turns to Trey. "Come with us. We'll open a bottle of wine and play Jenga or something."

I jump in first. "Trey's down here visiting a buddy from law school. I'm sure he's anxious to get back."

Hurt floods his face, and I feel as bad as I should. Assertive is one thing. Mean is another. MacInnes women are never rude.

Well, most other MacInnes women, and usually never…

He tries for a smile, but I'm not convinced. "Thanks for the invite, but I'll do as Cameron wants. I need to return a quick call, then I've got to get going."

Ally nods and goes back to the table where Lila's surrounded by five vending-machine copies of herself, complete with matching pony-tails of varying shades from blond to brown. As soon as Al's out of earshot, I reach out a beseeching hand to Trey.

"I'm sorry. I didn't mean to be so insensitive."

"Yes, you did, but that's you. Attack first so nobody can get close enough to see you're vulnerable. Remember, I've known you too long."

My attempt at a quip fails miserably. "It's not like I can forget."

He offers his arm to lead me back to the table that's now empty, except for Al, who's waiting for me, but Trey keeps me in place with a tug on my sleeve.

"I don't want to leave with this tension between us."

"I know, but we need to table this until Monday."

"If we wait, you'll be back under your armor, pretending you're fine. I know I'm being pushy, but you have doubts about me, and I don't like it. Talk to me. I'll tell you whatever you want to know. We'll find a computer, and I'll VPN into the office, show you my whole client list and all my associations. Whatever it takes to get this haunted look out of your eyes that's gutting me."

The correct term is fight-or-flight, but I'm feeling duck-and-dash. He's offering me what I didn't even know I needed from Johnnie until it was too late.

I put my hand on his arm, my breaths as erratic as my thoughts. "I promise I just need some time. It wasn't fair to chew on you. You couldn't have known the details of what happened."

"But I want to."

And that's exactly what I'm afraid of...

CHAPTER TWENTY-FOUR

ALLY

I'VE NEVER BEEN A MOTHER, but I'm a crazy-proud aunt, so when Lila collapsed, so did my heart. Those ten minutes until she was back to her laughing, if pale, self were some of the longest of my life.

In the weirdest way, the incident made singing with Zane a walk in the park. Knowing I was at least partially responsible for her dancing with abandon with her friends dulled the hard edges off of my brain and uncoiled my guts enough to put on if not a happy face, at least a neutral one. And I wasn't pleased to be indebted to Zane for anything, but I did owe him that night for being his usual crowd-pleasing self and making Lila one of the stars of the evening by association.

That was a week ago, and thirty pages of journaling haven't nudged me the slightest bit closer to Zen. If anything, my handwriting got faster and messier and more mistake-ridden until I threw the thing across the room, and it slid beneath the ancient cedar chest in the corner, where I left it, telling it to stay there and think about what it did.

Then my common sense tells me to get off my butt and get it before I forget and the next time I see it is for sale on eBay.

With a snarl, I push out of my chair and pull the chest out, finding the journal and a blanket that's clearly been there awhile. It doesn't take but a second to fold it and lift the lid to put it away, but instead of quilts, the space is filled top to bottom with letters. I stare, a bit confused, as Brian never came across to me as the writerly type. A scan of the neatly arranged envelopes shows, by quick calculation, almost half a century of correspondence between him and Violet.

I don't open any of them, but I pick up a packet from each neatly divided side, a smile and tears forming at the same time. The ones addressed to Brian in a feminine hand have an address of The Little House Down the Lane. The ones to Violet say My Lady's Castle.

Well, dang, Brian. Who knew a romantic lived in your stoic, almost-silent self?

I itch to read them, but I won't, although a love story between two people who lived a mile apart but regularly wrote to each other is almost too delicious to resist. Instead, I shut the top, replace the blanket, and head for the castle and the fountain of information who surely knows the answers.

At least this new mystery has stopped my mind from zipping around like a demented pinball in a retro arcade. I keep hitting the flappers in my head, but I can't get the damn ball to go where I want it to, so the reprieve's welcome.

I almost run to the gorgeous shouldn't-be-here testament to our impressive lineage. Pride swells inside me at the morning sun glinting off the beautiful blue-green schist stone. I'm grateful for whatever quirk of fate made me part of this sometimes crazy, sometimes confusing, always awesome genealogy. I vow to stop and say hi to Penny on the way out, but for now, I'm on a mission.

The back door to the main kitchen opens on almost silent hinges, but Eunice Greene doesn't turn from the enormous stove and all the accoutrement of this domain she's been in charge of for as long as I can remember. The room isn't different, but the petite woman bustling between the stainless-steel industrial freezer and the prep table with no-nonsense, efficient movement has an extra zip in her step. Bailey told me about Eunice's new workout addiction and an ever-increasing wardrobe of unique leggings and tops.

She glances over her shoulder but doesn't stop cracking eggs with her left hand into a mixing bowl and whisking with her right fast enough to make a KitchenAid jealous.

"Good mornin', beautiful. About time you made it up here. Sit, and I'll get you some coffee in a jiff."

I kiss her age-defyingly smooth cheek and take the chair she directs me to with a quick thrust of her chin. "Good morning to you, too. I haven't been avoiding the castle deliberately, I just—"

"Needed time to get your feet under you. I wasn't scolding."

I know that's true. There is no mistaking when Eunice Greene chooses to take you to task.

"I figured you'd be poppin' in soon. The magic calls you when it's ready, and it makes perfect sense you couldn't stay away today. I'm fixing a little bite for Juliette. She's coming to work in the gallery, so clearly you got your message in time to meet up with her."

Got my message? I start to pull out my phone, but I'm sure I don't have any messag—

Ah, of course. The mysterious magic of Castle MacInnes that the older generations swear is baked into the stones themselves, beginning with the chapel that's the heart and soul of our venue bookings. In the old days, prior to two hundred concerts a year, I'd play events big and small, happy to support the family and for the exposure. It's been a long time, though, since I've sat behind a solo mic with just my guitar and entertained lovely, happy, engaged—but mostly tiny—crowds.

"I'm not here to talk to Juliette. I came up to ask you about Brian and Violet."

"What about them?"

"Did you know they were... an item?"

"Lord, yes. Everybody did."

"I didn't. I knew Brian better than I knew Violet, but I never saw them together."

"That's 'cause they didn't want anybody to know their business. After Violet came back from France and giving up her babies, she was kinda broken, as can be expected, and Brian became her solace. As time went on, their relationship was a secret-not-secret, but everybody bought in on being a part of it."

I sit back in my chair, stunned. "Huh. Hardly seems possible that everyone bought in on keeping the secret, especially around here where everyone seems to know what color underwear you're going to put on before you do."

"Times were different then, and knowin' and talkin' about it's two different things. We weren't watched twenty-four hours a day by some device or another."

"I suppose secret love was easier to keep secret prior to 24/7 surveillance and social media."

Eunice gets her wicked grin. "Maybe you should write a song about them, changing names to protect the innocent, of course. Noelle and Juliette don't deserve to have their business known by every Tom, Dick, and Harry."

As if called by Eunice's mention, the door opens, and my stunning French cousin glides in, a big bag over her shoulder, her ebony hair pulled back in a simple ponytail that is ridiculously elegant. "Bonjour, mes amis."

Eunice points her spatula at the table. "Bonjour to you, too, missy. Sit yourself right there."

Juliette busses both of Eunice's cheeks and then mine, settling across from me as we watch the master pour her fixings into a skillet that has to be as old as the castle itself. God save the soul who washes that perfectly seasoned five pounds of cast iron with soap and water.

The enticing scent of caramelizing onions fills the room, and my mouth waters, anticipating one of Eunice's mind-bogglingly fluffy omelets with cheese oozing out the ends. There isn't a five-star Michelin restaurant on the planet that can hold a candle to Eunice's cooking, and she knows it, yet she's never strayed from her domain on this estate. My heart hurts for just a moment when I remember that Cammie said Eunice is training several recruits, but it'll hit me nearly as hard as losing Brian Steele when this kitchen isn't infused with her energy. Luckily, one of the recruits is a cousin of hers, so maybe there will always be a Greene at the helm around here.

But I'm done thinking about anything else coming to an end.

Juliette gets plates and cutlery, and I pour three small glasses of freshly squeezed ruby red grapefruit juice blended with orange, all from our own trees. Eunice pulls biscuits from the oven that are so good they should be illegal, and I wait, my stomach growling, as she joins us after one final round by the refrigerator for a jar of her peach marmalade. Our orchards have grown considerably, and we're almost as well known now for our fruit as our sheep... almost.

None of us are shy about digging in, and discussions about the weather and the upcoming games see us through scraping our plates clean. Eunice lets us take our dishes to the sink but then shoos us away.

"You two go on about your business. I'll finish up here."

I get in the first thank-you hug. "That was wonderful, as always."

"I had to make sure you two were fortified before you start your long day. Now git."

Long day? I planned to pick Eunice's brain about my discovery, promising myself I'd get back to Brian's to see if words might come again. Up to now, there's been a void in my mind, as if my brain becomes a black hole as soon as I even think the word *lyrics*, but Juliette and I leave as we've been ordered.

My cousin has this still center I adore. Even though we've just started getting to know each other, it feels peaceful, uncomplicated, to move together in unspoken agreement to the front entry so we can climb the awe-inducing staircase to the second floor and walk down the long hallway to the gallery with the quiet comfort of centuries baked into the walls around us. The wood floors have been worn smooth by thousands of feet, and they're kept buffed and breathtaking with loving care.

Juliette and I stand before the magnificent portraits of our ancestors in a moment of respectful silence. I don't know every detail of our history, but what I do know about Alisdair and Evajean—who seem to be staring right at me from their places of honor on the wall—makes me achingly proud to be a part of this family.

I gesture to the museum-worthy artwork. "I feel like they'll just leap from the frames and start talking to us."

"Bien sûr, these are magnificent. I have restored a number of pieces done by their youngest daughter, Gavina, and each one fills me with awe. She deserves to be known with the greatest of the realists, yet few outside the family know of her."

I glance over, tipping my head to the left. "Didn't you tell me you're planning an exhibit?"

"Oui, my sister, Noelle, and I are in the midst of the negotiations. It cannot happen before next year, but we intend to make it as special as she was." Juliette leads the way farther down the long wall and points toward another work. "Alyssa MacInnes was a formidable woman. Did you know?"

I admire the portrait of Alisdair's half-sister and the reason he survived to become the patriarch of a proud lineage. "Of course, I'm named after her, obviously. I've thought about her a lot, but don't know much of her story."

"Her diaries, much like Violet's, are treasures. It's a shame we don't create epistolary records anymore."

Hearing Violet's name makes me think of the treasure I discovered earlier.

"Speaking of her, I found a cedar chest full of letters, clearly from your... from Violet to Brian. Did you know they were a couple for the rest of their lives when she got back to Magnolia Bloom from France?"

"I did, but Violet's diaries don't go into a lot of detail, ending rather abruptly after they became secretly involved."

I look at a photograph of her on the far wall, moving closer to see her sitting at her desk in the turret, smiling toward whomever was taking the picture. "It appears she did continue writing, just not in a diary."

"Did you read them? The letters?"

"It didn't feel right, but you might consider it. Or, if you wish that to remain private, you can move or shred them before his house gets cleaned out. Suzanne, his great-niece, is going to do that pretty soon."

"Thank you for telling me. I'll stop by in a day or so and decide what I wish to do. The thought of destroying history troubles me, but to make public such an intimate thing... I don't know."

I look around the enormous gallery, from the twenty-foot-high ceiling to the yards-long walls, each person represented there with their own stories, most of them lost in time.

"We come from an interesting line, you and me." I hook arms with my cousin and lead her to the velvet settee stationed across from Evajean and Alisdair.

"Mais oui, a lot of love and a lot of drama, so it appears. So many people who nearly lost out on the chance for love."

I can't help but tease. "From what I've observed, you and Rory seem to have found your footing pretty well in that arena."

Her blush is utterly delightful, and a surge of happiness on her behalf rushes through me.

"He has become the center of my world. I never thought I would have that kind of connection with anyone."

"I believe you owe your thanks to our woolly busybodies."

Her laugh is soft and echoes gently in the cavernous room. "Indeed. And how are your two interlopers doing?"

"Getting fat already. I bet they'll be thrilled when shearing starts."

"You may find them naked and happy by the time you get home, actually. Rory mentioned rounding them up this morning."

"I'll be sure to send you pictures."

"That is fabulous, merci. Now, we must circle back to you. Mayhap I can offer unsolicited advice, despite my sister's voice in my head telling me to not be nosy."

I pick at a cuticle for a moment, trying to decide how much I want to share with her.

"Please do not let me press you, Ally. I used to be quite insular myself, until I came here. If you knew me a mere two years ago, you would not think me the same person, but there is something about this estate."

"The MacInnes magic?"

"Bien sûr. I would not have believed it had I not experienced it."

I hesitate, not wanting to insult her. It's more than we're newly met.

"Please understand, it's not you. I don't share with anyone, really. It's safer that way. Always has been, but becoming a public commodity has damaged me forever, I'm afraid."

"I will confess I was horrified to see your life taken apart like fresh meat by hyenas on the news. I don't watch it much... the news, that is. I'd rather stream a new series and eat my weight in buttered popcorn."

"Hard on the hips, but better on the psyche."

"Agreed."

True to her promise, she doesn't press, and it gives me the space to breathe. "It sounds ridiculously trite, but I'm lost right now."

"How could anyone expect anything else?"

My laugh is bitter, but not directed at her. "The world at large expects everything of me all the time, no matter the circumstances, hence my rabbiting myself home so I can hide."

"It has barely been a month, has it not?"

"Just about. I've seen Zane a couple of times, and we've spoken a bit, but it's all so new I'm still shell-shocked."

"Of course you are, and you must not punish yourself for taking time for you."

"I'm good at telling other people to do that, but I'm the worst at it."

"As we all are, I'm afraid. Does not your discovery and the stories of all these people surrounding us tell us that there is no such thing as normal? Our family is extensive and eclectic, and yet wonderful. Maybe that is the lesson for both of us, non?"

The quiet wafts through again, caressing my skin like a cool breeze on a hot summer day. It makes me want to go grab one of the mink-soft blankets off the big couches in the great room and bring it in here for a long nap.

"You want to know the truth?" I can't stop the words from popping out of my mouth. "I don't know how to be alone. Zane and I have been... were a team since I was nineteen. We were in the same music program in college, quit that, and started our music careers. In the early days, we were just kids, trying to keep our heads above water and make it in a brutal business, but through it all, we had each other.

Always. It didn't matter how exhausting a gig got, or what crazy thing happened along the way, he was always there."

"And now you feel like someone has changed gravity, and you have no footing."

I look at my cousin with even greater respect. "Exactly."

"I understand. My sister is my twin, and I had such a connection with her, but when your cousin Paige found out about Noelle and me, that we were the children your aunt Violet gave up for adoption, it changed everything. I came here and found a part of my heritage, so vastly different from the tiny vineyard where I grew up in France. Noelle was furious, believing I was betraying our parents by pursuing this. We barely spoke for months."

"I can see her point, though."

"I came to understand her perspective, but that was the heart of this journey. Noelle was and always will be a part of my soul, but I had to move in a new direction, which meant we were no longer living in each other's pocket, as the expression goes. It was not easy, but it was necessary."

"And you have Rory, which you wouldn't have."

"I shudder to consider having missed this chance. I came so close."

I finger-comb my hair back over my ears, a nervous habit telling me Juliette's words are hitting too close to home. "It's sweet of you to share this with me. I'm really glad you've found your happiness. Has Noelle?"

"Oui, thank goodness. She has started an entirely new level of her work and is dating a very handsome doctor from Germany. We visit each other every few months, sharing the trips overseas respectively."

"That's awesome."

She reaches across the velvet with her palm up. "I tell you this not as a history lesson, but in the hopes that you will know you are not alone."

"Nor unique, it seems." My voice makes it clear I'm poking fun at myself.

"We may all wish to be unicorns, but fate has a way of showing us we are not."

My phone buzzes in my pocket, and with apologies to Juliette, I pull it out and see a text from Cammie asking for a partner to play hooky with. She hit the margarita and taco emojis with gusto. She's headed toward the castle, and I'll need to get going to be back at Brian's when she arrives.

"That's my sister Cameron. We're not twins, but sometimes I feel like we should be." We stand, and I give Juliette a hug. "Thank you for telling me about Alyssa and about Noelle. I'll come by soon to see the painting and the diaries."

"Bon, I look forward to it."

I leave her to her work in the gallery and head out the back. My walk will have to be more brisk than the one that brought me here, but I don't mind as my feet feel a little lighter for the first time in weeks.

Maybe I can take a lesson from Violet. She found a way to start a new life after great heartache. Juliette did, too, and still maintains a relationship with her sister, not only as family, but in business. I'd need to think about that. Our situations are far from the same, yet there's a flutter of hope I don't look at, too afraid it'll die if examined too closely.

I make a promise to the tiny spark to hang on. Give me some time.

Let me prove, eventually, that I'm not irretrievably broken.

CHAPTER TWENTY-FIVE

BAILEY

MY OFFICE CHAIR is ridiculously expensive, and on most days I find it comfortable, but despite being swung around to face my window and tilted back to the maximum degree, it feels like I'm sitting on a cactus. I try losing myself in the cloudless, almost painfully blue sky, but my brain won't stop replaying Lila's almost-disastrous graduation.

In the six days that have passed, I've relived watching Zane lower her to the ground in an endless loop.

There's a double-tap knock on my door before it opens. I turn to find Jake in my doorway rather than a staff member.

"Hey there. What are you doing here?"

"Dang, Bailey. You sure know how to pop a guy's ego."

I scoff and wave him in. "Oh, please. Sit down, but I don't have long. I'm leaving in a couple of hours for Magnolia Bloom. The games start tomorrow."

"Thanks for reminding me. I'd completely forgotten."

I wrinkle my nose at him, aware he's smiling as he feigns shock. "Payback for you giving me a guided tour of the town I grew up in.

And an inside source told me Broder Engineering did all the work on the new stage."

Jake and I began a hi-how-ya-doin'? texting relationship after I'd returned home. I've found myself looking forward to a ping once or twice a day with him checking in, though I try not to read too much into it. We keep the exchanges to tidbit depth about what's happening in our lives, all surface level and light.

"My latest engineering masterpiece." He winks, and my heart skips in reply. "Kiki and her team have made some awesome changes not only to the setup, but the lineup as well. This will be the best year ever."

"From your mouth to God's ears, buddy. So, what brings you here?"

"I'm headed back to town, too, and thought I'd stop by and check on you, see if I could talk you out to lunch."

My skippy heart launches into a jog. Good grief, I do lunch almost every day, going so far as to eat food with other human beings, including handsome fellow medical professionals of different stripes. There's absolutely no reason to go high-school-girl giddy because the star quarterback has metaphorically leaned his broad shoulder against my locker and asked me out for pizza after the big game. Besides, I'm immune to wind-mussed hair falling over a regal forehead toward rich, almost-mahogany eyes.

"You're—" I clear my throat to get the pitch down. "You're sweet, but I need to finish up some dictation before I hit the road. I appreciate it, though." I steel myself against the disappointment flashing across his face, both flattered and bothered that I caused it. "How's Lem?"

I'm truly interested in knowing, but equally desperate to change the subject.

"Having a streak of good weeks, I'm happy to say. After I read those articles you sent, I worked with the housekeeper and Doc to change his diet and vitamins. After about ten days, it was stunning how much he perked up."

My mouth says, "That's awesome to hear," while my head struggles with wanting to urge him to be careful about reading too much into such a small data set. Diet, exercise, and supplementation have shown amazing results in the literature, but if Lem really is on the dementia spectrum now, nothing can fix it. Still, I wouldn't take these moments away from him for anything.

As if he read my mind, he continues, "Doc told me not to get my hopes too high, but we're going to keep trying. One blessing from this is Lem's agoraphobia is easing, and we've got him enrolled in a tai chi class in the park two days a week. He's quite the hit with the ladies and even found a fellow train enthusiast in the class."

Remembering how he lit up when I showed genuine interest in his hobby, I'm delighted. "That's wonderful. Loneliness and isolation are brutal for our elderly population even without the added element of mental decline."

"Which makes me determined to find other ways to get him out of the house. I feel guilty it took me so long to make this a priority."

Irritation hits me as I look at this genuinely kind man who defies several stereotypes, and I don't like him beating himself up. "Hell's bells, if anyone is a unicorn, it's you."

He fidgets in his seat. Apparently, I've hit a nerve.

"Come on, Jake. You own an insanely successful business, are enviously wealthy, have a schedule Doc tells me would exhaust most mortals—which reminds me to tell you about the pot calling the kettle names—yet you make time for an aging grandparent." I hold up a hand to stop him from demurring. "I deal with a lot of family members as I work with patients fighting a devastating disease. I see a range from obsession to aggravation when the reality of long-term care kicks in. But I can probably name from memory the folks who dive into the solutions with kindness and not from obligation."

"I don't—"

"Take the compliment, Jake. It's sincere and from someone who might not be familiar with dementia per se, but who definitely has seen all sides of this coin."

"Yes, ma'am."

I shake my head at his pretend contrition and let the subject go.

He decides it's his turn to skewer me. "Tell me how you're doing. Your text responses are pretty autofillable with 'I'm fine,' and we both know that's not true."

Guilty as charged.

Maybe, ironically, feeling lost and vulnerable makes me want to tell him what's really up instead of retreating behind the mask I'm well aware I keep in place. Or maybe, unironically, it's because it's Jake who's asking.

"I'm struggling. After the graduation bombshell, Lila pretty much opened a spigot of things she's been keeping in. It's been brutal sometimes, but also cathartic. The short version is, she's going to take a gap year to travel with her dad."

"Doctors Without Borders, right?"

"Yup. I'm proud of him. And her. I'm just glad she found her footing before I ruined her life."

Jake's mouth tightens into a thin line. "You weren't ruining your child's—"

"I almost did. It's humbling. But I'll fix it." I put my cap on my pen and straighten my desk. I'm genetically incapable of leaving with stuff lying everywhere. "For now, though, I need to get going."

Jake looks at me a long time before finally nodding, but I know the gesture isn't implying agreement. When he stands, I feel... bereft, which is an odd word to pop into my head, but it fits. I feel like something monumental has happened in the span of a few lines of conversation, but what it is eludes me.

"I hope to see you at the games. Maybe we can share a bag of kettle corn and watch the caber tosses or something."

He walks to the door, and I squash a ridiculous urge to beg him not to go. "Sounds good. Drive safely."

He pauses, studying the doorjamb as if it holds the answers to life before he turns back. "You have to stop, Bailey." His voice is low, but I hear him clearly. "You have to stop living for anyone and everyone but yourself. If you ever want to find out what life might have to offer you, personally, look me up."

Then he's gone, and his words echo in my head. *You have to stop living for anyone and everyone but yourself.*

My voice cracks as I manage to whisper, "I don't know how."

CHAPTER TWENTY-SIX

CAMMIE

FROM THE FRONT lobby to the back doors and the enormous expanse of stairs spilling onto the east lawn, there are MacInneses everywhere. Most of us in kilts, all of us bearing our clan colors somewhere on our persons. Kiki is sweetly nervous, as this is her first time leading the family out. We have our own rules on this side of the pond, and here, the chatelaine of the castle leads us for the parade around the grounds to start our annual games. It might not make sense to anyone else, but we all know the history of the women of this family, and we created our own vision of pride in our clan.

I'm jostled and turn to Ally. "Sorry. This is madness."

I look around at all the happy faces, hear booming laughter and animated chatter echoing off the enormous vaulted ceiling. "Every year. You've just been away too long, but I'm glad you're here now. And thanks for going to lunch with me on Wednesday. Fair warning that I'm taking advantage of having you close by while I can."

"No arguments from me. Have you seen Bailey?"

"Not yet. She got in late last night and stayed with me at my apartment. When I left, she was hitting the blow dryer."

"Your new place is a pretty sweet find. They did a super job converting that Victorian, not only restoring the exterior to its gingerbread beauty, but modernizing the interior."

I nod, adding a chuckle. "Let's just say my budget had me prepared to make some sacrifices, but I didn't complain that the bathroom has a Jacuzzi. Best thing is, I walk to work most days, breathing in the last of the magnolia blooms."

It's been less than a month, but every night when I push open the door and put my keys in the bowl on the antique credenza I bought in Atlanta, I feel like I'm home. Not like I'm-gonna-live-here-forever home, but my-soul-can-heal-here home.

Eventually.

I haven't felt an inkling of this peace since I left Dallas in my rearview mirror. I worry it's going to go away again after my blowup with Trey at Lila's graduation. I know I overreacted, but maybe I can be forgiven for being a little touchy, considering how my life has gone lately.

Kiki rings the bell, so we quit chatting just as Bailey rushes up, out of breath, but looking beautiful in her tartan skirt and MacInnes sash.

"What's up?" I ask as the procession starts.

"Had to take a call about a patient who had to go on a VAD."

I give her the *huh?* head tilt.

"Sorry, ventricular assist device. In this case, the guy has to go on the transplant list, and hopefully the VAD will keep him alive long enough to get a donor."

"That's super sad."

"It sucks."

We quit chatting as the pipe and drums hit full volume, and we're get busy waving at the crowds as we traverse the fields. I love the walkabout because I cherish being in the bosom of my family, and I adore looking at the people and kids and dogs, all the humans fluttering flags and strips of their clans' tartans. I heard through the grapevine that Fina Greene made sure she'd be home to call the roll. She might not be a MacInnes by blood, but she sure is by love, and while I'm thrilled she's now embroiled in a hot, international romance, I'm more thrilled she's here.

By the time the late morning sun's making us all fan ourselves and itch to get into shorts, the air's filled with shouts of laughter and encouragement for the field athletes, groans when someone obviously misses a mark, and the clanging of bells and barking of dogs as the sheep-herding events get underway.

Our trio has long split up, and I'm headed back to the castle to change. We've all stashed gym bags in Eunice's office and will use the staff bathrooms to clean up. Being family has its privileges, and access to the air conditioning and modern amenities is a perk I don't deny myself.

The games spread out over acres and acres of the estate, so I wonder just why the universe hates me so badly that I have to stumble across a canopy with a banner over the front lip emblazoned with Jonathan Arthur Dallas, Attorneys at Law, in royal blue lettering.

I nearly go to my knees seeing it. It's not like Johnnie and I made it to all the games, but we were sure to host a company event to coincide with the fun every so often. It was always a hit, but I guess I never dreamed the current HR manager would pick the estate this year of all years to team-build.

It seems especially mean, but maybe I'm reading more into it than I should.

When I feel I can walk without face-planting in the dirt, I turn, but it's not soon enough.

"Cameron! I didn't expect to see you." The too-bright voice belongs to none other than Stephen Kline, douchebag extraordinaire.

I turn back, forcing my face into a smile, even though I know it's morphed into a grimace. "Stephen. I can safely say I didn't expect to run into you here. Or anyone from the firm."

"I've been working with Trey Greene, and he mentioned it months ago. We thought it'd be fun."

I am many things, but dumb's not one of them, and a stump wouldn't mistake as accidental his oh-so-not-subtle use of *we*. I'm wondering if I'm imagining some kind of emphasis on Trey's name, though, but there's no reason for Stephen to know about my arrangements here.

Too-loud voices carry from inside the tent. I can't see the speakers, which means I don't think they can see me, but it's clear I'm the topic of conversation.

"Yeah, she's managed to get her hooks into another rich attorney. Can you believe it?"

I don't recognize the voice, but I feel blood rushing up my chest and into my cheeks, even though I'd give my soul to not reveal I'm affected.

"Hopefully, she won't kill this one. Trey's a nice guy and super cute."

I step back several paces as the blood that surged up races away with equal speed. Stephen shocks me even more by looking embarrassed, rather than gleeful, as I expected.

"Cameron, I—"

"Y'all have a good time. Kettle corn is fresh, and the lemonade stand is serving Eunice Greene's secret recipe. You'd better get some before it runs out."

My about-face would make a Marine proud. I keep my pace to a good clip, but I refuse to run, even though I'd race straight to DFW and crawl aboard the first plane on the tarmac if I could.

I make it to the staff locker rooms and strip, folding the plaid skirt and white blouse with shaking fingers before putting them in my bag. I manage to barricade myself into one of the shower stalls, barely finding the strength to turn both taps wide open and bracing my hands against the wall to let the pounding water cool my overheated skin.

And stifle the sound of my tears.

CHAPTER TWENTY-SEVEN

ALLY

I SEE Cam head for the castle, and I envy her. I'm going there myself to get out of my clan gear as fast as I can, but Suzanne and I had to postpone our talk until today, so that means we each have a turkey leg and are headed for one of the tables staged under every available shade tree. We're going to do a secret-not-secret set on the new stage this afternoon, but until then, I intend to be as cool as possible.

We've already covered the chitchat, so I dive right into what I've been wanting to say. "I'm not going to tell you to not pursue a career in music. It's impossible to describe what you feel when you see your creations alive in the world, but this business is the definition of insanity sometimes. If you're going in, go in prepared. I want to make sure you know that you can always call me if you have questions, or get in a bind, or anything, really."

"I don't know what to say. Thank you."

"Zane and I were lucky to have some awesome mentors in the early days, and I've never forgotten how much that meant. I don't claim to know everything about everything, but if I can help you, I want to.

Your uncle was so special to me, and I couldn't face seeing his ghost disappointed in me if I didn't reach out to you."

Suzanne's face goes soft with memory, but the sadness seems to be taking a back seat to the wonderful times she had with Brian.

"I'm not so sure I should claim any special treatment just because of that, but I do appreciate it." She takes a moment to chew a bite, then asks, "Is it worth it, though? If you could go back, would you change it?"

"I've thought a lot about that. The truth is, the bigger your career gets, the smaller your world gets. Your real world, the world that counts with people who know you, love you, and truly want nothing from you. It shrinks pretty damned fast, actually." I pause, take a breath, trying to find words both realistic and yet encouraging. "Don't get lost in glitz, and that can be really easy."

"I'm not so sure I'll ever have to worry about that."

I drill her with my hardest look. "Listen to me. You are *that* good, but talent doesn't always mean success. I think you have the whole package though, if you want it. But to answer your question, I think the thing I'd change the most is I'd take better care of my marriage. I don't take blame for the affair. That's a hundred percent on Zane and his choices, but I do accept my piece in us drifting apart. We both could have done things differently, but no, I wouldn't give it up, even for this ending."

"That's kinda profound."

"The good years made the public limelight bearable. That's the thing I want you to know. There's a cost to fame, and no one wants to believe the shadow side of the light. No one gets away without paying the piper, as it were, so what I wish for you is to stay strong from the get-go. Refuse to compromise on the things that are important to you. Make space to be reasonable, but never let a label take your dream away from you. I did, and I regret it."

"Really? But everything you write is amazing."

"You're sweet, but I let myself get boxed into a pretty, comfortable cage, and I don't mean my marriage. I mean professionally."

"What are you going to do now, if you don't mind me prying?"

"I'm not sure yet, but I'll let you know when I decide." I point my big bone toward the trash cans. "For now, I'm going to go get out of these fancy duds and enjoy the games until I see you for sound check. Deal?"

Her smile's as brilliant as the June sun above. "Deal."

I don't mean to sigh as I head for the back of the castle, but when I'm with Suzanne, I wonder if I was ever that bright and shiny. My guess would be no.

"Ally! Ally, back here."

I turn, recognizing Sarah's voice, and stop, waiting for my agent to catch up. It gives me time to see who's right behind her, and to say that I wasn't expecting Zane would be a serious understatement.

"Hey, you two," I say cautiously. "What are you doing here?"

Sarah frowns at me, putting her hands on her hips as she tries to catch her breath. "Trying to find you, since you won't answer your phone."

I have determinedly unhitched myself from the electronic leash that has controlled my life for far too long. I usually keep it with me, but if the ringtone isn't Cammie's or Bailey's, I ignore it completely.

I look from one to the other, and my oh-crap-ometer redlines. "This looks serious."

Zane answers first. "It is. Can we talk?"

I pluck at my skirt. "Listen, this might be summer-weight wool, but that's an oxymoron in Texas, so I'm about to melt. Follow me up to the castle and let me change, then we can have some privacy in the gardens."

Gardens might be a bit of an understatement to what comprises the back of the castle lawns, but they're blocked off for the big weekend. The head gardener would have a coronary if thousands of people tromped through her masterpieces, and I can't say I'd blame her.

I hurry through the kitchen and grab my bag from Eunice's office and head for the restrooms. I envy whoever's already in the shower, but while cooling off sounds lovely, I'm not going to make Sarah and Zane wait. I hurry, shimmying into my shorts and a tank top, and rush back out to where I left them stashed under an oak tree that's rumored to have been around when the Texas Declaration of Independence was signed in 1836. Whether true or not, the branches over my soon-to-be ex and our agent provide a heavenly cove of shade and peace. Adding in the water trickling out of the fountain a few feet in front of us, the setting would be worthy of a scene in a book except for the tense energy radiating from both my unexpected guests.

I take the cool concrete bench next to Sarah. "Now, give it to me."

"You know the new head of the label you were supposed to meet last month?"

"Yeah, the one who hates me."

"Yeah, him."

I wait for the rest. Am I supposed to be devastated by this news about a man I've never met? "And?"

Zane and Sarah exchange glances. "And he wants to write you out of the new negotiations."

"I thought he was just pushing to get the last track done."

"He is, but he's ramping things up."

I haven't thought a lot about the damned contract. I've been a little distracted, which means I'm not sure how to respond. Do I care? Should I care?

"It's pretty clear he's only a fan of the Z part of A to Z. News flash, you two. He's hardly alone in that particular belief."

"Yeah, but other people don't have the power to sideline your career."

"True, but the label is under zero obligation to sign me again if they think it's in their best interest."

Sarah looks at Zane again. "I told you she wouldn't be upset."

Zane looks at our agent like she's grown another head. "Of course she's upset. She's just being Ally."

Score one for Zane. And here I thought he was oblivious.

Sarah sighs and takes a long look over the gardens that could go toe-to-toe with Versailles. "I'm really sorry to hit you with this today, but we're supposed to have a meeting on Monday, and I wanted to give you as much time as possible to process."

I do a slow head roll and squint at her. "Really? You couldn't tell them to go sit on a tack and ask for more time? It's not like the fate of nations depends on this."

Her smile has that world-weary should-be-a-New-Yorker quality. "Nations? No, but the label has every intention of milking your breakup as a gateway to splitting you two up as a country duo. They feel Zane is more marketable as a solo artist, and an older man as a country superstar will sell more records if he's a hot new bachelor, unencumbered by a "woman of a certain age.""

"I'm thirty-seven for God's sake." But who am I kidding? After seventeen years, I should expect it, yet I find myself amazed at the sheer callousness of the execs.

Sarah plunges ahead. "There's lots to think about. These guys aren't the only label, and if you wanted to show a united front with Zane, they'd probably back down. But..."

But I'd have to want to keep working with Zane.

He moves from beside Sarah and takes the space next to me. "Would it be horrible to keep working together? We've been a pretty great team."

I know snorting is mean, but I can't help it. "We're not Fleetwood Mac, Zane. Even if I did cocaine, there's not enough coca leaves on the planet to give me Stevie Nicks-sized balls and guts."

Zane and I both have marveled at our favorite band's ability to work together despite all the drama both behind the curtain and playing out in the press... and that was before social media. We've speculated often about what they managed to hide.

As for us, we escaped the damage of drugs on both our bodies and our music, not because we were some paragons of virtue, but because we watched too many of our friends flame out. We had each other, and we may have given the makers of Titos and Deep Eddy Vodka a hefty chunk of change, but we saved a lot of money by avoiding drug dealers and rehab, enough for Zane to do crazy crap like buy a NASCAR team.

He clears his throat and starts to reach for my hand, then pulls back. "So, what do you think?"

I stretch my neck in a slow circle to see if I can get my shoulders out of my ears and to buy time to stop from saying something bitchy. "I have a short set to play with Suzanne, the girl you heard at the Moon a few weeks ago? And then I have to find a good bottle of merlot and a few hours to parse this out."

"Do you, um, want me to stay?"

Our few hours together at Lila's graduation broke the I-want-to-throw-something-at-you feelings in me. We haven't had a real conversation yet, but the tilt toward murderous rage is apparently gone. His simple question starts a thought forming in the back of my head, and it goes from crazy to good idea in a couple of heartbeats.

"Yes, I do, but more, I want Sarah to. I want you to hear this girl, because I think you'd be nine kinds of crazy not to sign her as a client."

Sarah's ears perk up like a Chihuahua that's heard the word *treat*.

I tell Zane the songs I've chosen, and he smiles bigger than our agent. "You'll let me tag along?"

I think about Suzanne and that there has to be some silver lining in this really crappy rain cloud. "Yeah, I will."

Sarah excuses herself to go get her computer from her car. I can see the wheels turning in her brain, the wheels that made Zane and me a lot of money and a lot of fame, but I know at heart, Sarah's a good person. While none of this is in my control, she'd be good for Suzanne.

I'm feeling very fairy godmothery as Zane stands and holds out his hand. I look long and hard, but I put mine in his and let him help me to my feet in that Southern gentleman way having nothing to do with me needing assistance.

"Would you walk with me for a little while?" he asks. "I didn't realize how much I missed the games until I got here."

I reclaim my hand, but move beside him and start back toward the festivities. "Sure."

"Have you had any kettle corn?"

The innocuous question is loaded, and we both know it. The last games we came to, we got the biggest bag of the sweet treat they offer and slipped off to *the* grove, where we ate until we were sticky, then we proceeded to lick the sugar off each other in a very NSFW manner. The only thing that kept us from completing the amateur erotica hour was the knowledge that photographers tended to follow us no matter how hard we tried to sneak away. Instead, we raced to the castle, where we'd booked the most luxurious suite available, paying full price. The afternoon of blazing-hot sex was worth every penny.

"I'm full of turkey leg at the moment."

Sad understanding replaces the hope that was taking root. I have to give him credit for trying, but I need to make it clear it's never going to happen.

I do give in to a cup of lemonade, as there's nothing loaded in that sweet-tart treat.

"Al." He stops until we've moved away from the line and are unlikely to be overheard, "Do you think—"

"No. I don't. I'm not nearly through being mad at you, and someday I might even forgive you, but... no."

He nods, blinking hard and fast. Using his napkin to catch a drip of lemonade off my chin, he adds a sad smile. "I'm sorry, Al. More than you'll ever know."

It's my turn to nod and blink fast, but I don't let the tears fall. "I am, too. I mean that."

We stop to watch a herd of kids chasing a passel of lambs in a pen. The problem with Valais sheep is they think it's all a big game and are more likely to run *to* the kids instead of away, knocking the squealing toddlers on their butts and causing shrieks of laughter that make me wince. You'd think someone who's been in the music industry as long as I have would have some hearing loss, but they manage to hit notes that could break glass.

"I'll postpone the meeting for a while." Zane is mesmerized by the field, his smile wistful, his voice subdued.

I can't think about the larger meaning behind his expression. We delayed having kids for myriad reasons, and now it seems it was a good idea after all.

"Why? You have your career to think about."

He turns and looks at me for so long I begin to think he's not going to answer. "Because I haven't stopped caring about you. Loving you. And I may be colossally dumb, but I'm not a monster."

I can't stop myself from reaching up and brushing my fingers through the lock of hair that falls over his forehead every time he's not wearing a hat or it's not cemented down with spray.

"I know, and it wasn't a trick question. You might as well take the meeting and see what they're offering, because if they want me out, even the great Zane King can't stop them."

"I can leave the label."

I'm touched, deeply, because the offer isn't some desperate I'll-get-her-back move. He means it. And maybe I'm crazy for not giving him a second chance, but Zane is who he is, and I am who I am.

"Don't. Not unless it's truly right for you." I slip my fingers into the curve of his elbow and start us down the path again. "Do you still have that buddy with the little sound studio in Austin?"

"Matt? Yeah, why?"

"We still owe the label one track, and I just figured out my plan." It's a song I wrote years ago when things were, ironically, wonderful. It doesn't fit the theme of the album, but if they're going to be a bunch of jerks, I'll do the finale of A to Z my way.

He cocks his head to the left.

I scooch a little closer and put my head on his shoulder, which is an awkward position to walk in, but it fits. "It's time to record 'I Never Wanted to Say Goodbye.'"

CHAPTER TWENTY-EIGHT

BAILEY

I HEAD for the border collie herding demonstration to meet Doc, as I promised. I've already spent too much time wandering the booths, watching the dancing exhibitions, and listening to the musical performers in an attempt to stop myself from rehashing my conversation with Jake. I know he means well, but he doesn't understand that even if I wanted to slow down, I can't right now. Maybe after I get my medical school loans paid off and see how Lila's choices for college pan out when she gets back. There are too many plates in the air for me to change gears.

Doc sees me and waves, and I'm delighted to see Lem standing beside him, watching the keen intelligence displayed by the truly gorgeous collies. The dogs' eyes are sharp and take in the whole field in front of them, the velvet tips of their ears twitching as they wait for commands.

Must be a good day for Lem, and I'm thrilled, needless to say.

"Hello, gentlemen."

Lem gallantly tips his brown derby that has seen better years but is clearly cherished, and Doc follows by touching the brim of his straw Stetson.

"Young lady, I need to buy you a turkey leg."

I ignore his pointed look at my too-thin calves. "Already had one. And it doesn't show yet, but eating ice cream every night to console myself with Lila halfway around the world has the scale inching up. On top of that, I'm looking into gyms so I can start getting some muscle built up. Eunice has made me promise I'll go with her to Quinton's box."

"You should. She has fun, but that lady's serious about her iron addiction now."

"It shows. I'll try to follow her example." I pretend nonchalance, but I'm not kidding myself... and probably not Doc. Seeking out a gym isn't because I've suddenly developed a desire to pump iron so much as something to keep me away from the too-quiet house in the evenings. To keep him from further comment, I smile at Lem. "It's so good to see you. Are you enjoying the games?"

"Wyatt and I come most years." He winks at me. "This year, I have the added bonus of a pretty doctor."

Doc chuckles. "You don't call a man pretty, Lem."

"Wasn't talking about you, you old fool."

My heart sings to hear the men bickering. It helps me imagine a lifelong friendship, and I hope the changes in Lem's regimen make it last a good long time.

Doc gestures to the food booths. "You two stay here and enjoy the show. I'll go grab us some waters."

Lem and I strike matching poses, our arms crossed on the top beam of the fence. "Man's a darn nuisance," he mutters, but I hear the affection in his voice. "Today's a good day, though, and I'm glad he fetched me this morning. I don't know how long it'll last, though."

His attention is on the flashes of black and white zipping around the enclosure, but I know he's not seeing the dogs. I nudge his shoulder with mine.

"Hey, we're going to do everything we can to make these days the norm."

"I appreciate you, sweet lady, but I'm mad because I don't know if I'll remember tomorrow what I'm telling you today. I wasted so much time, so many years, and I didn't see it until now."

"Wasted?"

"I've had a wonderful life, but I got so dang hard-nosed when I lost my wife. I set my mind and wouldn't let time nor tide sway me." He turns his head to nail me with a piercing gaze I haven't seen before. "Don't make my mistake. Don't get so locked up you think there's only one way out."

"I—"

Doc's voice breaks into the moment. "Everybody drink up. It's getting hot and gonna be a scorcher before the day's through."

When I glance at Doc and then back at Lem, his eyes have lost their previous intensity, returning to a soft happiness I don't want to risk breaking by asking him what he meant. Then again, maybe I don't want to know, and it's safer to chalk the moment up to the mercurial shifts common in dementia.

We move together from the collies toward the new fields and the impressive stage that's already hosted a number of performers, both local and rising stars. I made this date with Doc once we confirmed Ally was going to play, especially now that Suzanne's going to be joining her. Having Lem there makes the day even better.

I play the family card without remorse and get us backstage. Lem is captivated by the rat maze of activity, so we find him a chair and make ourselves as unobtrusive as possible in the wings. There's something special about seeing a concert from this vantage point, and I think I'm enjoying watching Lem as much as I am the performance. It's not that I don't appreciate my sister's amazing skill, but I don't have stars in my eyes about her. At the moment, I mostly have concern and worry, especially when I see Zane on the far side of the stage, clearly waiting.

What the heck? Ally didn't say—

"Ladies and gentlemen." Ally holds up her hand to try to stop the clapping and screaming. "Thank you so much, but I have another treat for you. We've told y'all about the MacInnes magic, and abracadabra, here's a very tall rabbit I've pulled out of my hat."

The crowd goes wild when Zane steps from behind the curtain, strumming a guitar, then stopping to give his signature two-finger touch to the brim of his hat, then saluting. He and Ally flank Susanne, and they launch into one of their most famous pop crossovers. I wonder why people even go to concerts if they're going to scream the entire time the performers are playing. Having the advantage of a fold-back speaker nearby means I can actually hear the trio despite the cacophony from the field, the main reason I wanted to be close.

Kiki didn't advertise Ally's appearance, merely noting a special guest on the program, and she was wise. We're at capacity, but it would have been a mini Woodstock with too many people for the space available if the public at large knew just who the special guest turned out to be. Still, this is the kind of touch that makes the lure of our games grow every year. You never know what prize you might get just for attending. Great marketing, that.

Not that I know marketing from manure, but I can appreciate genius when I see it.

Doc's eyebrows rise. "That girl's smile looks real, by golly. Nice to see."

I watch my sister and realize that there's always been something... reserved when she's onstage. I know her better than most and marvel that she gets out there, time after time, when she truly doesn't like crowds. Today, she seems... here. All here. And I should expect Doc, of all people, to notice.

Suzanne exits after two more numbers, leaving Ally and Zane in front of the microphones.

"We've got one last surprise, but you have to promise you won't tell anyone?" Laughter rolls through the crowd. "We'll be releasing an album later this month, but until today, we hadn't picked the last song. This will be it, and you're the first to hear it."

My heart just about breaks as the music and melody float over me. It's a song of deep and desperate love.

And of goodbyes.

Doc hands me a clean and folded bandanna, and I swab away the tears streaming down my cheeks. When the last notes fade and Zane reaches over and kisses Ally's forehead, I lose it. The whimpers I was stuffing turn into sobs, and Doc pulls me against his shoulder and lets me soak his chambray shirt. I know my sister had a great marriage once upon a time. Back in the day, she and Zane could heat up a room just by looking at each other. And to know, in the course of a four-minute song, that it's gone forever tears my soul apart.

Ally and Zane separate with him leaving by the opposite wing and Ally coming toward me. I grab her and squeeze her so hard she squeaks, but she doesn't pull away.

"God, Al, I'm so sorry." I can barely get the words out, my throat tight with the need to scream *no!* and *it's not fair* and *why?*

"Hey." She wipes the last tear off my cheek with a soft thumb. "I'm going to be all right. Not saying it's all right just yet, but it will be."

The moment's broken by Cammie's arrival, looking a little pale and much too stoic, as well as Daddy, all grins and pride radiating from his pearl-snapped shirt to his dusty boots. Soon, it's a family convention, and we have to move the herd to give the roadies room to do their thing for the next act. We adjourn to the family tent, and I'm disappointed Zane doesn't show up. I'd like to punch him one last time and then hug the stuffing out of him.

I'm in the back, watching from the corner, as that makes me the most comfortable, when a familiar cologne reaches me. It's a hint of leather and tobacco and something earthy like oak or moss. I'm not a scent aficionado, but I know what I like, and I sure like how Jake Broder smells.

I turn and try to hide my hesitancy. Our conversation yesterday didn't end on the brightest of notes, and as usual my brain has gone to the darkest place it can, certain he'll never want to speak to me again. Not that I can blame him as I reimagine myself as that pinball caught in a never-ending game.

"Hey, Jake. Enjoying yourself?"

"Always, but you look a little less certain."

I do? I thought I was doing a good job hiding the distress shredding me from gizzard to gullet. I mastered the doctor face years ago. Doesn't Jake know that?

"It's been an interesting day so far. Not what I expected."

"Thanks for taking Lem backstage, by the way. He hasn't stopped talking about it."

"He's such a dear. I'm really glad I got to see this side of him. Not that I needed proof, but I can see why you're so close."

The tent is crowded and noisy, mostly filled with laughter and joking. Jake nods toward the back flap right behind us. "Care to go for a stroll?"

My anxiety has been climbing by the minute, so I don't hesitate to agree. We head by unspoken agreement toward the lake. It's a bit of a hike from the fairgrounds, but neither of us minds, and with the afternoon sun sending long shadows over us, we stretch out on the dock where he tied off his impressive boat after displaying his equally impressive skiing skills.

The noise from the games is barely recognizable from this distance, and in typical Jake fashion, he leans back on his elbows and lets the almost silence glide over us. There are boaters on the water, but they're beyond our cove. Still, the waves lapping beneath the dock are a bit more energetic than usual, an interesting counterpoint to the soft and welcome breeze from the surrounding hardwoods.

And magnolias, of course. I look at the last of the offerings from the later-blooming species and wish they'd bloom year-round. I hate the sense of loss I feel when they go away, leaving me aching for next year before this one's even half over. It also signals how much I haven't gotten done and that summer's about to descend with a vengeance.

I'm sure my therapist would have a field day with that thought, but I don't see how it's unreasonable to be focused on my obligations. They're real, and I can't wish away my debts and duties to my daughter and my patients. I get all the New Agey mumbo jumbo about living for today, and that's all well and good for people who have the freedom to carpe their diem. I don't have that luxury.

"Do you ever get your brain to shut up?"

Jake's voice startles me, not the question so much as the fact that I was so far in my head I forgot where I am.

"It doesn't seem so," I admit, and even I can hear the melancholy in my voice.

It all hits me like a tidal wave. I'm not used to that. I plan carefully against it. Tsunamis are never allowed on my spreadsheet. Yet here I sit, unable to take a deep breath, wondering if I'm about to be my own patient, because it doesn't seem like there's enough air in the world right now.

Jake shifts back against one of the pylons and pulls me to him, letting me rest my cheek against the swath of his chest that is much too comfortable, much too inviting.

Much too forbidden.

Maybe someday in the future, when my life calms down, but there's no place for a tall, dark, handsome man who should be off marrying some bright young thing and making lots of happy little Broder babies.

And even if there was space for an us, the last thing Jake needs is the mess that is me. I'm not searching for a metaphorical fainting couch with my wrist flung against my forehead. I'm trying to be realistic, even if I'm so far into the future that Google hasn't made the calendar for it yet. I've had my child, the only one I intend to have. Jake hasn't even had the chance to get started.

Wrangling my thoughts back into at least this portion of the year, I tell him what I've been thinking about all day. "I want to help Lem."

Jake shifts ever so slightly, and my heart warms when it's clear it's because he wants more of my chest against his. "You already have."

"I mean really help. I've been looking into some continuing education in geriatrics and dementia. Life-spans for people with the diseases in my specialty have increased a lot, but I never I see anyone as old as Lem. Still, I don't think it would be too much of a stretch to add—"

"No."

I pull up. "No?"

"As much as I love Lem and would be thrilled to have someone like you on his team, I'm not about to let you use him as an excuse to ramp up your hamster wheel to infinity."

I move away, affronted. "Let me? I'm not sure you have that authority."

"Not in general, no, but I won't be a part of you running yourself into the ground."

I'm not about to tell him I've been mulling over talking to Doc and offering to come up to the Bloom once or twice a month to do clinics with him.

Jake's chest rises and falls with deep, steady breaths. "Bailey, you can't keep this up. I'm no psychologist, but even I can see you're trying to please some phantom that can never be satisfied. I'm not sure why. I'm sure it's none of my business. But I just found you, and I don't want to lose you, but it feels like you're trying for an early grave."

I pull my legs up and fold my hands over my knees. "Isn't that a little presumptuous on all counts?"

"Probably, but I didn't get to where I am by being shy. I try not to be a jerk, but I generally speak my mind. Right now, warning klaxons are blaring that I'm moving too fast, but for the first time, I don't want to take the see-what-happens route. I want to make things happen."

That suffocating feeling is back as he shifts, clearly getting ready to stand.

"So here it is, Bailey. I can't explain it, and I sure don't understand it, but I've fallen for you. Damned if I know how. But I'm laying it out, pure and simple. I want to be with you, but I won't be a weekend boy toy or a here-and-there lover."

I can't help myself. "'Boy toy' doesn't sound so bad."

He raises one dark eyebrow. "We'll circle back to that, but let me finish. I'm not saying you have to leave Houston, so don't think this is a relocation ultimatum. What it's about is I won't watch you kill yourself. So my question is, do you have to collapse, like Lila, or look back on a lifetime and have regrets, like Lem? In case you didn't listen, let me spell it out. I'm here if you want me."

"I'm not sure wanting you is the issue. I'd be lying if I said I didn't."

"My ego thanks you for that." He takes the long, simple braid I used to wrangle my hair away from my face and strokes the end with his thumb. "Until you, I never knew what I was missing. I thought I was happy dating now and then, just staying busy and with my projects. Now I'm hungry for more."

He leans forward, and those long fingers caress my jaw before slipping behind my head to pull me with aching gentleness toward him. I breathe him in with a ragged inhalation, trying to memorize the feel of his mouth slipping against mine all too quickly before he pulls away.

Then his thigh muscles bunch as he gets to his feet and walks away, taking all the oxygen with him.

CHAPTER TWENTY-NINE

CAMMIE

I STAYED in the shower until I was shivering, my skin pruning, but I got a hold of myself. At least enough that I can pretend to laugh as I flit between the different groups under our huge family tent. I see Bailey slip out the back and want to follow, but seeing Jake with her makes me stay and pretend to listen to a really bad joke Daddy's telling. Something about a pastor, a priest, a rabbit, and a typo.

I edge back to the train of red and blue Yetis and give a finger wave to Harville, who seems to have gotten himself tagged as temporary bartender, or cooler tender, as it were.

I change my gesture to include the whole faire. "Your wife is amazing."

His glance immediately finds Kiki, and his smile goes full wattage in pride and love. "That she is. So, what's your pleasure?"

"Do we have ginger ale? My stomach's a little wonky."

"We do, and I'm glad to have a second to talk with you. I had a minute with Ally at the dock party, so if I can snag some time with Bailey, I'll have officially worked through the Terrible Trio."

"I'm not sure you're getting any of us at our best, I'm sorry to say."

"That's all right. The good news is you have each other." He digs into a mound of ice and hands me a cold can. "So, how are you?"

It would be poor form to cuss in front of a preacher, no matter how appropriate several words that come to mind might be at the moment. "I've already spilled the beans that I've been better, but the last thing I want is be an Eeyore in the middle of such a great day."

Harville pops the tab on his own can and tips it at me. "You know, I read this great quote, and I wish I could attribute it properly, but the gist is this. Eeyore was probably clinically depressed, and I think Milne wrote him that way to make the point that all his friends accept him just as he is. No one tries to change him, or force him to cheer up, or be anything but Eeyore. Now, I don't think you're the blue donkey's metaphorical twin, by any means, but you don't have to put on a happy face. And if you want me to play Pooh, I can just sit with you and let today be today."

Tears spring to my eyes, forcing me to press my wrist to my nose to stop myself from dissolving into an inelegant mess. "So who sits with you?" I ask, trying to get a handle on myself. "Piglet?"

He looks across the tent at Kiki and his gaze goes long and loving. "Nah, I have a Tigger with a nuclear battery who keeps me together."

"Lucky you."

"You have no idea."

But I think I do. It was such a short time, and against the odds, but I had that with Johnnie. Imperfect, but wonderful.

Before I can get lost in the past, Trey walks through the front of the tent and responds to a chorus of hellos. As he sees me and heads this way, Harville drops his voice. "Take it from me, Cammie. Some of us are lucky to get more than one chance in this lifetime. You just have to see the gift for what it is."

Trey holds out his hand to Harville as he comes abreast of me. "How you doin', Preacher?"

"Couldn't be better if I tried." The men shake, and Trey takes a Dr Pepper, tapping his can against mine. "Having a good day, partner?"

No, I'm not, and we're not partners. That's what my brain says.

What my mouth says is, "It's certainly gorgeous. Did you watch the caber toss?"

"Yeah, and I ran away before anyone asked me to give it a try, forcing me to go crawling to my grandmother for help."

"Help?" I ask, injecting amusement into my voice. "She'd toss the biggest of the lot one-handed and win the whole shebang."

"True. So, what's been keeping you busy so far?"

I don't think nearly drowning myself in the shower is what he's looking for. "Just strolling. I loved Ally's set with Suzanne and Zane. That was a shock."

"Yeah, but man, it was great."

"Indeed. Listen, I haven't made it to the everything-on-a-stick booth yet. Wanna come?"

Smooth, Cameron, very smooth. But I need to talk to him, and in the middle of a sea of people who share DNA with me isn't the place.

"Sure. See you later, Harville."

He nods and gives me a wink as Trey turns away.

As we wend our way back outside, it occurs to me that there must be something in the Magnolia Bloom water. Southerners or not, the men around here, with only a few exceptions, are good guys. Oh, there's a fair share of testosterone and ego, I can't deny that. But in the end, I can look back and point to ten guys who would stop, drop, and roll if any one of us needed help. You wouldn't have to ask twice, and there'd be no tally stick waiting for paybacks. I wonder sometimes if the Bloom isn't in some alternate dimension, because the world would say, while it's not perfect, such a place can't exist.

But it does.

I keep my peace until we're blowing on our just-out-of-the-grease shrimp skewers, and we've claimed spots under a towering pecan that's going to drop nuts the size of golf balls in a few months. A pain slices through me when I realize I won't be here to see it, or take part in the annual shelling contest. I've never won, mostly because I can't stop myself from eating half my spoils, so my basket never comes in against the champions with better restraint.

I have, however, proudly brought home a ribbon in the watermelon-seed-spitting contest a time or two.

"Uh-oh." Trey's voice draws my face toward him.

"Uh-oh?"

"You're thinking."

I wrinkle my forehead. "Isn't that what we get paid to do?"

"At the office, yes, but you're supposed to be relaxing." Trey strips off a tail and offers me the plump prize.

"Thanks, I have plenty."

"So you going to tell me what's up?"

I groan loudly. "You know, you were this annoying in high school, but I'd forgotten."

"And you deflected constantly then... and now."

I put my empty skewer on the ground and dust my hands together, then do an in-depth examination of my nailbeds. "I'm leaving."

Trey does the same thing, wiping his hands on the one remaining napkin and resting his elbows on his knees. "When?"

Well, that's not what I was expecting. "When and not why?"

"I saw Stephen a little bit ago."

"Ah, the power of the grapevine."

"And knowing you for most of my life."

"What's that supposed to mean?"

"You run, Cameron. You choose the geographic fix. I'd just let myself hope that this time you'd choose differently."

As clearly as if he'd said it out loud, I hear *you'd choose me.*

"It's not that easy, Trey."

"It's not? Pray tell, why?"

"Because I can't do this again. Even if whoever was talking was being a giant jerk, the truth's there, and it hurts. Once again, I've run to someone else to fix my boo-boo. I can't stand on my own two feet."

"Says the woman who just spent two years cleaning up a massive estate and losing everything in the process."

I pluck a dandelion and blow the fluff into the breeze wafting past. "The truth is, I'm not the extrovert everyone thinks I am."

"Not everyone."

I close my eyes against the intimate I-know-you timbre in his voice. "Point being, it's exhausting to put on my competence face like a layer of my morning makeup."

"So don't."

"Says the man with a sterling reputation and a thriving practice."

"Which you can have, too."

"As I squat in your offices and take your leftovers."

His face goes red and angry. "Don't. Don't insult me, and don't diminish yourself. Not to me."

Guilt makes my cheeks heat. "I'm sorry, truly. I didn't mean that."

"I accept you didn't mean to insult me, but you can't help digging at yourself. I hate it when you do that."

"Which is another reason for me to take my friend from Denver's offer to come work for her. Colorado has reciprocity, so I can practice while I study for the bar there. Shouldn't take me long."

"It wouldn't. When you put your mind to something, you exhaust the Energizer Bunny." He points to my trash and gives me the gimme signal. I pass the stick and napkin, aware this is his sign the moment's over, kinda like the queen switching her purse to her other arm. In a way, I feel almost like this has been a royal audience, and I'm a peasant who's displeased the crown.

"Well, let me know when you're exiting stage left." He wraps the sticks and paper together as if being precise with the detritus of our overpriced faire food is of utmost importance. Then he nails me again with those beautiful eyes. "I didn't realize I was waiting for you until you came back, but then I saw you, and we started working together, and for a nanosecond, my world was pretty sweet. I wanted to see where this would go, but I won't chase you, and I won't beg you." He stands, not offering me his hand. "I'll only ask once. Stay, Cameron. Give us a chance."

And then he's gone. Walking away.

And he's taking my soul with him.

CHAPTER THIRTY

ALLY

WITH THE GAMES once again over and traffic returned to normal, the quiet around Magnolia Bloom is almost deafening, but at least the folks who raise a friendly hand to me as I stroll downtown are familiar. Bailey and Cammie are joining me in a few hours at Brian's, but I'm too antsy to sit still. My bag containing my newest bobbles from Traycee's Emporium are testament to what a bad idea it is to go shopping when you're feeling out of sorts.

Those aren't the right words. I'm not out of sorts. I'm pretty comfortable with my decisions, but I'm still... at a loss. So maybe they are the right words after all.

Gah!

I glance into Tara's hair salon as I'm struggling to find an inner thesaurus and Eunice looks up, waving me in. Tara has a skill with hair that her sister Traycee has with merchandise, and I've found it's impossible to get an appointment with her since I got here. I hoped to finagle one, but now it looks like I won't have a chance to before I leave.

Eunice is unable to give me a hug, as Tara is painting strands of hair and wrapping foil around the bits. It's no big deal. I know where to find her, as I have no intention of missing out on a final lung-mashing from Eunice.

"Hey, sweetie. I see you're busy with some retail therapy."

Tara points to the empty chair next to Eunice with the pointy end of her color brush. "Sit a bit. You need something to drink?"

I thank her but demur and confirm Eunice's statement of the obvious by showing off the polymer necklace and matching earrings by a local artist Traycee's showcasing. With her help, Happy June Clay's creations are going to take off like a rocket. Eunice and Tara ooh and aah appropriately, and we chat about nothing in particular as Tara finishes the last packet and sits Eunice under a dryer, leaving us essentially alone.

"My next appointment canceled," Tara offers as she washes her hands. "You interested in taking the slot?"

"I'd love to. This is serendipity."

"Happens all the time. What do you want to do?" She turns my chair to the mirror and stands behind me, doing that hairdresser thing where she fluffs and finger-combs my honey-blond locks, tiling her head side to side as if trying to read an oracle.

I don't hesitate. "Cut it off and take me back to my natural brown."

Tara lifts an eyebrow at me. "You sure? That's a lot of inches, and I don't want you cursing me to Eunice later, 'cause I can take it off, but I can't glue it back on."

"I promise, no cursing. And I'm sure."

"So, what kind of short?"

"Wash-and-dry-on-the-run short." I meet Tara's eyes in the mirror. "I'm going to be traveling soon."

She reaches for her tools and makes a *snick-snick* noise with her shears. "Last chance."

I shake my head and don't have a scintilla of doubt. "No, first one."

Two hours later when Bailey and Cammie come through the door at Brian's, they both stop in their tracks.

"Holy camoley." Cammie slaps a dramatic hand to her heart and looks around the room with exaggerated concern. "Who are you, and what have you done with my sister?"

Bailey gives a creditable wolf whistle. "Hubba-hubba."

"You both are nuts. Boo, open that wine on the table. Cam, grab the glasses. I'll get the snacks out of the fridge."

"Oooh, more charcuterie. You're singing my song."

We all laugh at Cammie's bad joke and settle ourselves on the back porch, all of us distracted by Waylon and Willie acting like fools. Lovable fools, but still, I'm sure if I ever wanted a preview of how teenage boys behave, these two are giving me a good idea.

I hope Juliette will forgive me for turning them back over to her and Rory. I know they're beyond rehabilitation into a herd as they're now sure they're basically human and deserving of nothing less than complete adoration.

I look at my sisters and pour the first round. "Thanks for coming over."

Bailey swirls with an expert hand, watching the delicious but not especially expensive legs paint the inside of her glass. "I wasn't ready to go back to Houston anyway."

Cammie leans back in her chair and sighs. "I got in a full day's work by lunch, so cutting out early wasn't a thing. But enough chitchat. What's up with you? New do and one hell of a public goodbye onstage Friday. I've got this feeling Boo and I are about to get a turn at adios."

"I wish I knew how to say it in Gaelic. I'm going to Scotland."

She and Bailey both drop their glasses to the table. Thankfully, neither breaks.

"What?" they demand in unison.

"I've been pretty busy these last couple of days. In a nutshell, I've asked Sarah and Zane to watch over Suzanne as much as they can. I'm meeting Zane in Austin tomorrow to cut the tracks on that last song, and then I'm going to hand-deliver the diaries back to Maggie that she sent over here with a portrait of Alyssa. Juliette's keeping a photocopy if y'all want to read them, but Maggie's insisting I stay with her for a couple of weeks until I decide where I want to land."

"Scotland? Like, forever?" I can tell Cammie's trying to keep the panic from her voice.

"I doubt it, but for a while."

I look at Boo, she looks at Cammie, they both look at me. Bailey toasts me first. "Good for you. I'll miss you."

"I might a little." Cammie pokes her cheek out with her tongue.

"It's not like you can't come with."

"Uh, yeah, it is like that." Cam gives me a signature snort I swear under oath I won't miss.

But I will...

"You can visit."

"If you're there long enough," Boo says, giving Cam an exasperated headshake.

"We'll just have to see." I top each of us off and hoist my glass. "To sisters."

"Sláinte," Cammie toasts, appropriately.

After my heathy mouthful, I cut to Bailey. "So what about you? What's the plan?"

"Between not sleeping all weekend and Mother Nature's Xanax here, I'm a little loopy, but suffice to say, my guts make a plate of spaghetti look like a ruler."

"That bad, huh?"

"Thing is, I'm reasonably smart."

Cammie throws in snort number two, and I give her an I-agree nod.

Bailey ignores us. "I know what I need to do. I don't even have to open a spreadsheet. But knowing and having the courage are two different things."

"Because of Jake?" I meet her eyes squarely. "It's not like it's not obvious."

"Part of it, maybe, but no. No matter how great a guy he might be, I've never once made my life choices based on a man, beginning with Lila's dad. I'm not about to start."

"Good girl." It might be redundant, but I clink glasses with her again.

"I've been telling myself for years I have to keep going until Lila's out of college, and my loans are paid off, and the mortgage, and—"

Normally, Cammie's the blunt one. This time, it's me. "And, and, and. We know."

"Well, I'm exhausted." She cuts me and Cam both a don't-you-dare glare. "Lila really brought that home, even if she didn't mean to. She's so happy spending time with her dad, and she says when she gets back, she wants to finish up an associate's degree at ACC in Austin. She wants out of Houston, which I can understand, and she has friends going to UT."

"Why doesn't she just go there straightaway, then?" Cam's tone is curious, not judgmental.

"She doesn't want to dive into a huge campus and thinks taking government and Texas history and whatnot in an auditorium of six hundred is silly. For her, not speaking for her friends. She already has a year of dual credits from high school, so in two semesters she'll have her associate's. Then she says she'll decide if she wants to finish out a four-year."

"If?"

"Yeah, I don't dare tell Mom Lila isn't sure yet she wants a bachelor's, much less an advanced degree."

As the only one at the table who never came close to finishing college, I have to pipe in. "I hope you're not going to push her."

"Not anymore. I learned my lesson in ten minutes of abject terror as my baby collapsed from exhaustion. I do worry about her future, but the only thing I really want is for her to be happy."

"Which is why you're an awesome mom." I wag a finger at her. "And why you need to apply a little of that wisdom to yourself."

Bailey raises both hands. "I'm trying. I swear. I've got some ideas churning in my brain, but I give you my word, whatever I end up doing, it'll involve putting some balance into my life. I'm just not sure what that means yet."

"Fair enough." I turn the laser on Cam. "What about you? You're wound tighter than a tick, too."

She gives us a quick recap of what happened at the games, and with typical Cammie honesty, she leaves out none of the harsh details.

I clench my fists, fighting a sudden urge for some swamp justice. "I may rescind my determined pacifism if I ever meet those women in a dark alley." We all know I basically risk anaphylactic shock if exposed to physical violence, but I might find my inner MMA fighter if I ever discover who hurt my sister this badly.

Bailey raises her hand again. "Count me in."

Cam blushes but, for once, doesn't pretend she's not touched. "Rude and mean I can get past, but the thread of truth gutted me."

I rear back like she slapped me. "You did not kill your husband."

"Not that, silly. The part where I ran to someone new."

I feel the furrows forming on my brow. "I'm sending you my Botox bills if you keep this up."

"What I mean is, I have to face that I've never truly stood on my own two feet, and as much as Trey's a gem for helping me, I have to grow up."

Bailey frowns this time. "You lived on your own in college and law school, so to say you aren't a grownup is crazy."

"You two are sweet, but I have to be serious."

"And serious means moving to Colorado?" I've pulled the cork on a new bottle and replenish all our glasses.

"Says the woman flying halfway around the world. I don't think you have room to pound on me."

"I'm not pounding. I'm just asking. You can walk down any random street and not be recognized. I'd like to go back to that."

If Bailey had a whistle, I'd bet money she'd use it. "Stop it, you two. Cammie, if you need to get away, I'll support you, but I don't think you have to move to Denver to do it." She gives Cam a crooked smile. "Not that you asked my opinion."

Snort number three fires off. "The whole reason we're here is to get each other's opinions, and I didn't say I *am* moving to Colorado. I said I'm thinking about it."

We take a time-out to demolish the charcuterie, play-fighting over figs and olives and perfect tiny pickles, before finally sitting back with satisfied sighs.

As the sun makes a final dive toward the horizon, I tap my glass with my knife, making the crystal chime. "It's been a brutal month-plus for all of us, and I need you to know how desperately glad I am that you've been here with me."

"Ditto," Bailey says.

Cam nods and raises her glass.

I groan. "Oh, please. Not another toast."

She pretends to be hurt, but I can see her smile as she drains the last ruby drops. "Okay, no toast, but the truth is, I don't know how I would've gotten through this without you."

"You did two years without us," Bailey reminds her.

"Yeah, but that was all on autopilot. When I got back here, I didn't have any armor left, and you two gave me the glue to hold myself together."

"That's a terrible metaphor, but back at you, kiddo." I don't mind when Cam sticks her tongue out at me. It means my baby sister's going to be all right.

We let the conversation turn to a recap of the games and other general subjects. When they're both starting to nod off, I send them inside to bed, as neither of them needs to be driving tonight. While they crash in Brian's room, I make a quick sink full of hot water to wash the dishes.

Sliding my hands into the silky suds, I feel sure of my plan. Scared, but sure.

As for my sisters? While I have confidence in them, I admit I'm worried. All three of us were pretty set in our ways until the universe decided to rather brutally end our delusions and kick us out of our nests with a solid boot to the backside.

Bailey's the most afraid. I get it that she doesn't make her decisions on romantic consideration, but still, even being thrown from the saddle myself doesn't mean I want her to be alone forever. I'm not talking white dress and picket fence. Just connected to someone.

I already know that's what I'll miss most about Zane. What we had. And I know it'll take me time to grieve what we lost.

Now Cammie? She's the one furthest along this path of all three of us. My baby sister is both the closest to her goal and the most guarded, and I don't want her to waste years thinking that physical distance is going to solve a mental issue. Or a heart issue. She seems to be the only one who doesn't know she's loved Trey since they were teenagers. It doesn't diminish what she had with Johnnie, but Trey's been waiting for a long time.

Lord knows I'm the last one to offer advice, but I know how hard it is to refuse to let other people's opinions rule your life. Cammie'll get there. If she doesn't, she's in for a lot more heartache than she realizes. She's going to regret it forever if she gives up on Trey a second time.

I put the dishes in the drainer and turn out the lights, satisfied things are as put together as possible, and I'm not talking about the décor. My sisters and I spent too long thinking we would be bothering each other to reach out for the very strength we have, have always had, but let slip away.

No more.

Lyrics start forming in the back of my head, in that place where I know they're percolating but aren't ready to pour from me yet. It's the first time I've felt that knowing in a long time. My sisters have given me back my music, or at least the promise of it.

And I'll return the favor, the love, for the rest of my life, and make sure we never drift apart again.

CHAPTER THIRTY-ONE

BAILEY

TAKING Monday off to spend a glorious day with Ally and Cammie meant the rest of this week has been a nightmare. Being short-staffed means a lot more rounding at the hospital than usual and lots more interaction with the families of the patients, most of whom think they know more about pulmonary hypertension than I do, thanks to WebMD.

I know there's a term for when you become aware of something and then suddenly see it or feel it everywhere. Like the tag in the back of your shirt that never bothered you, but now that you've noticed, you can't stop fidgeting like a three-year-old in church.

Except this isn't a label I can remove, hopefully without damaging a piece of designer clothing. This is my brain, which is determined to be irritated at every text, every email, every page, and every call from every charge nurse at Memorial Hermann who apparently thinks I'm the only one who can authorize med changes.

I can't even drive home with Hayley Williams blasting out of my kickass audio system. Instead, I take five different calls, including a heartbreaking consult that I don't think's going to end well. By the time my garage door descends behind my back license plate, I'm exhausted.

Finished. Finito. Pure done-in.

I've barely cued up a movie and put the lap blanket over my swollen ankles when Lila's ringtone jerks me upright. I scramble for the phone, madly swiping to connect the video call. I've been extremely proud of myself for leaving her alone, letting her initiate most of the contact between us so she doesn't feel me hovering.

"Hey, baby! How's Guatemala?"

"It's amazing. Incredible. It's so cool what Dad and these doctors are doing. There's a lot of poverty here. I mean a lot, but I don't think people know there's a lot of happiness, too."

"It's pretty complicated."

"Dad says we might not be able to fix everything for everyone, but it's never a waste to make someone's life better."

"Sounds like someone's becoming a social justice warrior."

"Maybe a little. I think the term's gotten hijacked, which is unfortunate. I've met a lot of cool people from some different aid agencies, and I'm thinking I might be good at a nonprofit. There's so much going on behind the scenes, and I had no idea. I'm pretty good at organizational stuff." She wrinkles her nose at me. "I did learn from the best."

I strive for upbeat-mom voice, not oh-crap-mom voice. "Don't follow too closely in my footsteps, sweetie. We've already seen that's a mistake."

"Nah, we both just needed a little shakeup. Kinda like this trip making me see there's some really crappy people in the charity world."

"I'm sure that's true, but there're some miracle workers, too."

"I'm finding that out."

"The important thing is you're finding out how to define your own happiness. That's all that matters."

"Mom, are you watching *Dead Poets Society* again?"

I reach for the remote and turn off the television. "No."

"Mmmm… Well, point is, I'm seeing the ones that are all flash. It makes me so mad to know how much money they raise that doesn't get to the end cause."

"And you want to be one of the others."

"I think so. I'm not sure yet."

"Just enjoy what you're doing. You'll figure it out."

"That's what Dad says."

"Oh, Dad's become a savant now?"

Her laugh makes my heart smile. "Hardly, but we've had some long talks, and he's told me a little about you two."

"Uh-oh."

"Nothing icky, I promise, but it seems Dad was a bit of an asshole."

"Back in the beginning, but he's a different person now."

I get an eye roll as only the young can manage. "Kinda on the nose for the people-can-change lecture, innit?"

"I wasn't going to lecture."

Teen sighs ensue. "That wasn't meant toward you. My thoughts meander lately."

"You're allowed. You're only seventeen, remember?"

"Mah-ommm, seventeen and a half."

"Mea culpa."

"You're forgiven. I gotta go. Dinnertime."

Thankfully, my girl's not prone to skipping meals. One less thing I have to worry about.

"Have fun. Tell Dad hi for me."

"Will do. Love you."

"Love you more."

And the moving picture of her on the screen is replaced with my favorite shot of her, her arms around the neck of her best friend's golden, both their faces alive with happiness.

I should have gotten her a dog.

I should have gotten me a dog.

Instead of letting us experiencing the pure innocence of a pet, I told her, and me, that we didn't have time to take care of an animal. My one overly ambitious attempt to have an aquarium proved I'm the Dr. Kevorkian of fish. I remind myself that doesn't necessarily extrapolate to mammals.

I don't think my child meant to send me down an existential rabbit hole, but instead of turning the television back on, which is, um, definitely not *Dead Poets Society*, I stare at my reflection in the shiny glass of the monster display.

First my sisters, then my kid.

I get it. Everyone comes away from their childhood with mental boo-boos. Otherwise, how would we keep therapists in business? I know on a top-line level that my mom's obsession with education is from her own family of origin crap and so on down the line, but it's sobering and a little embarrassing to see how much I let it control my life. I'm a grown adult, for Pete's sake. I shouldn't need a seventeen-year-old… Excuse me, seventeen-and-a-half-year-old to be a Buddha to me instead of the other way around.

My job, not hers, and I've done a pretty poor one at it.

Digging out from under the blanket, I head to my ridiculously large kitchen that hardly sees me except when I'm doing exactly what I'm doing now… grabbing a bottle of water from the fridge. No wine tonight, thanks. I've had my limit with my sisters, which was the perfect place for it.

Time to be clearheaded.

And, for the love of God, stop thinking.

Stop dreaming about how much I want to ditch the big city and the big salary and the big everything and maybe, just maybe, find out what being a small-town doctor's like. Doc has been a master at the occasional just-checkin'-on-ya text, with updates on Lem or other clients in his clinic. I'm not blind to what he's doing, and I've been in the biz too long to go all *Dr. Quinn, Medicine Woman* in my head, but I also have enough experience to know just how detached I've become. From my calling, my patients, my… everything.

And ego check—the world of pulmonary hypertension is not going to implode if I change tracks.

I snuggle into my nest on the couch and pick up my phone, opening my contacts list with two clicks.

I dive right in when he answers. "Hello?"

I can't blame him for the tentative tone.

"Any chance, by some magical coincidence, you're in Houston again this weekend?"

"Actually, I just hit the outskirts of Clear Lake. I'm going to watch my buddy try for a brain injury playing rugby tomorrow."

"Just watching, though, right?"

"I rather enjoy my face and having all my natural teeth, so I'm fine with being head cheerleader."

I enjoy that face, too. And those teeth. And those lips. "I bet you'd look cute with pompoms."

"You should come see."

I twist the fringe of my lap blanket between nervous fingers. "Any chance you might want to stop by The Woodlands?"

We both know my house and Clear Lake are diametrically opposed on the map, with Houston in the middle, but he chuckles.

"I might be talked into a little detour."

"I could bribe you with some really excellent microwave popcorn."

"What red-blooded American man could turn that down?"

"I'm only worried about one."

"You're in luck, then. I happen to have plenty of gas to make it all the way around the loop."

"It's a date." I use the term deliberately and send him my address so he can plug it into his GPS.

"It's a date." There a softness in his long pause, and it makes my insides go squishy.

Panic makes a push to edge out the hope trying to spring through, but I manage to keep my voice in its normal range. "Jake?"

"Still here."

"You know I'm a mess, right?"

That laugh, all deep and gentle and warm, floats through the speaker. "I have a little clue. And spoiler alert—I'm not perfect, either."

I think he might have some work to do to prove that, but it's okay if it's not tonight.

"See you in a bit. Don't get a ticket."

"It'd be worth it."

The line clicks off, and I bite my lip, wondering if I've lost my mind on many counts. Radical career change. Radical income adjustment. Radical romance.

I hope.

I race to my bathroom, stripping like my clothes are on fire and jumping in the shower. Even if he drives like Ally, I have an hour to put myself together.

And get ready to change my life forever.

CHAPTER THIRTY-TWO

CAMMIE

I WAIT until late in the evening to haul the boxes and rolls of tape I bought at the moving and storage place up to my office. My temporary office. My no-longer-mine office.

It's been a long week. Luckily, I've had back-to-back-to-back closings, so I haven't had time to think when I'm at work.

Trey has been one hundred percent Trey. His usual affable, smiling, polite self.

Blast him.

Why can't he be all chest-beating-be-my-woman? Instead, he's all patient and unflappable and acting like everything is just fine.

Except nothing is fine. At least not for me. Even Eunice has been short with me, telling me I'm being blind as a wombat at midnight.

I think she means blind as a mole, but I'm not about to correct her. Not when she's got her spoon in hand, and I feel like I'm nine again and going to feel it against my backside if I don't straighten up.

I chalk her lack of usual willingness to play Switzerland in any discussion up to her being more than a little partial to her grandson.

Not unexpected, but it also means I can't pour my heart out to her for that very reason.

It also highlights how small my world became when I married Johnnie. I was perfectly content in our little bubble, but the end result is I find myself reluctant to get out. I'm usually wiped out at the end of an average day and don't mind going home to my apartment and relaxing with a good book or a movie marathon. It wasn't until just recently that my routine no longer works as well as previously planned.

Even my revived friendship with Jolene hasn't made up for unappealing dinners for one, no-longer-engaging novels, and restless walks around town after the sidewalks have been rolled up in the evenings.

"So, slipping off in the middle of the night, eh?"

I don't turn around at the sound of Trey's voice. I actually expected it, not only because the security system no doubt alerted him to an after-hours entry, but the little *beep-beep-beep* told me someone else came in.

I finish taping the bottom of the box, then face him. "No skulking or slipping. I just couldn't sleep."

"Welcome to the club."

"I'd rather revoke this particular membership, if you please. I won't even ask for a refund."

"Me, too. Let me know when you find the out clause." He points to the floor. "You gonna put anything in those?"

I look down and realize I've put together five boxes. All empty. "Eventually."

Trey takes one of my guest chairs and runs his hand over his entirely too-sexy evening scruff, and the fatigue in his beautiful eyes makes guilt wash over me like someone opened a floodgate at the dam.

I sit down in my chair, not because it's behind the desk, but because it's the closest, and my knees are a little weak.

"Who are you going to give your power to in Denver?"

That wasn't the opening salvo I was expecting. "Oh, please. No armchair New Age pop psych. Leave that to the new palm reader over on Fifth."

"Honest to God, the name on her birth certificate is Crystal, and she's really sweet. I don't buy into her thing, to be honest, but she had me review her lease, and come to find out, she's pretty smart, if you don't judge her by obvious prejudices."

I give him an arch look. "Subtle, Trey. Super subtle."

"You brought her up, not me." He shrugs. "How do you want to phrase it, then? You're leaving here because you think people are judging you while simultaneously saying you don't care."

"I'm a woman. I get to be a contradiction."

"Bullshit. You've never played the chick card, so you don't get to now."

I toss a pen at him, old memories surfacing like bubbles in a glass. "Not fair. You've known me too long."

He catches the projectile, but we're both glad this time it doesn't squirt ink all over him. "And yet not long enough."

"Man, you're playing dirty tonight."

"Man's gotta do what a man's gotta do."

"Oh, you get to play the dude card? Double standard much?"

"Desperate times and measures and all that." He lobs the pen back at me in a gentle arc.

I put it back in its assigned place.

"Cameron, don't go."

"You said you wouldn't ask again."

"I lied."

I put my elbows on my desk and press my thumbs under my eyebrows, pressing hard to stop the blasted tears trying to escape.

He slides the box of tissues from the little table between the guest chairs across to me. "You came home for a reason. I was hoping I was one of them."

I grab one and blow my nose before it leaks. I didn't realize it at the time, not explicitly, but he was definitely one of the deciding factors for moving back to Magnolia Bloom. If I were being honest, he was probably in the top five.

Fine. The top one.

I just didn't acknowledge that to myself. Or anyone.

"I'm scared."

Two words. Whispered. My entire soul cut open and laid bare right in front of him.

"That's reasonable."

"I need to know I can make it on my own. Stand on my own two feet."

His lips quirk. "What, you think I'm going to throw you over my shoulder and drag you to Harville, demanding he marry us at dawn?"

Not so sure about the marrying thing, but tossed over his shoulder? That might be fuel for some sweaty dreams.

"I've never quite pictured you going all caveman on me."

"You do things to me no one else ever has. It might embarrasses us both if you knew the directions my mind's gone in."

Maybe, and maybe not. And maybe we might have matching GPS destinations. "So, tell me a couple."

"You open your own firm, and we go toe-to-toe for billable hours. Or you join me, become partners, and we take the legal world by storm. I don't really care." He meets my eyes. Hard. "As long as you stay."

"You don't fight fair."

"Nope."

I feel my smile waver. "I'm still a little broken, you know."

"I've been told I'm good with fixer-uppers, and a couple of folks question my man card because I'm too patient, or so I'm told."

"From this vantage point, I can assure you your man card is perfectly safe."

His grin is adorable. "Well, thank you, ma'am."

"Problem is, I don't deserve you."

He stands and comes around to my side of the desk, pulling me to my feet and into his arms. "That's such a stupid phrase. You deserve the best of everything, and I'd like to be a part of it."

I reach up and trace a hint of gray in his beard. "You've waited a long time for me."

He nods. "Honestly? I didn't realize it, exactly. Not until you came back. Came home."

"I'm glad you did. Wait, that is." It's so hard, so gut-slicingly hard, to say the next words. "I love you, Trey. I have since you gave me your juice box at Kinder Kastle Daycare."

"Took you long enough to say it."

I play-punch him in the shoulder. "That's not what you're supposed to say back."

He kisses me, long and soft, then long and hard and desperate. Kisses that have been waiting, stored up and growing, and now they've been released, and I can see all the way to forever to learn every inch of this man.

"Good God, Cameron, if you don't know how much I love you by now, then I rescind the partnership offer. I need someone with a brain on my team."

I grab his head and pull him back, making sure I show him with lips and teeth and tongue and ragged breath just how much brain I have.

"Come home with me." His voice wobbles, but his eyes are bright with an intoxicating mix of love and fire-hot desire.

"Oh, yes, please."

It's a mad scramble to turn off lights and lock doors, and it's a good thing there're only two full-time police officers in Magnolia Bloom, as I'm afraid my first client would be my partner, for a speeding ticket far in violation of the posted limits.

Trey has my full approval, though, and we shed clothes the second the door closes and locks behind us.

And I find out just how amazing a long wait can make a union of two souls destined to be together...

... and two bodies that've known, all along, they were perfect for each other.

CHAPTER THIRTY-THREE

ALLY

SIX MONTHS ISN'T NEARLY enough time to take in Scotland, I'm finding out. Having an enormous extended family has let me see the land of the Gaels, from Lowlands to Highlands, with tour guides who are thrilled to have one of their own to enthrall with stories both historical and fantastical. I started with couch surfing with Maggie. She was delighted to have Alyssa's diaries back, saying she wanted to read them one last time. She's quite frail now, but I can still see the woman who reveled in being called a witch, both in jest and in fear. From the home she's had outside the hamlet of Inchree since before her children were born, she sent me off to explore the Glen Righ forest, just as she had my cousin Paige, I'm told.

Apparently, the waterfalls of Glen Righ are magic healing portals. Maybe there's some secret wave between here and Lake Maggie, and we just don't know it.

I consider the beauty all around me as I sit with Maggie and take little bitty sips of the tea that's more Balvenie than Darjeeling.

"You going to come hear me play tonight?" I try to get Maggie out as much as possible. I know our time is coming to a close soon, and I want to take every second with her I can.

"I am indeed. Yer cousin Finn says he's goin' to have a microphone for ye this time."

"It's really all right if he doesn't." Finn's bar is a tiny thing, and I don't need the amplification. Even more, there's something amazingly intimate to have nothing between me and the patrons but my guitar. "Let's go get ready, then, and we'll head into the village."

She happily complies, not needing my help even at almost a hundred years old. She might be slow, but she's still independent, and I hope I'm half as gutsy as her when I hit her age.

Aware I have a fragile passenger, I keep my driving sedate. I love the tiny Corsa Maggie's hilarious granddaughter Lexi has lent to me. I'm pretty sure I'm going to buy a car in the next few weeks, as I don't appear to be going home anytime soon.

My head barely clears the doorway of Finn's Place, a not very originally, but accurately, named establishment. Being a typical American, I'm still not used to how small most buildings are around here, and how old. Most of the taverns I've played at are as old as my country, and of course I've stood awestruck in thirteen castles and counting so far.

"Alyssa!"

The chorus comes from the group at the bar as I get Maggie settled in one of the ancient but marginally comfortable chairs close to the roaring hearth. Winter in Scotland has left me literally breathless many times now, as I'm nowhere near acclimated to a cold so deep I'm immobilized by it. This Southern girl loves visiting, but she's not sure she could live here forever.

I call roll as I wave. "Ian. Brodie. Fergus. Hey, Shannon."

They all lift their respective pints and turn back to their conversations as I set up. It doesn't take but a few moments, a far cry from years of roadies sweating themselves out of their T-shirts, practice with choreographers, program review, sound checks, lighting adjustments...

I play my first set with half the crowd that files in listening, half completely uninterested in me being anything but background noise. And I'm fine with that.

More than fine. I relish it, dive into it, cover myself in the pure joy of just singing.

When I take a break and gladly accept both the glass of water and the perfectly drawn Guinness Finn hands me, a stocky Scotsman with shockingly red hair takes the stool beside me.

He lifts his beer toward mine. "Do dheagh slàinte."

I touch rims with him. "To your health as well."

"Anyone tell you you sound like that American country singer? Can't remember her name."

I hide my smile by brushing off my Guinness mustache with a napkin. "I've heard that a couple of times."

"You sing good, lass."

"Thank you. I'm working on it."

He holds out his hand. "Seamus Tavish."

"Alyssa MacInnes."

"Ah, one of Maggie's girls."

"Tangential, but yes, related."

"Scary how many of us are around here, but I think we're safe."

There's a delightfully devilish twinkle in Mr. Tavish's eyes. He's not the first man to flirt with me these last few months, but he's the first one to cause a little hey-there interest.

The divorce is done. I put Trey on retainer, but Cam understood it probably wasn't best to have her on the job. Family and all that. Other than a few back-and-forths that edged toward tense, Zane and I came to an agreement with surprisingly little acid reflux. Trey scolded me I gave up more than I technically had to, and I told him I'm more than happy with how things turned out.

Mostly because I've come through this not hating Zane, and that's the biggest prize of all. I had no intention of going all War of the Roses when I could end it with a friendship and plenty of assets in the bank.

My phone vibrates, and I excuse myself, leaving Mr. Twinkle Eyes as I take Sarah's call.

"Good to hear from you. How's things stateside?"

"Busy. I've got Suzanne booked to open for Miranda Lambert in March."

I desperately wish I had someone to high-five with this news. "Holy camoley! That's incredible."

"I'm considering it a coup. We've kept her busy in small venues, but this might put her on the map."

"Thank you so much, Sarah."

"I'm thanking you, too. Not enough to share my management fees, but I might send you an Edible Arrangement some time."

"You're a peach, for sure." I let the humor die off. "How's Zane?"

"He's good. Client confidentiality and all, but we negotiated a pretty sweet deal for him going solo."

"He'll kill it, I know."

"Yeah, he will." She pauses. "He misses you."

The pang contracting my heart is real, but smaller than the ones I started with. "I miss him, too. Us."

"Can—"

"No, Sarah, I can't. I wish him all the good things, but no."

"I get it. We got sidetracked, though. I didn't call to talk about Zane."

"Do tell, then."

"You might want to sit down. I'm holding a letter for you."

She lets the moment expand.

"Enough with the dramatic pause. What is it?"

"An invitation to be a member of the Grand Ole Opry."

I have to stand there for a second to parse out what I'm feeling. Unbelievably honored. That goes without saying.

But I can't tell Sarah that there's an equal measure of *it doesn't matter*. I get that it's rare for someone just under forty to be one hundred percent certain about anything, but I know, soul-know, that I don't want to be in the limelight any longer. I love performing, and I'll probably do small gigs until I'm put out to pasture, but I have zero interest in chasing that brass ring ever again.

"Ally?"

"Sorry, just overwhelmed. This is pretty awesome."

"Will you come home to accept?"

"Of course I will. It's an amazing honor."

She holds the line for a good ten seconds. "But it doesn't change anything."

"Nope. Sorry."

"Eh, I'll live. It's not about me anyway."

"Says no agent ever."

"This one just did."

"Just take care of Zane. And Suzanne."

"I will, as long as they'll let me." I hear the clicking of a keyboard. "Dumb question, but have you checked the charts?"

I let silence be my answer.

"Leave it to me to have to tell you that 'I Never Wanted To Say Goodbye' charted on release day and is on track to equal, if not beat, 'I Will Always Love You.'"

I do the slow blink, even though there's no one to see it. To match Dolly's legendary song is the Holy Grail for most of us in this genre, and I'm speechless.

"Wow," is all I can get out.

"Wow is right. Congrats."

"Thank you. And give Zane an attaboy for me."

"You know, the old label isn't the only game in town. If you want me to shop your ballad album idea—"

"No."

She huffs. "Dang it."

"I'm sorry, Sarah. I'm just not interested."

"Okay, then. I'll send you the details for the induction, and I look forward to seeing you."

We do the usual goodbyes, and when I return to the bar, there's a fresh beer, and Mr. Twinkle Eyes is still warming the seat next to mine.

"Good news?"

I nod. "A bit." I take a good, long sip of the fresh pint and give him a smile. "Thanks for the refill, but I need to get back to work."

"You should keep at it. You could be a big star with that voice."

I almost draw blood biting my lip not to laugh. "I'll work on it."

Maggie gives me a wave as I pass by and take the chair again, checking my strings and flipping through my notebook to see what grabs me. That's been my current system. Rifle through and sing whatever falls open last.

It's worked so far. So many of my songs have never been recorded, because these are the heart songs that weren't considered pop-y and dance-y and chart-y. They're the songs I always wanted to do and let myself be drawn away from. I don't blame Zane. He had a vision, and it was a good one. It was just different than mine. Certainly mine now.

I make sure to put in plenty of toe-tappers, as I do know how to read an audience. I can get away with my ballads very early and very late in an evening, but in the middle, drinking Scots want to clap and cheer. Come to find out, I don't mind writing and singing up-tempo when it's what I want and not what I'm expected to do.

Who'da thunk?

When I take Maggie home, I have an invitation to dinner from Twinkle Eyes MacTavish and hope that I'll have enough time, if it goes that far, for him to like Alyssa MacInnes before he finds out I'm Ally King. Good news is, American country music isn't a huge thing in small Scottish pubs, and as that's all I want for the foreseeable future, I'm fairly insulated from the glare of my previous life.

Previous life. Six whole months ago.

Apparently, a lifetime can pass in two seasons.

Not only for me. Bailey has officially become Doc's partner, with his intention clear as daylight that he intends to retire in short order. I haven't seen them in person yet, but when we video chat, I can see the fifteen pounds good food and good sex with Jake have put on her. She looks healthier and happier than I've ever seen her.

Cammie's my big shock. No Denver for her. Instead, I about fell down when she let me lend her the money to buy into Trey's practice. Full partner, market value. I was a little stunned at the number, but then, the ins and outs of law firms aren't exactly my bailiwick. Contrary cuss demanded standard interest and all the blah-blah-blah, but she made my entire year letting me do it.

I cried when she sent me a picture of the new plaque.

MacInnes and Greene, Attorneys at Law.

Yeah, I was surprised, too. Didn't see that coming.

I think she knows it helped me as much as it did her, because I no longer feel I have to buy my sisters' love. That was dumb all along, but sometimes I'm not the brightest tulip in the garden.

As they love to tell me.

And, turns out, I have to get busy writing a love song to play at her and Trey's wedding. She's asked me and Boo to be co-matrons of honor. I cried. Boo cried. It was a soggy-sister mess.

Boo and Jake seem to be edging toward… something. Some days, she's all bright and shiny-eyed. Others, the wariness is back, but Jake's patience is apparently bigger than the average bear's.

I crawl under the covers in the little house I rented about a mile from Maggie's, the air bitterly cold despite the ancient radiator's valiant attempts to combat the storm that's settled in and seems determined to stay. I turn on my heating pad and snuggle down, listening to the snow pelt the roof and hope I can get out of my door tomorrow. Maggie and I have a date to go into town for the church social.

Just the kind of wild life I want.

Funny how life changes. How nothing turns out how you think it will.

But it's how it's meant to be.

~

THANK you for reading *SPRINGTIME IN MAGNOLIA BLOOM*. Next up in the series, *MOONLIGHT IN MAGNOLIA BLOOM*, is out now. Keep reading for a sneak peek at Chapter One.

MOONLIGHT IN MAGNOLIA BLOOM – Chapter One – Lexi

. . .

As God is my witness, I'm never flying overseas again. As soon as I find the strength, I'm texting my American cousin that I plan to live at Castle MacInnes for the rest of my life.

A dozen or so hours ago, I locked the front door of my beautiful home in Bearsden, which is a stone's throw from Glasgow, excited to begin my new adventure. I've never been to America. The farthest I've traveled is once to London and once to Paris, but those are a lot closer than Texas. Now I'm half afraid my hindquarters are permanently adhered to an airline seat, so the patina of travel has worn off.

"Ma'am? When we get parked, you sit tight. I'll get your bag down from the overhead."

To my delight, my companion from Heathrow to DFW is a bona fide Texan. As we traded bits and pieces about our lives, I discovered DeWayne Tomlinson is forty-one, has recently been promoted to lieutenant colonel, and is stationed at RAF Lakenheath. He's headed home from England to celebrate his promotion with his family in Dallas. To my delight, he's even been to the Highland Games at Castle MacInnes a few times, giving us plenty to talk about.

"You're a true gentleman, DeWayne. Thanks for making the hours fly by, no pun intended."

"My grandma'd have my hide if I didn't treat a lady like a lady, especially a beautiful one."

It's easy to dismiss his flirtation, and he's done quite a bit of it during our long voyage across the Atlantic. I even teased back a little, although I'm hardly known for my skill in that arena. It's easy because it's all in fun. He can't possibly be serious, so I appreciate the distraction.

Despite my companion's efforts, though, I'm so ready to be off the plane, I could weep.

Rest assured, I'm not the weepy type. I'm a born-and-bred Scot. Weepy isn't allowed unless you're full-out steamin', and then only for a moment before your mates toss you into a bed to pass out. Soon as you sober up, it's back to stoic. Still, if I don't get my feet on solid land soon, I might throw a flakie that would impress the most exhausted wean. Much like a fatigued five-year-old, I'm dangerously close to lobbing my too-long-empty stainless-steel mug at the bulkhead. Not at the flight attendants, mind you. They all deserve medals for putting up with cranky people.

Truth be told, I've never behaved badly in public, but it's fun to think about.

Having my handsome, self-appointed guide stick by me all the way to baggage claim mitigates my Negative Nellie inner monologue, and by the time he pulls my two big suitcases off the carousel and grabs his duffel, I'm back to my more genial nature.

He straightens to his full, military-trained posture. "It's been a pleasure, Lexi. I expect a call when you get settled. Dallas is only a short drive from Magnolia Bloom, and I'd love to show you around my beautiful state."

"Two hours is a short drive?"

"Depends on which side of the city you start from, but in Texas, that's a quick jaunt. Hardly long enough to get down a whole soda and pack of peanuts."

"Regardless, I'm sure your family will keep you far too busy for you to be traipsing over half the state with a stranger, but I do thank you for making this a lovely trip."

"Half the state?" He coughs a laugh as he hands me back my phone. He's entered his contact information, seemingly not trusting me to get the details correct. "Lexi, half the state is a good seven hours with stops, so you can do the math if you have a hankering to go from Louisiana all the way to New Mexico. Heck, DFW alone is the size of Manhattan."

"You're bammin' me."

He raises his right hand in the on-my-honor position. "No, ma'am. I swear on a case of cane sugar Dr Pepper."

Goodness, he is serious. I tasted this elixir he waxed poetic about on the plane, but I'm not sure it's the mead of the gods he claims it is. I refrain from sharing my opinion of the sacred drink of Texas, though, as the service cart had no Irn-Bru for me to challenge with. Too bad, that.

I see he's stalling and decide it's time to stop this nonsense, fun as it is. "Thank you for everything you've done, from keeping me occupied to playing my personal valet, but you need to get going."

"I'd rather not leave you until your folks get here."

"Traycee and Bethanie will be here shortly. They said to wait inside, and they'd fetch me. I believe that's the term they used."

"I'll stay, just the same. My grandma—"

"Would skin you alive. Sounds painful."

"She might lower my punishment to a whuppin'. You don't know wounded pride until you have to go cut your own willow switch to get your hide tanned with."

I firmly believe DeWayne is playing up his Southern roots a tad, but I do appreciate his unflagging amusement. "I'm sure you're past corporal punishment, but I dinnae want a newly minted lieutenant colonel getting a thrashing on my behalf."

"I appreciate you having mercy on me."

Before he can come up with another ridiculous Texanism, I hear my name and turn to see a lass with her dark hair piled in a high, messy bun, wearing a loose cotton top and shorts. Her summer wear should've been a clue, but I'm distracted by her companion in a dressier sleeveless blue neck tunic and cropped chinos. Her hair is pulled back as well, but fanning out behind her head is a short afro framing her beautiful face and high cheekbones.

I give a last wave goodbye to DeWayne and lift a hand to indicate they've found me, taking a look around to notice the range of dress, from pajama bottoms and fuzzy slippers to coordinated outfits seeming straight off a runway. I wish I could chalk up my stretchy pants and top and my needs-a-good-wash hair to normal travel wear. Unfortunately, as my chic welcome delegation stands before me, their smiles wide and warm hospitality practically shooting from their bright gazes, I feel an exhaustion more than jet lag.

My abnormal lack of concern comes from the lonely hollow I've been living in, created by the absence of my husband. I can imagine Douglas, his voice booming as he charms these two lovely women who've come to collect me, and to be honest, I miss having his strong arms to haul around all this luggage.

I have no regrets about my life choices. I'm happy with the way I look, in general terms. I'm not one for limelight, so you'll never catch me in a hot pink tracksuit, and I'll never be caught in an airport in bunny slippers, but what I see in front of me is effort. Optimism. Hope in turquoise and pale yellow and denim.

My current gray-and-basic-black theme is probably worth a session with a therapist.

I'm not the moody sort, but I zero in on their lipstick and how the pop of color brightens their smiles, which reminds me I haven't put on makeup since the funeral.

It's been a long time since I was lit up from the inside, much less shined from the outside. At Heathrow, which I am certain is the training site for the devil's minions, people had been too exhausted, angry, or both, to care about fashion. It seems the rules in America—or Texas, at least—are different.

"I recognize that look. Dehydration and too much airplane food. I'm Traycee Everson, the woman who's going to get you to the Bloom in one piece because I'm the better driver. Welcome to Texas."

Bethanie rolls her eyes and gives me a smile, one even warmer than I saw on our video chat, and herds us all toward an escalator. "Let's get to the tram and out of an airport twice as big as Magnolia Bloom."

"Okay, right, first DeWayne saying it's bigger than Manhattan, now you."

"Crazy, but true."

"My poor brain's beyond visualizing the immensity of DFW, but I can at least tell you that while I appreciate the name badges, remembering names is my superpower." I'll easily recall Traycee's because I've never seen it spelled so uniquely.

Both ladies glance at the lanyards hanging around their necks, share a look, and Bethanie points a thumb at her compatriot. "Traycee owns the Emporium, which I promise will be your favorite shop by Friday. She presented at a Women in Business marketing conference in Dallas, and I'm her lucky sidekick. Since we were close, we were tagged to grab you. Hope you don't mind."

"Och, nae, although I'm looking forward to meeting Kiki. We traded a hundred emails as I finalized my itinerary."

The girls relieve me of my bags, which certainly makes things easier, but despite DeWayne's delightful company, fatigue is creeping in, making me feel crabbit and old. I promise my better angels I'll be back to my usual self soon. I might be within a wink and a nod of fifty, but I've always felt like a bit of a poster child for the positively peri-menopausal, full of energy and determination. Just not today.

I guess losing your husband of almost thirty years long would take the wind out of anyone's sails. I'll chalk it up to exhaustion, but right now, I agree with my brothers-in-law, who called my Douglas a fekkin' bawbag for having a heart attack and leaving me out of the blue. I'll pull up my knickers and get on with getting on later. For right now, I'm tired, sad, lonely, mad, lost, and about thirteen other things I'm sure my brain would supply if I could get a strong cup of tea in me, and maybe a scone with clotted cream.

Do they even have clotted cream over here? I might pitch another imaginary flakie if they don't. I force my mind away from childish meltdowns and content myself to listen as Traycee takes up the conversation.

"Kiki would've been here if she wasn't under doctor's orders to slow down. To keep her from being the world's crankiest pregnant lady if she's put on bed rest, we're your temporary B-team. We're delighted, though, and are happy to get you caught up on all things Magnolia Bloom."

Fear shoots through me, burning off some of my fatigue. I feel I already know Kiki from our chats, so even though I've never met her in person, concern overwhelms my self-pity. As a mother, I remember the terror even the thought of losing a baby causes, much less being in any real danger. "Please tell me Kiki's all right."

"She is, and little Kiki junior is plugging along on schedule. Don't worry. Doc says if she takes it easy, they'll both be right as rain. Not much besides a scare of this magnitude could manage such a feat."

With what I've gleaned from my conversations with Kiki, I can safely agree. "She does seem something of a dynamo."

Bethanie directs us down yet another wide, bright white walkway. "She's done amazing things for the estate, and I'm thrilled she let me add the castle as one of my marketing clients, but the fundraising gala for our new regional hospital is taking all the available oxygen right now. Which is how we were tasked with picking you up. We try for a conservation of energy, and folks coming into the big city often grab everything from bags of feed to lovely cousins arriving from exotic foreign lands."

Even tired as I am, I have to laugh. "Of all the things Scotland gets called, I'm not sure 'exotic' is one of them."

Traycee lifts a perfectly penciled brow over captivating gray-green eyes. "Regardless, I want to visit. I haven't been to Europe yet."

"Well, both of you have an open invitation to Bearsden—and by extension, Glasgow—any time. Right now, I'm so tired I might start greetin' and I think I'm out of tissues."

"No crying allowed on our watch, so just hang tough for a little longer."

After gesturing with a perfectly painted purple nail toward the sign saying Skylink, Traycee gives me a compassionate pat on my bicep. "It'll take a hot minute to get out of here, but I promise we'll have you home and settled as fast as we can."

They make good on their claim, navigating through the airport and into the car park with admirable ease. Before I can really take it all in, we're on the road, and I learn Bethanie and Traycee aren't related to my crazy brood of relatives, but Magnolia Bloom is a close-knit community and stays connected in many other ways, both through history and the fact that the MacInnes estate is the second-largest employer in the area. The Broder Factory, I'm told, holds the top title, but everyone's connected somehow, mostly with the insane growth of the smaller shops making the quaint city a tourist destination, and the castle is the crown.

When Traycee tells me she hopes their little town of five thousand won't disappoint me, I chuckle. "I was born in a place called Pitlochry, which boasts a grand total of less than three thousand, so I adore small places."

We settle into a comfortable silence as the miles fly past, and finally, Traycee points toward an enormous iron gate with turrets visible to the east. "We're almost there. We'll drop you straight into Eunice Greene's capable hands to get you a bite to eat and settled. All I ask is you promise you'll say hi to Penny in the morning."

"Penny?"

Bethanie gives me a horrified glance. "Kiki hasn't told you about Penny the Dragon?"

"Och, aye, she did. My head's mince right now. Sorry."

"No sorries allowed." Traycee's voice is stern, but her eyes are dancing. "Kiki'll take away my honorary MacInnes badge if we don't give you platinum service."

I'm not the overly touchy type, but I can't stop myself from putting a hand on Traycee's arm and giving it a quick squeeze. "You're a lean-nan, Traycee, you are."

She lifts one of those perfect eyebrows. "I assume that's a good thing?"

"Indeed. You're a sweetheart in any language."

"Back at you, Lexi. We can see you're wrecked, so we'll have you on solid ground in no time. So you know, we're sorry we're dumping you right into the middle of the gala, but we're sure glad you're here."

"I'm happy to take the little things off Kiki's list to help her out."

Bethanie gives me a confused frown. "Um, little things?"

"Sure. I've run a business with a thousand moving parts, so I know it's the small jobs eating up your time. I'm happy to free her of them so she can take care of the important ones."

Bethanie's expression goes perplexed and worried. "Lexi, we don't need you to take the margins on this. We need you to take over."

I blink suddenly dry eyes. "Take over?"

She nods. "The gala. The whole kit and kaboodle, except for major contracts. For the most part, those are done."

My headshake is frantic. "You're off your trolley, lass! I've never planned anything bigger than a birthday party. Piping and fittings, I know. Toilets and faucets, sure. Chandeliers and seating for five hundred, not so much."

Bethanie's quiet for a long moment. If she's hoping to make me feel better, it doesn't work. I almost didn't make this trip to Texas, but in the end, the chance to fly away from the malaise I've been in danger of adopting too thoroughly was irresistible. It's normal to feel lost and bereft, considering I thought Douglas and I were all set to enjoy retirement, although what the darn fool and I would have done to fill our days is a mystery.

But I was willing to give it a go.

Facing a future alone was never in the plans I made, yet it seems the cards I was dealt were reshuffled, including my image of what the next couple of months were going to entail.

They say the universe will deliver the same lesson to you over and over until you learn it. For the life of me, I have no idea why the powers that be determined a past-her-prime widow needed to flirt with a serviceman. Or why they planted the idea of adding something tangerine to my boring, sensible wardrobe.

Or why they believed a woman whose life revolves around P traps, backwater valves, and closet flanges can pull off a high-profile gala.

The Magnolia Bloom series:
This series is being produced in audio,
available from Chirp, Audible, and many other audio retailers

Magnolia Bloom Beginnings, A Three Novella Box Set – the Origins of Magnolia Bloom
  Return to Magnolia Bloom, a Magnolia Bloom Novel Book 1
  Mistletoe and Magnolia, a Magnolia Bloom Novel Book 2
  Springtime in Magnolia Bloom, a Magnolia Bloom Novel Book 3
  Moonlight in Magnolia Bloom, a Magnolia Bloom Novel Book 4
  Sweet Dreams in Magnolia Bloom, a Magnolia Bloom Novel Book 5 –March 2021

. . .

IF YOU ENJOYED *SPRINGTIME IN MAGNOLIA BLOOM,* please leave a review on your favorite sites (Amazon, Goodreads, BookBub). It's the most amazing thing you can do to help an author! THANK YOU!!

PLEASE SIGN up for Paula's newsletter at https://www.PaulaAdler.com to receive Eunice Greene's famous Chicken Salad recipe, Paula's next free novella, updates, and information on all future publications. You can find her on Facebook at https://www.facebook.com/PaulaAdlerAuthor, and by email at Paula@PaulaAdler.com. She answers all emails personally.

ABOUT THE AUTHOR

Paula Adler is a born and raised Texan who doesn't care what the DNA test said… she's way more than 12.6% Scottish! If she's not writing, you'll probably find her on a dance floor or SCUBA diving. For more information, please visit https://www.PaulaAdler.com

THE MAGNOLIA BLOOM SERIES

This series is being produced in audio, available from Chirp, Audible, and many other audio retailers

Magnolia Bloom Beginnings, A Three Novella Box Set – the Origins of Magnolia Bloom
   Return to Magnolia Bloom, a Magnolia Bloom Novel Book 1
   Mistletoe and Magnolia, a Magnolia Bloom Novel Book 2
   Springtime in Magnolia Bloom, a Magnolia Bloom Novel Book 3
   Moonlight in Magnolia Bloom, a Magnolia Bloom Novel Book 4
   Sweet Dreams in Magnolia Bloom, a Magnolia Bloom Novel Book 5 –March 2021

If you enjoy the Magnolia Bloom series, please leave a review on your favorite sites (Amazon, Goodreads, BookBub). It's the most amazing thing you can do to help an author! THANK YOU!!

Please sign up for Paula's newsletter at https://www.PaulaAdler.com to receive Eunice Greene's famous Chicken Salad recipe, updates, and information on all future publications. You can find her on Facebook at

https://www.facebook.com/PaulaAdlerAuthor, and by email at Paula@
PaulaAdler.com. She answers all emails personally.

P

Made in United States
North Haven, CT
29 October 2021

10672985R00146